About the

Richard Jobson is a singer and lyricist with Scottish punk band The Skids. He published a series of books and spoken-word records before becoming Sky TV's movie critic and writing/directing six feature films, including his memoir, the award-winning *16 Years of Alcohol*.

THE SPEED OF LIFE

THE SPEED OF LIFE

RICHARD JOBSON

Unbound

This edition first published in 2018

Unbound

6th Floor Mutual House, 70 Conduit Street, London W1S 2GF

www.unbound.com

ISBN (eBook): 978-1-911586-83-8

ISBN (Paperback): 978-1-911586-82-1

Design by Mecob

Cover image:

© Shutterstock.com

Printed in Great Britain by Clays Ltd, St Ives Plc

Dear Reader,

The book you are holding came about in a rather different way to most others. It was funded directly by readers through a new website: Unbound.

Unbound is the creation of three writers. We started the company because we believed there had to be a better deal for both writers and readers. On the Unbound website, authors share the ideas for the books they want to write directly with readers. If enough of you support the book by pledging for it in advance, we produce a beautifully bound special subscribers' edition and distribute a regular edition and e-book wherever books are sold, in shops and online.

This new way of publishing is actually a very old idea (Samuel Johnson funded his dictionary this way). We're just using the internet to build each writer a network of patrons. Here, at the back of this book, you'll find the names of all the people who made it happen.

Publishing in this way means readers are no longer just passive consumers of the books they buy, and authors are free to write the books they really want. They get a much fairer return too – half the profits their books generate, rather than a tiny percentage of the cover price.

If you're not yet a subscriber, we hope that you'll want to join our publishing revolution and have your name listed in one of our books in the future. To get you started, here is a £5 discount on your first pledge. Just visit unbound.com, make your pledge and type BLUE-GREEN18 in the promo code box when you check out.

Thank you for your support,

Dan, Justin and John
Founders, Unbound

Super Patrons

Julie Atkinson
Phil Barton
Paul Beazley
Johnny Beskow
Jon Birkett
Philip Bowman
Rob Bridle
Iain Brown
David Brown
Andrew Bucknall
Mark Chadderton
Juan Christian
Harry Concepcion
Murray Craig
John Crawford
Brian Crosland
Michael Daly
Ian Davis
Steve Denison
Robert Dorrens
John Dunton-Downer
Edward Durdey
Mark Ellins
Jonathan Field
Mark Finnigan
Stu Fletcher
Frank & Liz Fraser
Mark Frendo
Doug Futers
Phil Gallagher
Alyson Gates
Tony Gaughan

Paul Germaney
Olivia Gianelli
Georgina Godolphin
Johan Goeminne
Colin Graham
Antony Greatbanks
Chris Greenwood
Andrew Gregory
Jorgen Gustafsson
Matthew Gyves
Melinda Hajdin
Adrian Hall
Alexander Hastings
Chris Hay aka Ernest Penfold
Sean Hewitt
Scott "Hissy" Hislop
Alan Hotchkiss
Nicholas Hughes
Paul Hutchinson
Mark Huxley
John & Judith Ireland
Edie Jobson
Gavin Johnston
Mike Jones
Jukka Junttila
Dredd Kennedy
Rachael Kerr
Dan Kieran
David Klimek
Steve Leslie
Andy Leslie
Chris Eggboy Lewis
Terence Magennis
Gaynor Maher
Colin Malcolm
Jimmy McCarthy

Elliott McClements
Gary Mccrindle
Calum McDonald
Rob Milne
John Mitchinson
Åke Noring
Justin O'Connell
Dermot Christopher O'Connor
Sara O'Hagan
Mary O'Neill
Mark Oliff
Tim Parry
Colin Patton
Andy Pearl
Lindsay Peebles
David Pinder
Justin Pollard
Paul Price
Steven Price
Paul Richardson
Gayle Riley
Brian Russell
Steven Sander
Glen Scott
Donna Louise Scott
Graham Shirling
Carole Siller
Graham Stewart
P-O Ström
David Sutton
Richard Taylor
Trevor Thompson
Gordon Tosh
Peter Trenholm
Ian Walker
Dave Watson

Fiona Williams
Mark Williams
Andy Woods (ADW Decorators)

There was a storm. Ferocious electrical cracks split the blackness as the conical ship continued its journey. Debris clouds swarmed ahead, offering an impossible passage for the slick, shiny machine already battered by its entry into a solar system recycling the story of its own beginning. Neither stars nor sun could be seen as the storm gathered itself for another surge both deadly and beyond beauty.

Rocks the size of mountains swirled and sprung loose from their gravitational pull with a devastating energy. They moved in arcs as they shot out from the nuclear-misty cascading clouds. No sound. Only silence. Great movements and fireball trails gouged lines into the neck of the black universe. There were colours; they held their violence with a simplistic snap of gold and red, vibrant in its terror.

The ship moved into the swirl – not the heart of rock clouds, but into the grey. The sensory navigation system collided with hot winds, using nuclear thermals to swish a path that was inelegant but somehow capable of avoiding smashing into objects that shot near and past. It was a scene that needed sound. But still there was only silence. The outskirts of the grey clouds had an explosive glow but that began to fade as the ship pushed further into the storm. The energy sensors sucked in the storm's force, using the increased power to glide faster, shaving the edge of the rocks with an engineered skill.

Inside the ship, all was calm. Translucent, skin-coloured tubes pushed liquid into ferns with silver tentacles, which gently moved backwards and forwards creating a mild breeze. The liquid moving through the tubes was a deep red, eventually turning a plum-bruise hue as they fed into the system. The tubes were attached to the circular walls, moving through the ferns at irregular spots. As the liquid left the plant, a small bubble suggested there might be oxygen present as it became a brighter red before darkening again.

Smaller plants grew out of the ship's wet and silver-tinted interior casing. They seemed to inhale the breeze created by the ferns. Nothing was rigid or manufactured in appearance. Everything looked alive, feeding on the flowing liquid before then sharing it with the next organism in a systematic loop. The tubes carrying the liquid also made small movements which suggested they, too, fed and inhaled from each pulse pushed through its delicate skin.

Shadows and silhouettes were projected against the interior cylinder from the chaos going on outside the ship. At times, the grey cloud would submerge the concave walls in a deep darkness but then the burning tail of a meteor would illuminate the ferns and tubes, causing them for a moment to breathe deeper and exhale the liquid, causing a slight discolouration which was just as quickly corrected. It looked and felt like an adjustment to the enervating light of near collisions.

Everything seemed to work together, everything was linked. In the middle of one of the walls was a rectangular shape cut into the side. Inside, a chain of organic matter was anchored. There, lay two creatures in a small pool of the same liquid that was flowing through the tubes.

There was nothing to separate them – they were identical. Dressed in tight-fitting single body suits, it was impossible to see anything different in their faces. Their bodies were the same size, their hands seemed to be exactly the same and there was no obvious indication of gender. They could have been twins, male or female or even male and female. Their faces were angular, thin and pointed but somehow, despite their angularity, they retained a glow of gentleness. Their eyes were closed but when the ferns blew a breeze in their direction their eyelids would flutter at great speed like a hummingbird holding an aerial position. The effect of the fluttering eyelids caused the liquid in their bath to push small waves against the sides of the container bath then back over their bodies creating a simple but beautiful cooling system.

They seemed unaware of the dangers the ship was sailing through. The interior world remained calm and controlled. They both smiled at the same time and opened their eyes. It was here that the first difference could be seen between the two of them. One had deep blue eyes, the other had bold green eyes. They both looked ahead, watching the flickering images play out a deadly narrative across the concave walls.

Blue held Green's hand. They simultaneously shifted their gaze to the window of the ship and looked out at the universe in uproar.

The view out of the window was violent. This was their welcome. Fire raged red and blood orange and a shivering blue, all combining to create a lifeless skin that was their entry point to a destination that had been set, locked and unchangeable. The fires reflected in their eyes and were digested without terror. They had reached entry point, they had awoken, and everything had survived to this point.

This new experience – violence – was confusing but their internal data constructed a narrative that showed this was the new world they were entering. The data told them that this new world had been born from explosions and fires and that it was deep in the DNA of the peoples they were about to meet. These new people had fire and explosions inside them; it was their natural state and this was the source of their creativity. It was the reason for their journey. This was the world that had created David Bowie.

The ship heard this thought and flickered a response that spun and echoed around them as they held hands, watching the fires and explosions bounce off the ship's skin.

Green and Blue sat up from their liquid bed and pushed their faces against the window. There it was. The fires were gone. The explosions over. There it was. The Blue Planet. They looked at one another. Smiled, then kissed. And David Bowie continued to sing 'Wild is the Wind' not knowing two star-crossed lovers had travelled distances beyond his wildest imagination to see him perform his songs.

They lay together in their new home watching television. The choice of channels available was as long as it was beyond logic. They liked the random and system-free nature of what was offered as entertainment. Some of the channels were bundled together in categories such as sport or movies but again what was called football didn't seem to have much in common with darts and movie thrillers were completely unrelated to movie comedies. The repetitive and predictable storylines and characters in the many movies they had watched since acquiring their projection system were easily read but still absorbing in their noisy banality. The language of symbols used by the creators of the stories was crude and unsophisticated for a people who prided themselves on how clever they were; ancient myths and iconography seemed to lie at the heart of everything they wanted to say to one another. The only transference and freedom they had found so far in this beautiful but backward planet was music. It was after all the sound of David Bowie that had brought them here.

Music was truly sensory and unpredictable. It was something new to them. Something truly ancient, but able to be pushed and caressed into new shapes and sounds. They loved sound. The sonar excess of their new surroundings was now a vibrant part of their lives here.

The house was in a street set back from the main passageway of London's Park Lane. It was tall and grand with stucco balconies and floor-to-ceiling windows. When they had first walked past along the street they could see that the windows had been closed up with shutters and that there was no visible sign of anyone living there. They decided immediately that this would be their home.

They easily navigated the alarms and even found a CCTV camera that was quickly rearranged into a feedback loop of different images that would change but never show the new inhabitants moving around. Occasionally a security company's car would pull up outside the house and the driver of the car would look up at the building for a few seconds before moving on. They always left by the back garden gate and had yet to meet or see anyone who lived in the neighbouring houses.

The interior space was enormous. Floor after floor of grandeur. The furniture and artwork, including sculpture and paintings, had been covered in white cloth to protect them from dust, but they had removed all the cloth and revealed a mix of 20th century modernity and antiquity ranging from the Renaissance to the Victorian era. They had been immediately confused by the iconography and how it had been placed in each room but they slowly immersed themselves in the history and peculiar notion of creating an environment and atmosphere to present art or taste – ideas that were new to them but were easily reconcilable to the way this world worked through privilege, status and knowledge. Without an understanding of who they were and where they came from it seemed that these people were lost on the periphery, unable to understand the power of choice and fulfilment. Green and Blue realised that they needed to know more about how this came to be and if it had always been that way. They started to digest the rows of books on the first-floor library.

The philosophical argument about who these people were and what the point of their existence might be was examined in enormous detail through the different enlightened periods of what they called civilisation. They started at the beginning and soon realised that the various ideas at play were all the same. Although the words might be different, the repetition of principle and reason was no different. They were all, in their similar routes to their version of truth, mad.

So, there it was, the very thing they craved the most, truth, was the same thing that destroyed them. They had their favourites: Green preferred Hume and Blue was amused by Nietzsche; neither of them felt tickled by the French but held on to Descartes because in their own way they knew that that was the right thing to do. They realised that at some point it would be worthwhile to talk to someone who felt they knew about the meaning of this terrible angst.

They had listened to a man on the radio and saw him a few times on television drily battling his way through the confusion of these ideas and decided they would meet him. He seemed to be some kind of professor of thought, a writer of many books. They were certain they had encountered him before, and in human terms he was unmistakably unlikeable, which they thought made him a good choice as he was lost in the fog of thought and was clearly mad. But, like Bowie, they would have to find him.

They turned their attention back to the projected TV image on one of the bedroom walls. A man pranced around a stage talking very quickly and then the camera cut to members of the audience laughing. This was comedy. Laughter seemed very important to the way the people here communicated. They loved to watch people laugh. It was beautiful. The laughter.

Although they had quickly understood the science of language, they still could not work out how certain combinations of voice sounds mixed with body movement and facial – especially eye – gestures could create such a special home for laughter. The man making the audience laugh on the television was introduced as a comedian, which they understood, but it was an experience they needed to feel as a live event, something they needed to share. Maybe they could do it with the Writer, maybe he could help them understand the part of the experience that they were missing. The man on the screen was jumping and skipping and delivering his words in a high-pitched voice that lacked the sensuality that they liked in these people, but the audience roared with laughter. It was perplexing not to understand the context in which comedy was presented.

Green decided to change the channel as the comedian slowed down and tried to be serious. A movie sparkled with an actor's large white teeth, which seemed to be the point of focus rather than the actor's eyes. The idea that the eyes were the window to how people thought was made more difficult with the less emotional white teeth. They tried. Overanalysis had caused long hours of failed equations and newly adapted philosophical wanderings. They remembered the Frenchman Baudrillard's ideas but it all became an unsolvable riddle. They knew who they would ask. More than ever they needed the Writer. It had become clear that everything had a meaning but some meanings were less resilient in their construction than others. The white teeth movie fiasco they now knew to be a superficial way to navigate the viewer away from the eyes, as the eyes were doing nothing other than looking at other actors' white teeth. A certain kind of popular movie concentrated on teeth and shiny kitchens. The connection was an agile seduction of the viewer into a smash-and-grab eating disorder.

Later they discovered another comedian who they faked laughter with as part of the soundtrack of the evening – a kind of laughter practice. The comedian attempted to make them stop thinking about what was actually happening. He made disparaging comments about comedians who hopped and skipped about, talking in a high-pitched voice. He suggested that if you were watching him, then the hopping-skipper was not for you. He was saying that you had made a choice.

Green and Blue up to this point had thought that everything was for everybody but slowly it dawned on them that this in fact was the opposite of what life here was about. Nevertheless the idea that life should be for everybody lay deep in the consciousness of how the people communicated, whether they were for it or against it, the two standard positions of how people presented their point of view.

During the commercial break they watched people using money to buy objects. They looked at one another. They would need to find money. So far they had walked into shops and just taken what they liked. It was done at such speed that the people working in the shops couldn't see what had just happened. They were uncomfortable with just taking things as they realised that the cause and effect of their actions would create a problem for the people working in the shops. Having money meant that they could start to pay for whatever they wanted. They discussed the simplest way to make money that would cause the least harm and decided on gambling.

They researched how gambling worked and what would be the easiest route for them. In one of the desk drawers in the house was a few hundred euros. This would be their starting sum. To gather the sums they had in mind they felt it would be better to move from different gambling environments and stick to cash deals as they had not worked out how to create a credit facility. Sport was the most obvious area to begin. It was competitive, therefore making it possible to gamble on a series of possible outcomes. The problem with sport was that what should be an obvious outcome never quite worked out that way. There were always unknown elements.

They worked hard on an equation that might correct the unknown. The focus here was always on available information. They decided to work on the possibilities thrown up by examining the statistics related to the narrative of the unknown. They chose football and decided to bet carefully on a series of outcomes on the upcoming fixture between Real Madrid and Bayern Munich.

The television was linked to a variety of boxes that spewed out the information they wanted. The managers, the diets, the history of each club were placed beside the weather, the location, current events and, most importantly, the fragility of each of the players who might play.

Their research told them that the German team, Bayern Munich, was less vulnerable to the unexpected but less capable of doing the unexpected, unlike the Spanish team Real Madrid. It was going to be wet, which suited the North European mentality. Although their players were international, the German team had adopted German principles, which prized craftsmanship above artistry.

Blue read aloud Nietzschean aphorisms to present the case for Bayern's lack of doubt. They agreed that the vulnerability lay within the Spanish camp. Their superstar team seemed unstoppable but Blue and Green agreed that they had broken connections that could be exploited by robust pressure. They found the best odds and placed their bet on Bayern to win 1-0 in the Spanish capital. Their second bet was on the goal scorer. They found ridiculous odds on the win being secured through a penalty kick. They decided that this was how Bayern would breach the Spanish defence and how their mercurial German captain would calmly, after much hustling, hit the back of the net with the ball. They would use the remainder of the money on the second two bets.

The bookmaker's shop had a glass front with lots of numbers proposing various gambling positions on a variety of sporting events. Inside, people stood at counters looking at gambling data, analysing the shifts and pulls that linked their experience with luck. Green and Blue entered the shop. They tried to slide along the back wall in an attempt not to bring any attention to themselves but they had no idea of their beauty and their peculiar radiance.

They were an unusual combination in a space that only ever saw the same hunched shoulders and grey fatigue. The betting shop was a busy station for the hopeful. Blue and Green didn't look like they were addicted to anything other than each other. People assumed they were nervous of this type of environment and, instead of guiding hostile glances in their direction, preferred to smile, amused by their odd eyes and suits and the way the two of them held hands in a manner that they had all but forgotten or had never known.

The gamblers prepared their bets, took them to the counter and came away with a small receipt. A man with a beard and yellow teeth asked them if they needed some help. They smiled at him and nodded their heads. He showed them the process, which they understood quickly enough.

Is everything here so simple, they wondered? This routine gambling which devoured more money than it spat out had had a crippling effect on the people in the room – another offer of choice which was in essence the opposite. Concerned, the man with the yellow teeth asked them if they were sure. They smiled gracefully as he shrugged and watched them as they placed their bet.

The person behind the counter didn't at any point look at them. He took their euros and gave them a receipt. Blue and Green were enchanted. This was their first interaction with their new hosts and it had been a great success. Tomorrow, they would start their search for the history of David Bowie in his home city and in the evening they would watch the match. Their long journey was beginning to make sense.

The interior walls of the house began to change, their cool chalky smooth surface becoming covered in a moss-like fungus. The clear tubes from the ship moved in and out of the dark green fronds and appeared to move back into the walls, where a series of long cracks with many small tributaries climbed the building like a wisteria looking for light.

Small flurries of movement accompanied a light ochre liquid that slipped through the tubes, slowly changing colour to a deeper red as it moved along and up the walls. The house was breathing out the floating molecules of dust, then just as they were about to reach the floor a small breeze would pull them back up again diffusing the light, creating a sparkling atmosphere that danced with a new life.

A gentle sound, like a low single cello note, vibrated around the house with an elegant subtlety. The lighting in the various rooms was softer than it should have been. There was a distant echo of scurrying feet: the mass of many mice leaving the building. And the sound, the long cello note, rumbled and rolled, continuing up the beautiful oak staircase. More cracks appeared along the walls. The tubes quickly followed and then the liquid flowed. To the naked eye the changes were an interior trompe l'oeil, a forest of winter branches and ancient trees. The outside world had no influence on the evolution of the house. Occasionally the lights from a passing taxi bounced off the house steps and front door but failed to upset the atmosphere inside, where a warm glow seemed to lift the house from its foundations.

Blue and Green were draped in long coats they had found in their new home. They were ill fitting but their pale demeanour gave a gothic romantic lilt to their appearance as they strolled through Brixton market. In a fight to be heard, the roar and rouse of market people shouting and selling their wares made a tinny din as Blue and Green fluttered through the various avenues and stalls, sharing their thoughts:

'How do they see us?'
    'As foreigners.'
    'That's one of their least words. Least something words.'
    'Effective.'
    'No. It's entirely effective.'
    'Then... I mean, it doesn't sound nice.'
    'I agree. But, I don't think they see us as that.'
    'No?'
    'No.'
    'Then what?'
    'They're not being hostile.'
    'Are they hostile to foreigners?'
    'That's what happens.'
    'Why?'
    'They're tribal.'
    'Primitive.'
    'In a scared kind of way.'
    'I don't like that word either.'
    'Yes.'

'It's sharp.'
'Yes.'
'Can you feel it?'
'I can.'
'Do they feel their words?'
'They must. That's why they write songs. Poetry.'
'Yes.'
'Is it onomatopoeia?'
'Not quite.'
'Because it's not imitative. That's no reason.'

A dog barked at them as they continued to flutter and stroll through the market. It followed them, confused and nervous, yet still inquisitive about their smell. It wouldn't come close and remained at a safe dog's distance from their touch.

'Woof.'
 'Bark. Bark.'
 'Grrrrrrrr…'
 'Yes.'
 'That's closer. They like animals. They are animals.'
 'Yes.'
 'Why dogs?'
 'Friendship.'
 'Yes.'
 'Sex?'
 'No. I don't think so, but maybe…'
 'Protection?'
 'Yes.'
 'Why do they need protection in such a wonderful place?'
 'From each other.'
 'Why would they hurt one another?'
 'Choice.'
 'Yes.'
 'Primitive.'

'Historically.'

'I see.'

'Their anger is caused by choice or the lack of it. Will they always be angry?'

'Maybe.'

'Are you scared?'

'Woof.'

'Bark. Bark.'

'Grrrrrrrrr…'

'No.'

'No fear.'

'No fear.'

'Do you like dogs?'

'They like us. So, yes. I return their like.'

'And how will we deal with the ones that don't like us?'

'Deal.'

'Everything here is wonderful.'

'Everything.'

'Even the ones who will not like us?'

'Even the ones who will not like us.'

'I agree.'

'Does happy imitate happy?'

'Happy is an adjective.'

'Then we are adjectives.'

'Do we need a dog?'

'No.'

'No.'

They walked out of the market along a street lined with rows of terraced houses on either side. They all looked the same. A variety of cars and vans were parked closely together on the road. Some of the houses were being renovated and had workmen coming in and out carrying tools or bags of debris. The sharp slice of a drill cut through the air.

'This is where David Bowie was born.'
  'David Jones.'
  'Can you feel him here, present at the market?'
  'Distantly.'
  'Me too.'
  'Did his family wander through these streets?'
  'I think so.'
  'They must have done.'
  'Why wouldn't you?'
  'Brixton is perfect.'
  'Yes.'
  'I would be an adjective here.'
  'I agree.'
  'We are foreign adjectives in Brixton. And we're not scared.'
  'Something we love was born here.'
  'Yes.'
  'David Bowie.'
  'David Jones.'
  'David Bowie.'
  'Yes, David Bowie.'

Blue and Green stood outside 40 Stansfield Road and felt the wonderment of the movement of history create a story that had a beginning. If any of the passing people on the street had looked up they would have seen a warm glow emerge around them, and then fade as quickly as it had arrived. Their thoughts were submerged into the liquid patterns of the past and for as long as the glow prevailed then the past became the present. They saw the young David Jones standing at the doorway looking out towards them. He waved and said hello and then just as quickly faded into the light.

They settled in front of the television to watch the football game between what had been described as the best two teams on Earth: Real Madrid versus Bayern Munich. Green held the coupon from the bookmaker's shop. The pre-match rituals unfolded and the closeness of the television cameras to the sell-out crowd in Madrid made an already hostile atmosphere feel unbearably near.

The walls of the room had now been completely invaded by the tubes and ferns and the once-clean surfaces had disappeared beneath this now-living, breathing force. The tubes had now moved through the floorboards, moving in and out of small patches of young but quick-growing ferns. The room had a mellow glow although there was no lighting on apart from the spill from the screen of the television.

'Stay' by Bowie floated its charm around the room, underscoring the titanic battle about to erupt on the silvery-green grass. They stopped watching the screen as the rhythmic guitar blazed over the percussion creating a further tremble to the already heightened anticipation of violence. They held hands listening to the voice of the man whose birthplace they had visited earlier in the day. The music moved around them, dancing with the liquid pushing though the tubes.

The match had started and although the rules and tactics were not obvious, they were both enchanted by the idea of eleven players attempting to outmanoeuvre the other eleven players to put the ball into the net. In such a gender-specific world they wondered how many of the twenty-two players were men and how many were women. The clash between the two teams was an unstoppable absurdity which had great moments of fun; the teams were in fact delicately wrapped individuals who were doing everything they could to shine above their fellow team-mates.

'We should go.'
    'Yes.'
    'Participate.'
    'Yes.'
    'Learn to shout.'
    'Scream.'
    'Passion.'
    'Like love.'
    'Like love.'

The teams were coming out for the second half. The noise was only apparent to them through the contorted faces of the many thousands who had gathered in the arena.

'Slip Away' from *Heathen* provided a golden-age cinematic sound that flickered and scratched into a typically gracious Bowie chord sequence, building to the epic chorus line. They danced along with the man responsible for their journey, their terrifying interstellar trip, their long dreams and exhausted fluids.

'Like love,' Green said.

'Yes,' Blue replied.

'Let's go.'

'Participate.'

As they danced, they closed their eyes, holding each other tightly. The fluid turned crimson red and the glow held its magical warmth. They opened their eyes and ears to a raw cacophony of tuneless aggression. They were there in Madrid, in the stadium, speeding through the match, as if they had arrived on a different timeline.

The faces then became enlarged – mouths had an operatic boom. The stadium was a circular tub and thump, reverberating into the sky. They could feel the tremors underneath them. Their feet bounced in time to an ancient gypsy beat – nobody was interested in the two identical beings with different eyes. All that mattered was the game.

The crowd moved together: standing, sitting, shouting, screaming, hoping, holding, loving, jumping, landing, eye-closing, eye-opening, arms outstretched, arms in the air, hands over their eyes, clenching hugs, ironic asides, bitter social division, political implosions, xenophobic dreams, explosive awakenings, triumphant melodies, fear, terror, astrological projection, fatalism, misanthropy, anarchy, alluvial earth, castles in Spain – and then, after all the insanity, tears.

The German team, Bayern Munich, was awarded a penalty. The captain of the Bavarian team held the ball without anxiety, knowing inside him what he needed to do, and would do. Throughout this ongoing drama, a culture's thousand years of fear and loathing spat hatred at the German captain.

Green and Blue watched him in slow motion as he ran towards the ball and casually placed his kick in the direction of the corner of the net. The crowd were silent. The Germans embraced. Green and Blue left the dream of the stadium knowing that they now had money. And money, it would seem, in this beautiful world, offered the opportunity to make more money. Gambling was not luck – it was analysis and data-led, leaving very little to chance. No impulse. No improvised thinking. No random God-like wishfulness. Gambling was not jazz.

They had a method. They knew it worked. Money in this place would never be a problem. But then, they had only a few moments ago planted themselves into another situation at different time-frames, some fast, some slow. They had food. They could travel easily in the slow orbit without moving and they understood money was only really of use in a world of things. But that was this slow-orbiting planet. They had made a decision to buy things. Start small: clothes, yes, clothes would be the first thing that they would buy.

They had walked through Bond Street, which was close to their house, and had seen the presentation of clothes in the various stores, with a near-religious self-regard. It would be the place they would start spending their new-found wealth. After all, had Bowie not loved clothes, created style, invented new fashions and been an arbiter of cool through his manifold character?

The labels available were endless. Designer. Celebrity. Celebrity-designer. Luxury. Refinement. And once again, the fatality of choice. They considered the words of one of their favoured philosophers, David Hume, and wondered if this shopping expedition might have taken them into the world of vicious luxury; whenever luxury ceases to be innocent, it also ceases to be beneficial. Now that they were here and actively participating, should they not also be alive to virtue and present acts of duty and generosity?

Their small fortune was about to be spent on clothes. They needed clothes, but did they need to buy them here in one of the city's most expensive streets? Consumer morality was a piercing challenge as it valued sanity over fun.

They agreed that they would postpone any decision on the matter until they met the Writer – he would surely guide them. Should they follow human morality or try, as they were currently doing, to digest and evaluate life here as a work in progress? They were aware, though, that they had made their first compromise – which was an entirely new and strange experience.

After all, they were not from here, so why the rush to acclimatise and assimilate with such clunky ideas about life's purpose? The elegance and simplicity of sensation, which had guided them to this planet through the music and words of David Bowie, were being assaulted by the learned as being superficial.

'Surely, that's the point?' Green said, breaking up their shared thought management.

'Yes.'

'They feel sensation is not enough.'

'They exhaust themselves with unhappiness.'

'Yes.'

'Sensation is beautiful.'

'Inspiring.'

'Sensual.'

'I like that word.'

'Sensual.'

'It does things to me.'

'Things.'

'Steals a breath.'

'I know.'

'Touches.'

'Yes.'

'Inside.'

'It's strange how they live outside.'

'Yes.'

'Everything they have is inside.'

'Like us.'

'Yes.'

The staff in the store had been watching Green and Blue in a bemused, near-hypnotic state. The other customers had been forgotten. Nobody was quite sure how to deal with them as they wrapped the clothes around themselves, rubbing the cloth against their skin, behaving like children. Green and Blue had simulated their response to these new experiences into what they felt was the most natural and normal human response – innocence.

They moved back into the silent mode of sharing their thoughts as they took various clothes from the rails and were directed into a changing room lit with grey neon strips.

Inside the changing room they stood facing one another. The clothes were hanging on the various hooks all around them but they didn't try them on. They continued to stare at one another. They slowly closed their eyes and took turns projecting each costume onto one another: shirts, knitwear, jackets, shoes, coats. Everything they would need.

Green helped Blue out of the costume they had been wearing since they arrived. The material was wet inside and had a translucent membrane on the outside. Green pulled out the last part of Blue's leg and rolled the material into a small ball. Blue stood naked in front of Green.

The body was slim and pale with a slight hint against the austere neon lights of blue veins pulsating beneath the skin. Small breasts with oversized nipples pushed out freely above a concave stomach. The body was hairless and appeared wrinkle free. It was impossible to suggest Blue's age. Green's hand moved across Blue's face and then down across the shoulders and rested on one of the nipples. Blue shivered. They looked into one another's eyes as Green's hand moved between Blue's legs and stayed there, gently caressing the flat patch that curved away from the lower stomach. The shiver moved through the body, increasing the colour of the blue veins against the torturous grey neon.

Blue smiled and pulled back Green's costume. The move was quick but elegantly simple. The costume was wrapped into a small ball as before. Blue touched Green's face in a way that caused Green to shake. Green's skin was the same colour apart from the veins, which were a very light green. Blue's face touched Green's nipples which stood out from small breasts and then moved onto the stomach and then slowly down below. They appeared neither male nor female but shared the sexual organs of both.

They continued to touch one another. The colours blue and green became deeper; the veins moved as liquid almost rolled through in a small wave-like motion. Their faces were now as close as they could be as they breathed into each other's mouths. Through all of these changes they remained utterly silent – no sounds from their breathing, touching, rubbing, fluttering and shivering. It was all done in silence as though the exterior world was locked out of an interior secrecy; a world of intimacy that travelled inwards, bypassing the crude exaltations and theatricality of their new neighbours. This was something that they shared with no-one.

Their interior communication took them through experiences that their many parents shone light on. Moments of shared beauty and happiness that flowed between silver oceans, mellifluous stars and a crackling tundra that stretched for thousands of miles reflecting the black sun's whispering clouds. This is what they were born from and carried through. All of their parents, many hundreds, waved back at them, smiling at their children's journey as it was revealed exactly in the same way as had been predicted. And here they were. Standing together, connected and tingling with a clear understanding of who they were. Their message to their families was as simple as it was beautiful. We are here but one day we will return. The ferns blew and the colours changed in their interior cosmos.

They believed in their journey. They believed in this planet, although its many contradictions bemused them. They would continue to search for David Bowie. Their engagement was easy enough, the need for some kind of assimilation was the only way forward: each experience had to be new, like this one, wearing clothes.

Could they see the clothes back home? What did they think of them? But the contact was gone; they were no longer inside one another. The veins cooled their colours and the warmth of the glow became faint. They held one another in a clasp, an embrace, in a similar way to how their hosts showed affection, but it felt insignificant. They told one another that they would try again when a connection to their home was within reach.

They left the high-end, four-floor Dover Street market dressed in their first choices. Blue had a bag by Azzedine Alaia and a Comme des Garçons overcoat over a Celine dress and Adidas shoes by Pharrell Williams. Green was in Saint Lauren trousers, a Julien David shirt and the same Comme des Garçons overcoat, and a black backpack by South2 West8. The odd combination of Japanese and European fashion all came together in polytonal fun.

Green's bench-made English shoes from Trickers finished off a monochrome toughness. Little gems of jewellery from Diane Kordas and Repose jingled like jazz as the Mayfair and Piccadilly streets played host to this new look. The clothes lay on top of their wearable skins, which couldn't be seen amongst the wools and silks. As they walked people stopped and thought which band? which film? which TV show? where, when, how...? Human greed, solipsism, the search for the self were all displaced for a moment by genuine wonderment.

They stopped in front of a large glass window. Inside was the opening night party for an artist's new exhibition. They quietly worked out the narrative: who was who, what people wanted from one another, what kind of relationships were beginning or ending.

A security guard watched the two of them, engaged by their similarly angular faces and comical concentration. He was waiting for them to come in. After all, they looked like they should be coming to this event. What he didn't know was that they were mystified by their own reflections in the glass. They shared the absurdity of how they looked and squeaked an echo into the star-strewn night sky that projected a newly discovered happy laughter. The security guard's smile ushered them in.

The gallery was lit with hanging bulbs, which had long, near-invisible threads which disappeared into the roof. The bulbs seemed to be moving from side to side with the faintest of touches from the light breeze when they opened the door. The effect of the lighting was startling inside the gallery, creating shadows that bobbed and weaved along the floor, and casting unflattering deep black shadows on people's faces, emphasising their sunken, tired eyes which both aged them and made them look liver-ill. Green and Blue entered the ghoulish environment of the Art World in their subdued fashion ensembles, causing the light bulbs to swing rather than sway.

They were immediately drawn to the long white walls, which had bright blue and green spots of different sizes spread all over them. At the far end of the room was a video installation showing blue and green spots raining down on a night-time cityscape. It was clumsy and cheap-looking but it still had people standing in front of it, seemingly engaged with the work's deeper meaning. Green and Blue stood next to the people viewing the large screen, watching the spots slowly fall and disappear off the bottom edge of the screen.

A man stood next to them, watching as the video looped its mundane tune. He looked at their clothes, the colour of their skin and eyes. He studied the detail of how the light did not have the same effect on their faces as on the other people in the gallery.

'Are you artists?' the man asked.

They didn't turn away from the installation but smiled and shook their heads.

'Students? Actors? Models? Designers?' he asked slowly.

Again they shook their heads but remained engrossed in the movement of the raining spots.

The man came closer, his voice dropped to a whisper.

'Do you know what this is about?'

They continued to look ahead, the blue and green spots reflecting on their faces, showing veins of blue and green beneath their skin.

'It's an exhibition about grief.'

They both collected the meaning of grief and turned to look at the man for the first time. Like all of the others, his eyes were sunk back into his head, the drooping light bulbs continuing to age and cast

21

deep shadows. He wore a black wool Nehru-collared jacket and his skin was grey and white. His eyes were deep watery black and glistened when he moved his head.

'Why?' Green asked.

'Why do you want to be sad?'

'We love your friendships,' Blue said softly, rasping the 'r's and sizzling each 's'.

The man couldn't take his eyes off the odd-sounding twins as he offered them another explanation.

'When a friendship ends then there might be sadness. No?'

'Why?' asked Blue. 'Why not make new friendships and never forget the one you have lost, so by making a new one, you should be happy. The memory of the old friendship should be a joy. No?'

'That sounds too easy,' he countered, gurgling the words from the back of his throat as if trying to clean them before making his point.

'Why is it easy?'

'Because it's deeper than that. It's love.' The words creaked and croaked before they eventually arrived.

'But if you go deeper then the love will make you happy.'

He looked at them, not quite sure which one of them had said this, or maybe they had said it together. He tried to clear his throat.

'Are you some kind of neo-hippy?'

'What's a hippy?'

'You must know. No? Peace and Love. That's what they believed in.'

'But what's wrong with this idea?'

'Nothing.'

'So…'

'They don't work in reality. '

'Why not?'

'The world's too cynical. People don't want those kind of ideas to work.'

'Really?' said Green, amazed by his certainty.

'You don't believe that.'

'Maybe I don't want to, but like I said, it's the world.'

'Which world?'

'The only one.' He looked at their confused faces.

'This one. There are no others.'

'You're sure?' asked Blue.

'Certain.'

'You seem certain about so much.'

'You have to be.'

'What's it based on?'

'Experience. You're both young. You'll change. We all do.'

'From what to what?'

'From uncertainty to certainty.'

'Why does that matter so much?'

'Knowledge is certainty.'

'No,' said Blue, 'knowledge is uncertainty.'

'Yes,' agreed Green, 'The more you know the less certain you should be.'

The man shook his head and laughed. 'I don't like philosophy. It's not practical.'

'But everything here is philosophy.'

'You really believe that?'

'We do.'

'You're both rather lovely.'

'I think you might be, what's the correct word…'

'Patronising us.'

'No. Never.'

They wandered along the side of the walls looking at the spots, unaware of the other people in the gallery looking at them with a haughty art-world curiosity. The man continued to follow them.

'This is art,' he said.

'Something to adore.'

'Or hate.'

They were both taken aback by the rasping charge of the word the man had snapped at them.

'No.'

'Why no?'

'We don't hate.'

'We don't understand it.'

'Really, come on. You must.'

'We don't know how to.'

'You don't know what you're missing. Anyway, you'll soon learn.'

'No, it's not possible.'

He stopped in front of them. 'You mean it.'

'Yes.'

'Where do you come from?'

They looked at one another and smiled.

'Do you really want to know?'

'I do.'

'We come from far away.'

'Far, far away.'

'Russia? Argentina? New Zealand? Greenland?'

They shook their heads as they looked at the different-sized spots on the wall. The man wouldn't give up and gently nudged people who wanted to talk to Blue and Green out of the way.

'So why are you here? For this? For the art?'

'No.'

'We came to discover David Bowie.'

'Bowie?'

'Yes.'

'And have you found him yet?'

'Little things.'

'It's exciting.'

'But you will never meet him. Not now.'

They didn't answer and continued along the walls occasionally putting their hands through the light beams and reflecting them against the shapes on the wall, as if trying to find a way to touch the art.

'He's a recluse. I mean he still works, and the work is good, really good, but he won't be interested in meeting you no matter how far you've come. Anyway, stick with the mystery – it's always better.'

They looked at the man as if seeing him for the first time. They knew he had more to tell them. They considered the nature of what people called coincidence and fate. This meeting had not happened by accident; they recognised that, within their knowledge of Bowie, the man in front of them was part of their story.

'You're quite extraordinary, the two of you. Can I take a photograph?'

They continued to hold his gaze as he took out his mobile phone and framed them against the the floating blue and green spots.

'No smile? I would have thought that you would be used to having your picture taken.'

'No. This is the first time.'

'I think you might be playing with me.'

He looked at the image and was surprised to see that all the other people in the gallery were out of focus and that the spots from the video installation were translucent and at the front of the image. Blue and Green looked back at him as if he weren't there, as though they had forgotten where they were. Their skin texture reflected the blue and green spots and a thin trace of vein lines spread like branches of a delicate Japanese cherry tree. The photograph, although untreated, was unusually rich in colour with a milky Polaroid shine.

'What did you think of him?' Blue asked.

'Who?'

'Bowie.'

He looked up from the photograph, immediately confused by the quality of the image and the faked theatricality of the gallery.

'What was he like?'

'How did you know that I've met him?'

They held his gaze, watching his amazement as their veins pushed liquid through their body at a visible speed. He looked up at the lights, looking for some kind of reason and logic.

'He was unusual. I don't mean in a weird way. I mean he was unusual because he is who he is, but he was happy.'

'Why the but?'

'I don't know. Maybe that's what you need to discover. I don't think you will.' He looked at the photograph again. The image had become cloudy and was starting to fade. 'Wait here for a moment. I want you to meet someone. You'll like her. She'll love you two. Wait a moment.'

He started to walk backwards, unable to take his eyes off them. He raised his voice so they could hear him over the gallery din.

'Bowie was funny. In a British, take-the-piss kind of way. He said 'I like your spots'. I told him I was a fan but he wasn't interested in that. He wanted to talk to me about my spots. Now, please don't move. I'll be right back.'

St Anne's Court in Soho was a narrow passageway between Wardour Street and Dean Street. A burger restaurant pumped out tinny drum and bass music that lent the evening a tension it hadn't asked for. Blue and Green stood outside Trident House at No 17. The door was painted red and looked cheap and forgotten. Behind the door was a warren of small offices and sound studios. All the lights were off. The edit suites and colour-grading rooms were busily uploading digital material without human help. Blue and Green smiled at the primitive nature of what their hosts thought was cutting-edge, the future.

Soho was still the heart of London's media world, but No 17 in a previous life had been the home of Trident Studios. This was where Bowie had recorded *Hunky Dory*, his first album of merit that showed his prolific skills as a songwriter. Blue and Green created a barrier that bounced the drum and bass attack into the subterranean vaults of Soho, where it scared the rats and corroded the ancient stonework. They concentrated on the period of May and June 1971.

The light changed. It became dim and sulphury. Windows were framed around red lamps and St Anne's Court was suddenly empty of people. There were no bars or restaurants blaring out music, only an occasional taxi driving down the one-way streets on either side of the passageway, reminded them that the city was alive. They connected their hands and pushed into the time-frame as producer Ken Scott opened the door of No 17 and looked up to the sky. In the background a skeleton version of 'Life on Mars' slipped out behind Scott and into the mist of Blue and Green. Mick Ronson joined Scott, smoking a cigarette, looking in the same direction above the mist into the night sky. The sky had a sepia tint and, like a photograph developed in reverse, Ken Scott and Mick Ronson began to fade but their voices continued through the now grey mist. Ronson wanted to use a string arrangement on 'Life on Mars'. He was convinced it would elevate the song. As the image faded, Blue and Green held onto Ronson's northern English accent as he sang the line, '"And she's hooked to the silver screen' and then bam – heavy strings.'

'Really?' Scott whispered up into the sky.

'Really. "But the film is a saddening bore" – bam. Come on, Ken, try it. Just try it. The song's pure cinema.'

'What does that mean?'

'Fuck knows, but it sounds good.'

And they laughed together as they closed the door of Trident Studios. But Blue and Green followed their footsteps whispering 'Try it, try it, try it, try it, try it…' and then the Mick Ronson 'bam' became once again the drums and bass escaping from the vaults where the tortured rats squealed in pain and now relief.

From the window above, the ghost of Ronson's strings echoed through the Soho night as Blue and Green walked across Wardour Street where the bars ebbed and flowed with anxious people in a hurry to go nowhere in particular. They watched how people needed to be busy even when they were 'socialising', 'relaxing', 'chilling'. And then 'bam' went Ronson's ghostly strings. 'Is there life on Mars?' was the question. But the answer didn't matter. It was all so beautifully fake. The faker. The fakers.

'This is all fake,' Blue shared with Green.

'Yes.'

'Beautifully fake.'

'He said the song was pure cinema.'

'He did.'

'Does that mean it felt like it should be in a movie?'

'No. I think he meant that the song was a movie. But in fact he didn't know what he meant.'

'Another of their great qualities.'

'Yes.'

'This was a great moment in Bowie's life.'

'The most exciting time.'

'The beginning.'

'He's about to become what they call a star.'
'This was the moment.'
'The time.'
'Changes.'
'It's all about to happen.'
'And we caught a glimpse…'
'Of how the others must see the faker.'
'It's less structured this moment. *Hunky Dory*.'
'Structured?'
'It's a word they use when something makes sense.'
'It's a terrible word.'
'Yes. You're right. It's terrible.
'What was that sound? Was that us…'
'Laughing?'
'Yes.'
'Let's do it again.'
'Did you feel it?'
'Yes.'
'We laughed.'
'How do we explain that?'
'Maybe we're becoming like them.'
'Looking for structure.'
'There…'
'We did it again.'
'We laughed.'
'We laughed.'
'Alien laughter.'
'That's funny.'
'I agree.'
'But it didn't make us laugh.'
'No.'

The backstreets of Soho mixed street food, bars spilling out onto the streets and late-night shopping. Small retailers illuminated their windows, inviting a final hour's sales from the anxiety-ridden hipsters. Blue and Green stopped outside the lingerie store Agent Provocateur and were baffled by the straps, garter belts, corsets, nylon stockings and whips. The female mannequin in the window was fetishised from head to foot and behind her a tired-looking shop assistant in a short pink apron was as theatrical but maybe a bit less demanding. She looked out at Blue and Green hoping they might come in and save her from the slobbering boredom of men buying lingerie for their girlfriends or wives. But for the moment Blue and Green preferred the cool breeze of the streets and gave her a simple but all-consuming smile that made her step back and sit down, not quite clear about what had just happened. Blue and Green were sharing their thoughts as they listened to the sound of Bowie's 'Quicksand' from *Hunky Dory*.

'Why did Bowie like Aleister Crowley?'
  'Maybe part of sensation as shock.'
  'That's all?'
  'It's their fear of the inside.'
  'And love of the outside.'
  'Quicksand.'
  'I like it.'
  'On the surface.'
  'And it's structure.'
  'I felt that.'
  'Me too.'
  'In the stomach.'
  'Yes.'
  'Are we laughing at Bowie?'
  'No.'
  'You're right.'
  'We're laughing at ourselves.'
  'Aliens laughing at aliens.'
  'Bam – now that's a movie.'
  'With strings.'
  'Stop it.'
  'I know.'
  'Too much laughter.'
  'Anyway the strings are…'

'Beautiful…'

'Indeed.'

'Why explain the inexplicable?'

'What's wrong with sensation?'

'They exhaust themselves with unhappiness.'

'More laughter.'

'More…'

'Laughter is a pure flame.'

'Kept alive by an invisible sun within us.'

'And then…'

'And then…'

'What is this place? The London Palladium.'

'Home of vaudeville.'

'The beginning of Bowie.'

The London Palladium growled with fantasy success lighting. I'm here, it said, I can make dreams come true. This was the home of variety, a peculiar form of entertainment that was born in the working men's clubs all over the land but in here it meant something else. This was where career entertainers knew they had made it to the top. The top, thought Blue and Green, what is the top? Magicians, comedians, baritones, animal trainers, impersonators, black and white minstrels, dancers as glitter balls, gymnasts, circus clowns and latter-day sociologists all had something in common here – this is where they all smiled the perfect smile. The freeze across the face. The imposter of a smile. The terror of a smile. This was a place made for smiling. Blue and Green could feel the history of the smile in the brash lighting and echoes of ovations and squeals of delight. They smiled together at how ridiculous it all was.

But it was as much a part of Bowie as were Genet, Burroughs, Ballard and Brel. The echoing laughter and vaudevillian smiles of history sailed around the building and drifted into a time-frame too cynical to understand what it meant to the people who loved it, breathed and absorbed its Englishness. Like Bowie.

Blue and Green heard the distant jingle of the singer Antony Newley and understood it was the starting point of a new identity. And that, mixed with miming Pierrots and Harlequins, engaged Bowie's cheap theatricality with something much more elusive and upmarket.

Bowie, they realised, understood he was a product and he fought that idea in all of his creations but paradoxically needed the adulation. It was from this chaos that a new reality would be born – the reality of Ziggy Stardust. Like us, Blue and Green shared, trying to make sense of this strange place. Yes, they smiled, this place is strange, as they crossed Regent Street through the faint drizzle of persistent London rain. They looked up to the sky, looking through the undemanding and windless haze, and allowed their faces and hands to be sprinkled with its weightless touch. Like children, they sang a note to the heavens, a thank you to nature. They ran from the ghost of Antony Newley as he performed an inelegant ballad to beauty. It was perfect.

They watched a long queue that stood outside a store with only a logo illuminated to distinguish it from all the others. The mood in the long row of people was subdued. The entrance to the store was roped off, with guards blocking the way.

'Why are they standing in the rain at night – what is about to happen inside the logo shop?' shared Blue and Green. They pulled up their collars simultaneously and in the eyes of the people queueing they appeared to dance alongside them. Blue and Green listened to their thoughts – a mixture of anticipation and excitement and even dread. It had something to do with an object they used for communication. They appeared to be waiting to purchase the latest updated version of what they called a mobile phone. They would be the first. The first until tomorrow to own the new phone. It was so important to them that they were willing to stand unhappily in the rain: for an object. Blue and Green watched the rain dampen the clothes and hair of the mobile phone fans.

'It's a passive object.'

'They are in love with a clumsy object.'

'A mobile phone? Why not people? Ideas? Not an object. It's not art.'

'It's important to them.'

'Today. But what about tomorrow? The next day?'
'It's part of their new techno-religion. The new cult. The future.'
'They love the future?'

They walked down the wide, eye-catching curve of Regent Street knowing that objects had become personalised art devices for this new expressionless era obsessed with the salvation of algorithms and genes. The people were deeply mistaken but Blue and Green did not feel it was their place to tell them that they were only replacing the deity of Man with the tyranny of machines. It was all the same thing in the end: the need for an explanation. A reason. It all made perfect sense to Blue and Green and at the same time made no sense whatsoever. It was just another reality.

'Are we as obsessed as they are?' Green asked.
  'No. This is more important than obsession.'
  'Do we need to choose a path? There are so many.'
  'Yes. Let's try and follow events. What they call history.'
  'According to whom?'
  'Bowie.'
  'Like here. This spot.'
  'Yes. 23 Heddon Street.'

The rain continued to cover the now emptying streets as Blue and Green stood next to the steps outside what had been the entrance to K West Furriers, thinking about this part of their story, their path to Bowie. These were the steps where he had announced the arrival of the alien rock star Ziggy Stardust and the Spiders from Mars. A super-star arrival with a B-movie name. All the experiments from the past with their music hall vernacular and chirpy cockney cheekiness were banished into the ether. Bowie's new reality – Ziggy's reality: David Jones was no longer. David Jones had died on these steps. Bowie was no longer kidding. This was it – the big gamble. Adulation was nor-mal in Ziggy's world. Blue and Green shared glimpses of history and allowed themselves to almost float above the street as they trespassed through time and found the corridor that took them to the door that was Heddon Street, 1972.

The sound of the traffic pushing through the rain disappeared, but the fine drizzle remained constant, spraying a delicate gloss on the empty cardboard boxes and tightly parked cars. The voice of a photographer directing banal instructions into the night air was the clearest of sounds. 'More like that, no that, yes, that works, leg up, one leg up, more dynamic, that's it, that's it, that works, yes.'

But all Blue and Green could see was the imprint – the negative of a photograph still cut out, leaving only a blank space. This was where Bowie stood. But he wasn't there, only an outline. He had been removed or hadn't yet arrived in the picture. Or maybe he had already gone. The photographer continued with his gruff directions about the light, about the rain, about the street below his studio, about the hair, about the make-up, about the man, about the alien, about Ziggy Stardust. But Blue and Green couldn't pull the image of Bowie into the outline – it remained stuck in the time-frames they had crossed and Bowie's enigma was never clearer. Only one sentence could be heard falling from his lips: 'I think this works best for me. This is what I want.'

And that was the end of their voyage into Heddon Street's secret history. The rain was the only reminder of where they had just been, their attempt to glimpse the beginning of David Bowie as Ziggy Stardust had gone. Blue and Green looked disappointed. He had made a declaration.

'I wanted to see that.'
'Yes.'
'We need to use more energy.'
'Is it not dangerous?'
'Yes, but…'
'Why are we here?'
'Yes.'

The movement of people coming towards them felt awkward and

anonymous. So many people moving at the same time but with no point of contact.

'Why don't they stop and dance?'

'Why don't they hug and kiss?'

'Why don't they become friends and find something they can share together?'

But the waves of people continued past them with only the occasional glance at the two confused creatures, who were not moving at all but seemed to be standing asleep in the middle of a busy underground train platform. This was life underneath the city, subterranean tunnels pushing people in different directions away from and back to places that were their anchor: these things they called homes.

Green and Blue controlled their tight space and shared their thoughts about this system of bundling people together in a space without any clean oxygen. Oil and damp air clung in black spots all around them – this was the opposite of the gallery spots. There was no fakery here, nothing was theatrical, this was a version of movement that was outdated and corrosive.

Why was movement more important than health and happiness? Again, the systems they were learning seemed contradictory and inelegant. Why underground when overground would have been so much more beautiful? Why hide what everyone wanted to see and share? The exploration of the mass beneath the surface made no sense; it was more difficult and dangerous and would need vast resources to be maintained and modernised.

Is it to do with buildings and land and property and ownership? The currency of thousands of years of poor thinking; asset-driven melancholy.

'Can we help?'

'I don't think we can,' replied Green as a train squealed to a halt and the doors slumped open.

'It's part of how they think.'

'It doesn't make any sense.'

'No.'

'Surely they must know that?'

'I think they must.'
'Will they help themselves?'
'Only when there's nothing left.'
'When it's too late.'
'That's part of their story.'
'And now ours.'

A young couple, male and female, sat opposite them. The visible skin of their arms and neck was covered in tattoos: Celtic crosses next to Arabic slang and ancient names in Gothic script. They were both listening to music and watching the small screens of their mobile phones, oblivious to the rest of the people on the train. The young woman was laughing at something she was watching and nudged her friend to look at her screen. Their lips were both shining with black lipstick and as they laughed together their mouths revealed industrial-scale metalwork. The young man put his arm around the young woman and kissed her neck and gently bit her ear. She pushed him away but he came back for more. This time he kissed her on the mouth. The kiss was long and juddered into a slurpy clumsiness with the disorienting rattle-and-shake movement of the train.

Green and Blue were engrossed as they watched the young couple create a musical beauty amongst the biting metal shrieks of the train and the plumes of chemical oil spots. The indifference and arrogance of love had delivered a surprising reward in an unlikely place. They shared this revival of optimism – the truly magical alchemy of these peculiar people – a quality worth travelling the thousands of years it had taken them to get here.

'But look.'
'Is it them helping themselves?'
'No. Sharing.'
'Down here without real light.'
'Yes.'
'I wonder why darkness is their favoured atmosphere?'
'Maybe they don't understand light.'

'Yes.'

'But we're here.'

'Nobody else wants to look at them.'

'Fear of intimacy.'

'They don't believe in their love.'

'Deep down they do.'

'Inwards.'

'Unable to be outside.'

'What would David Bowie say if he was watching this?'

'He would love it.'

'Yes.'

'They are in all of the songs.'

'Yes.'

'All of the atmosphere.'

'Yes.'

'What would he say to them?'

'Thank you.'

'Yes.'

'Thank you for being alive.'

'Yes.'

The train continued through long dark tunnels and the only sound was the looping, slicing crash of metal on metal and the rapidity of air being sucked and pushed. The kissing couple looked at their devices, acknowledging nothing about the world around them.

An older man holding a guitar case scratched his beard as his gaze wavered between the kissing couple and the strange twins sitting opposite them. He raised his eyebrow in a gesture of what he thought was cool understanding and Blue and Green tried to do the same back to him, forgetting for a moment that they didn't have eyebrows. The musician looked a little glum and had the air of exhaustion that was common amongst these city dwellers, they thought.

'Why are they so tired?'

'Exhausted.'

'Why don't they stop?'

'They don't know how to.'

'No.'

'They have to keep going.'

'Strange.'

'They're scared to stop.'

'Why?'

'Because they will have to start again.'

They continued to watch the people getting on and off the train: old and young, black, brown, white, pink and red. They knew that each of them had a story; some didn't know how to tell it and others knew only that it defined them, it was all they were interested in. Their life was all about finding a way to tell their story.

'I like them.'

'Me too.'

'They're all lost.'

'Yes.'

'Are they pessimists or optimists?'

'They want to be happy.'

'Yes.'

'But don't know how to be.'

'But everything around them is telling them.'

'How to be happy?'

'Yes.'

'Stuff.'

'Success.'

'Is that how they measure it?'

'We need to ask.'

'Hammersmith next.'

'Yes.'

Cars whizzed by in the direction of Heathrow airport on the Hammersmith flyover. The acoustic ring rose and fell onto a murky concrete walkway that shouldered the underground train station and shopping mall. They could see people hanging around in the sodium splash from the overhead lights. All kinds of small dramas were unfolding around them but they kept their attention on the building directly ahead of them, the Hammersmith Apollo. Formerly known as the Hammersmith Odeon, this was the world-renowned venue for live acts ranging from bands to comedians. The latter seemed to have taken the place over as a home for celebrity comedians with their own TV shows, comedians they had watched recently – they had been left confused by what comedy actually meant. But this was not why they had come into the dull thud of West London. They had come because this was where Ziggy Stardust died.

There was no event happening at the venue on the night they stood outside, silently focused on the building's enormous history. Their concentration made them oblivious to the cars and people that moved around them. On closer inspection passers-by may have noticed the veins pulsating in their necks up to their cheekbones. They would have seen colour vibrate blue in one of them and green in the other. They would have seen their hands gripped together and how their eyes became grey, black then either blue or green. They were a lantern of glowing tones that created a beautiful warmth on a cold street. They closed their eyes for a final concentrated push that would take them to the same West London spot but this time in 1973.

The murky sodium light was re-engaged with a jagged, brightly lit Hammersmith Odeon. Young women hugged and laughed together and their male counterparts stood tall in platform boots, mascara and spiky-topped hair. The young men retained a sense of their masculinity in their fearless glare at the watching world. The young women didn't suffer any testosterone-laced pressure but needed to feel that their Ziggy-influenced ensembles were standing up to the competition.

Blue and Green stood amongst them and felt the febrile tension of anticipation and the excitement of shared identity. This was the David Bowie Fan Club – and they were part of it.

They held on to the moment although it came in energy bursts and almost faded back into the empty street that they still stood in. In slices and unprovoked cuts, their journey into the venue became a series of flashes and still images. People moved then stopped as if on the timeline of a film editor's machine.

Blue and Green moved around the stillness – the people around them were breathing or at least their blood continued to flow but their movement was restricted to a thousandth of what it should have been. It was like being in a sculpture museum; figurative and life-like figures stuck in time, frozen to the spot but remarkably still alive. And then, just as quickly as the Bowie fans had stopped, here they were moving again at normal speed and as alive as the atmosphere around them.

They followed an excitable group of teenage girls into the main auditorium. The lights were being lowered and a man walked onto the stage and sat at a piano. The noise dimmed with the lights to a reverential hush and the tension mixed with the sheer physical mush of the audience to create a blanket of whispers, nervous titters and short breaths exhaled into the new heat.

Was it Bowie? Was it him? If not, then who, who, who…? What's going on? Is Bowie about to appear? Is that Ziggy? Is it, is it, is it? The thoughts became breaths then shaped words then whispers that feedback-looped the room and swung around the auditorium and up into the balconies before sliding along the walls and down and round again like a smoke-born snake.

Blue and Green wanted to tell them that no, this was not Bowie. Not Ziggy. This was Mike Garson, the band's pianist. He would play a medley of the tunes that everyone in the room knew. The hits. He would sit there alone and play the hits. And after working out that this was in fact somebody else, not Bowie, they would realise that this was just the beginning.

This was to get them in the mood. Then, just as everyone relaxed into the hits, a collective, meditative swoon swung with the whispers as people began to sing along with Garson's playing. It was vaudeville. It was theatre. It was the fun before the arrival of the messiah.

Blue and Green smiled their beautiful smile and sang along with the piano man, even though nobody could hear them. They concentrated hard to keep themselves present in 1973 in Hammersmith at the Odeon. They worked together as they stood outside the building pushing energy from deep within themselves to create the historic tableau. They couldn't leave now. Not before the arrival of Bowie. Ziggy.

This was why they had come. To understand. Nothing existed like this in their world: fakery, seriousness, abstraction, fun. This was fun. This was the strange race regressing into their innocence and engaging with a caprice that in later life becomes a forbidden fruit.

This was a cry from them that they had an identity and never wanted to grow old like their young parents. This was a cry that they would never die; that Pop was eternal and their loving chalice brimmed with hope that beamed from within.

Blue and Green could feel the surge of a sexually motivated physical collision amongst the audience. They could feel the confusion and the sudden understanding that they were no longer alienated – that there were others who felt the same way, felt the same things. It was a wondrous event that shook West London but in reality shook the world.

The room staggered into a juddering forward movement. At times the whole space almost faded into blackness but would then snap back into real time, only to get stuck in a single frame of time-travel reality. The stage had gone from being lit by a single spotlight on the piano of Mike Garson to total darkness. He was coming. Ziggy was about to enter. Bowie was here.

An audio earthquake boomed in the shape of the Walter Carlos theme for the Stanley Kubrick film of *A Clockwork Orange*. The boom shuffled along the floor, the walls, the roof; it rippled up through the audience's legs and arms and pushed the skin on their faces back as if caught in a ferocious wind machine. It spun around the Odeon at a fraction of its original speed – there was no music, no percussion, no tunes – only the whoosh and sizzle of war sounding torment.

Green and Blue carefully navigated their way through the still image in front of them with its slow, slipping sound. Arms were aloft, girls hugged, boys kissed, poets danced and young philosophers were becoming serious. A flash of light indicated movement and sure enough people made slight gestures, breaking their frozen, photographic lifelessness into a sharp mobility. But just as quickly as there was a light movement, the people in front of them were stuck again. The atmosphere, which was sparkling and celebratory, faded into a milky sepia tint, but Blue and Green pushed for more of their energy than ever before to keep these jubilant movements alive.

He was coming. Ziggy was coming. Bowie was here.

The band, the Spiders from Mars, stood under the lights armed with their instruments in silhouette, presenting a stroboscopic apocalypse and churned a soul-searching riff, a thumping grind that barked into the auditorium.

And then, there he was: Ziggy, Bowie, Jones. Already, Aladdin Sane.

It was triumphant, messianic, unashamedly sexual and it was right there in front of them. Bowie, no, Ziggy moved at different speeds – super-slow, then quick, then at real-time cinematic frame speed. They stood directly in front of him below the stage. Security guards looked anxiously at the screaming horde of liberated teenage angst moving towards them. Blue and Green stood below Bowie, looking up at him. He wasn't Ziggy, they were too close, he was Bowie. He was taller, thinner and even more beautiful than they had imagined. He was a sphinx, an ancient storyteller, a philosopher and, like them, an alien. They couldn't maintain their real-time connection so words and music sprawled like a whirlwind in the middle of the room but this time it didn't matter. There would be other events, other opportunities and they would be better prepared. They would need to rest for longer.

Above them, Bowie lifted his arm as he held the microphone stand and pushed his hip forward with camp arrogance and looked down into the worshipping crowd. He focused his changing eyes on the two creatures who had broken through the security line and who were smiling joyously back at him. He held their stare, knowing that he had met them somewhere before.

It didn't take him long to remember seeing the same two creatures outside his Brixton home as a small boy. It was the same two wondrous beauties who shared their magical smile with him as if they were the only people in the room – and, for that moment, they were. He put out his hands towards them, beckoning them closer but the slow-motion action staggered to a single frozen frame. A photograph from Hammersmith Odeon in 1973.

People would ask: who was he reaching out to? what was he thinking? was it part of the unfolding drama? who was he looking at with such fear and hunger? It would be interpreted as his audience. As his lovers: the David Bowie Fan Club. And in so many different ways they would all be correct.

The image began to slowly fade in front of them but they were joyful. There he was, there they were: united in love. This was the currency they had believed in, the one that had brought them here. The search for one person's history, a person they had chosen to believe in beyond all others, the search for the meaning of love.

They were aware of the wars, the violence, the inhumanity of a wretched species. But they were also aware that this same wretched species could show endless compassion and love. They chose not to look at the dark side, the cruelty, the hatred, the incoherent systems they called society. They chose not to look at the denigration of others, the genocide, the religious totalitarianism. None of this was part of their journey and this was by design. Although they knew that they would encounter all of the shadows of the madness that was particular to this planet they had decided to sidestep the horror. This was a world of monsters, but they were not afraid of them.

Bowie sang about monsters, about armageddon and end-of-days apocalypse. His playful mythology was graphic and delightful rather than destructive. It was serious but without any use of intellectual intimidation or snobbery. He was their fun prophet who imagined a world transformed by technology and romance – a world threatened by its own people's tribal sense of mutual destruction. But within that world there was sweetness and youth and understanding and a desire to care. That's what they wanted to touch and understand. That's what they wanted to know more about. To send home. To send home.

There it was, they had shared a thought they had both hidden. They wanted others to understand why they had come here. To

understand what they had found out about these unremarkable people
– that they were in fact remarkable.

They lay next to one another back at the house. The lights were low.
A gentle yellow and white glow moved along the walls and floor. No
sound could be heard. Nothing. No breathing. No rustle of growing
ferns. No buzz even from dimmed lights.

The room engaged the sound of silence, leaving the exhausted couple to gather the lost energy of visiting Ziggy Stardust in 1973. They
slowed their shared thoughts and consumed the information that had
so delighted them in a less frenzied breakdown of all of the most
important elements. Something else had happened, Blue thought.
Something else. Something was wrong.

'I know.' Green agreed.

'I don't think it happened like we thought. I think we got caught
up in the event and missed something.'

'Yes.'

The mathematics of their memory banks engaged the various points
of view that had been so recently recorded. Their exhaustion slowed
the process down. Fluids moved in and around then through and into
them quicker than normal, feeding the tiredness with soundless yet
thrumming transfusions.

When they had returned they were jubilant but knew they had
to switch off and prepare to rest. It was at their most vulnerable
and weakest moment that they were simultaneously disturbed by an
understanding that something else had happened. Something they
had missed. What was it?

Had they been there? Yes. Had they moved around the audience?
Yes. Had they understood the excitement? Yes. And then there he
was: Ziggy. Standing under a spotlight in front of them, breathing
deeply, sucking in the atmosphere of the room, looking out over the
audience. A performance. Then he had looked at them. Stop. Then he
had looked in their direction. Yes. But was he looking at them? Was
it Blue and Green he had recognised? Yes. But then, before the image

froze, he looked over their shoulder at something else. Who? How could he have been distracted at that crucial moment? He recognised them but then saw something else.

The thrumming of the fluids grew in response to their exhaustion. They tried to manoeuvre the scene. They took a recorded still from Hammersmith Odeon in 1973 and attempted to shift the point of view so they would have the same sight line as Ziggy. The memory became a plate which they were burned onto – a metallic sizzle corrupted and burned the image into near-destruction but they had managed to turn it around. It was incalculable how quickly the image was created and it had already begun to decay. They gathered one small section of the crowd as the image dissolved: young women screaming; young men smiling. This was all that the yellow spray from the spotlight revealed, beyond that was only darkness. Silhouettes. Shapes. No movement.

But they both knew that something was there. Somebody. They couldn't hold on to the image, their strength depleted through the sheer willing of moving through the memory of time. The shadows and shapes disappeared with the screaming fans. The memory was destroyed in recall and would never be available to them again. But they knew that something was there in the darkness of the now-faded image. Somebody.

They both knew that they needed to rest but couldn't find the appetite for their version of sleep. They lay together, eyes wide open, consciously slowing down the movement of fluid, calming the air in the room until not a spectre of dust remained. They emptied the less important memories of their evening in 1973, freeing the organic memory fluids back to a colour that was safer, less dehydrated and thin. If there was an anxiety present then it was sidelined for the moment as the process of rejuvenation and restoration became more important. They knew they had pushed themselves in a way they were unaccustomed to. The joy of the concert at Hammersmith Odeon had overwhelmed them and once again logic became secondary to impulse. They had stayed longer than they had prepared for – a harsh lesson. The maintenance of recreating time was a new experience – they had hoped it might be easier but the sheer weight of exhaustion told them otherwise.

And now something had developed that they could never have prepared for. They looked at one another. They needed to rest and realised they must sleep. It was time to dream.

The city grew out of the ferns and trees. Everything was connected naturally. The trees were 600 metres high. The ferns were shaped in circles and conical tunnels. Green and blue rivers ran through the ground level at a gentle pace then flowed over and around the ferns then up and down the trees. A silver sun was the gravitational pull that shaped this living, breathing planet.

Solar mercury bursts occasionally puffed out of the elegant silver shine of the sun's beauty. The mercury was sucked in and injected into the city's undergrowth. A natural warm glow of light sat like a bubble, consistent and ever present. The spaces between the trees were buildings made of long grass that retained a grey dullness, responding to the light without reflection or creating shadows. There was no darkness in this city – it exuded heat and light, and a warm moisture that had a thermal tingle – almost as if the lines had been drawn from the ground to the sky beyond, which was a deep near-impenetrable black. The trees, the ferns, the rivers, the buildings all moved in unison as if an imaginary musical wind had called their tune.

The sounds were subtle and difficult to locate. They were there, somewhere, but the minor booms and gentle whistles provided no clues as to where they had come from. It was a jungle without a roar – a luscious, mercury-reactive home for subterranean families who worshipped its kindness and immediate response to their needs.

The inhabitants of the planet rested in the underworld darkness illuminated with fissures of silvery light from a river of pierced holes in the ground above. They lay amongst ferns and fluids of blue and green, holding hands or gently touching their fingers against each other's skin.

Nothing seemed to hold the city above – there were no posts, nothing but space, cavernous space that curved like a perfect, never-ending landscape into the distance. There was no uniformity to where people lay together – some groups of two and five and then ten and more, many more. There was a silence and then a long, uniform hush, as a collected breath was taken. Within the hush there was nothing discordant, nothing that got in the way of its musical beauty.

The ferns whispered along with the hush and the fluids rippled the flowing applause of water on stone. The people of the planet lay together with their eyes closed. They waited for the mercury sun to fade so they could look at their beautiful planet without dying.

Their siesta took months before this paradise could be touched again. But months meant nothing in seasons that lasted a thousand years. They would never understand the shortage of time that caused all of Earth's anxieties. They had no measure of time. There was no need.

In the middle of a group lay a glowing couple. Liquid transfusions poured through the ferns and in and out of each of them with an immeasurable sigh. They held hands and smiled as they imagined a planet so far away that they would need to move through universes and galaxies to get there but it would be worth the risk. They had first heard the music from the crashed satellite.

The news was difficult to understand, the peoples and their customs even stranger and their version of food and movement was so primitive that they began to wonder if they could possibly really exist, but then… But then they had heard the music of David Bowie and it all made sense. Not the wars, not the religion and starvation and cruelty; not the humour, the fashion, the aspirations and disappointments; not the correspondence, the books, the ideas and the breakthroughs; not the emperors, the kings and queens, the generals and the rebels; not the drama, the science, the philosophy and the philanthropy.

No, none of these – this mixture of achievement and destruction was all staggeringly digested and understood in minutes. None of it left a mark on them like the sound of Bowie. It didn't make sense. Their reaction had been instant and impulsive. This was a response they had not known they were capable of making. The music and the words touched them. They could not explain it. It felt like sex and an eternity of foolishness that they had evolved into a gentle communication. It was love.

A rotating, broken satellite came crashing out of the solid black sky with burning collapsing metallic plates sparking and igniting as it eventually became a fireball. It slammed into the trees and bounced a dance all the way to the bottom and was then punched up into the air by one of the rivers and thrown against the ferns, which gathered together and catapulted the satellite onto rough, ash-coloured ground. Its parts were torn to pieces but its cargo remained safe – an audio-visual box showing a series of looped images from Earth.

The images buzzed and clicked as the Writer introduced imaginary recipients to how Earth worked as a collision of culture and science that attempted to eliminate stupidity but had lost the battle. He talked of tribes, unhappiness, meaningless contributions and reductive societies driven by futile systems such as capitalism and the new communism alongside religious fascism and totalitarian atheism. Each branch sprang another as his stream-of-consciousness essay evaporated into nothing other than language.

Language here on this new planet held no value and was not important for the inhabitants to understand their purpose, which was to live. As the Writer ended his essay to other universes, a compendium of photography showed the planet in static beauty; theatrical colours and shapes which looked like musical notation to the new people looking on and trying hard to understand what it all meant. A montage of images showed Earth's version of success.

The music that accompanied the images made no sense to the new viewer.

'Fame' by Bowie slammed Blue and Green in the stomach.

They had listened to the Writer talk about the ribald overuse of irony as a way to detach from a world that had become closed. So, this was irony – they deciphered and understood, but again irony seemed so primitive – surely 'Fame' by Bowie wasn't irony, it was a hymn to emptiness?

These people hated the ritual of religion and its codes but used its tools to spread their unhappy message. Fame. Others around them dismissed the message, the image and the song but Blue and Green were touched. Something moved inside them, something rich and delicate and sensual. They had discovered an inexplicable human trait: fandom. Stupid, innocent and beautiful. A love pact made through an adoration of creativity. It seemed to Blue and Green that there was some kind of transaction at play – you do something, I like it, it means something special to me. Love: the only religion that worked on this strange blue planet.

They watched the film again. The images flickered into action then slowed down. The history of Earth from what they thought was the Big Bang through their evolution from stardust to water and then the first signs of life. The film quickly moved into the human part of the story as if the rest of it was less important. Again, the film staggered through different frame rates as it slowed down, stopped and then started up again. The beginnings of man in Africa, the Chinese dynasties, the pre-Columbian tribes of South America and then the beginning of Europe. The film moved slowly through the Greeks and Romans, barely touching the Egyptians or Assyrians. Kings and conquerors: voices of reason, voices of dissent.

New ideas: from Charlemagne to Gutenberg and from what was left of the holy Roman Empire to 16th century Florence and Machiavelli – somehow, history was neatly joined nose to tail in a seamless move from chaos to order then back to chaos.

These were the people of chaos. The people who mistook survival for a reason for living. How could that be enough? Blue and Green gasped for a moment at the sheer weight of this thought. The ferns shimmered, the fluids quickened but nobody seemed to notice that their dreamscape and shared thoughts had caused them to think in a way they had never done before: negatively. Were these people lost? Hopeless? Loveless? But again, they thought of Bowie and the enchantment returned. It was at this moment that they knew that they would have to understand this world – not through the march of history but through one person, through his creativity. That's what these people did best – maybe better than us, they thought, maybe we can learn something: how to be creative. 'What does that mean?' they shared. 'What does it mean?'

The images continued to flicker on and off, and their people had grown less and less interested in this message from another universe. Some began to share ideas on the satellite's incredible journey. They reached the conclusion that it could have taken a thousand years in planet Earth time or as little as a few years if it had bounced its way through one entry point and was then sucked into another. Nobody seemed to consider them worth a visit.

A few listened again to the Writer's disenchanted voice describing a dying pointless world. The general feeling was that they were too primitive and weren't worth it. Blue and Green continued to focus on his dry monotony as they shared a plan in which the Writer's thoughts and words might be useful.

As 2015 slowly came to an end, the citizens of London walked around the streets looking at their mobile phones, bumping into one another and walking in front of speeding bicycles as they raced taxis, buses and cars in an attempt to stay alive. Social media made everyone relevant and at the same time misunderstood what relevance was. News became a headline and information was cheap and fraudulent, as it was now the currency of people in a hurry to be part of the great nothing. There were no pauses in people's lives. They read a few lines on Twitter and Facebook, connecting with opinions and links to suggested pop antiquity, which rolled on and on in an unstoppable inferno of what would become the new knowledge. The sheer weight of information, in small neat slices that led to more opinions and more people, had prevented the possibility of silence and solitude ever being part of people's lives again. But that in fact, thought Blue and Green, was the strange paradox. The somnambulistic relationship these new-knowledge people had with their devices was an attempt to defy the great modern malaise, loneliness.

Blue and Green had tried to connect with the Writer through social media but soon realised that the thought professor had turned his back on this wasteland of flushed egos and tipping-point insanity. Like the master, Nietzsche, he had turned his back on the 'modern' world. As people searched for relevance, they had blindly allowed their sense of story and words to fold into a clumsy urban haiku that was, in fact, anti-creativity. Blue and Green regarded the Writer's decision to search for silence as decadent: he had ploughed his route in a completely different direction to the great continuum, although he continued to observe this mass movement of incendiary loneliness destroy itself from within. Like a character from a Huysmans fin de siècle novel, he had felt obliged to freeze-frame the gluttonous hordes of reality as they cannibalised creativity in a series of cultural ram raids. There was nowhere for him to retreat to and hide other than the imagination: comedy, satire and graceless laughter became the excesses of a drowning man.

He was walking but they couldn't find out where. In the pyschogeographic realm it might have been somewhere in London's Thames Valley or the jutting Kent coastline or even the bleak Saddleworth Moor, with its haunting, mystical landscape and barbarism. Or was it a remote, uninhabited island off the coast of north-west Scotland, reachable only by a small boat? They couldn't be sure and discussed whether they should imagine themselves into his walk or wait for his return. They looked at Skype as a way to talk with and see him at the same time, but the only writer available was not the one they were after. The Skype writer, a stand-up comedian, was keen to befriend them but they had taken the view that comedy was full of hate and couldn't be trusted. Their decision was random in way that they had never tried before. They employed a Bowie-style automatic line of questioning which they sent into the great cavernous ether of social media in the hope that a connection could be made or that he might even answer their questions:

Question 1: Do you prefer illusion to reality?

Question 2: Is artifice the mark of human genius?

Question 3: What is imagination?

Question 4: Does everyone have an imagination?

Question 5: Please explain what love is.

Question 6: What do you think of David Bowie?

Question 7: Is laughter important?

Question 8: Why are people so violent?

Question 9: Are we all fake?

There was no immediate response, which they had expected, so they took the opportunity to rest and share some thoughts on what their next move should be. Where should they go? New York, Berlin or Los Angeles? They looked at one another and realised that the Writer would never answer their questions as he would see them in the light of mass observation as part of a fan-fetish syndrome that was both adolescent and silly in a bone-numbing kind of way. There was no room for fandom in the world of the graceless: blind faith, cult-love, slow beginnings, unquestioned devotion, pop-scions, lost children, ersatz disciples. And the lists that humans love to guide them would grow and grow in the temple of Self in a denunciation of their votary of David Bowie.

They also knew that they had begun to understand the answers to all of the questions they had sent him. They no longer needed guidance. They had removed themselves from the story for a moment and tried to understand something that didn't matter – the reason why humans did what they did. It just didn't matter. What was important was that what they did do was inexplicable and beautiful and deranged and simple and complicated – that's what was important, not what would always come later, the denunciation and overbearing essay. The moment, they decided, was more rewarding than history's recalibration of the truth – that was why they had to be there, be in amongst Bowie and the people around him: the smells, the colours, the lives and the dramas. They needed to be in the moment.

The next part of their journey would of course have to be Los

Angeles, as that was where the next important part of the Bowie story took place. They didn't need to read books on Bowie's life in LA – they were imagined copies of a life, doomed essays of qualification. No, they needed more than that. They needed presence. Truth. A world of Anti-History.

1 January 2016

They had wandered away from the busy streets and now stood by the river watching fireworks explode in cascading colours of gentle violence. Their hosts were celebrating the end of 2015 and the beginning of a New Year. What was it, they thought, the end or the beginning? Measurement was ridiculous, especially of time. It seemed again another evocation of ritual and their new favourite comedy word, structure. People around them hugged and kissed to celebrate this peculiar junction in measured time. They drank from bottles and cans, sharing toxins and bacteria as London's great river sped past with an anonymous grace. The alcohol raised emotions with a blunt stupidity but nobody seemed to care. It was a time to cry and laugh, not at the absurdity but at the excuse for connection.

A date. A simple date reduced the people around them to a helpless drunken sentimental mass of confusion and hope, the two contrary products of alcohol's immediate effect. It was hysterical and oddly beautiful. Human beings anchored by crisis, forgetting who they were, finding each other – even for the briefest of moments.

Maybe they are celebrating the fact that they are still alive. 'A reaction to their mortality,' shared Green.

'Yes,' thought Blue, 'it's a space in time when they're not afraid.'

More fireworks exploded above them like dead stars fading into darkness after a wistful illumination. London was at peace, although it sounded as if it were at war. Its people worshipped a measurement in time as an orgy of goodwill punched through the damp air. Everyone had a song: a favourite song. Nobody was challenged with the usual tribal impatience. Tonight everyone was equal. Together. And the songs kept coming. They both knew that their time in London was coming to an end.

'Before we go,' thought Green, 'can we listen to how they dream? Choose one of them and follow their story.'

'Why don't we follow the Writer's dreams? We can ask him about LA. What we should expect. What to look for. What we will need to do to connect with Bowie.'

They decided on the banks of the Thames to sleep with the Writer. Share his dreams together. Inhabit his dream. His dream world. His paradise. They would never meet him but they could meet his dreams.

In his dream, the Writer's car floated above the ground and set down again to manoeuvre around the gridlocked traffic. The noise from downstairs in his home in London as his children and their friends celebrated the entry into 2016 funnelled and coughed into his dream. But the tinny din wasn't enough to wake him and his two companions, Blue and Green.

'What do you want?' he asked them.

'To guide your dreams to Bowie,' they replied together in perfect synchronicity.

'Why Bowie?'

'It's the choice we made.'

'It's not a bad choice. Bowie is important. It's his birthday soon. When you meet him remember to wish him happy birthday. People like that. I do. I think I do.'

'You said he was important. Why?'

'He caught the death of feeling. Understood it. Understood how to fake it. Feeling. Learned how to act it. Be it.'

'Is that creativity?'

'That's exactly what creativity is. Bowie had an eclipsing effect on pop culture. He's baffling and indiscreet but frighteningly connected to the masses. Not bad for a South London dystopian-romantic. But look at this place. The land he once lived in.'

'We know, that's why we're here.'

'But it was a long time ago he was in LA. The 1970s. The era of *Crash* and the Thin White Duke.'

'*Crash* by J.G. Ballard. He does for you what Bowie does for us. Yes?'

'Well, it's mutually exclusive. Look, I like you. But I think you should get out of my dream. I don't take drugs any more. My dreams are more sensual – not as morbid as people think.'

'No. Not morbid. But we want the truth about LA – explain the myth.'

'Help you understand the horror.'

'The horror?'

'This is paradise. An evil one.'

'Is this what they mean by Hell?'

Yes, this is another version of Hell. Man-made, built through corruption and for the corrupt. It's a desert utopia by the sea. Paradise. But an evil one. It goes on forever. There is no convergence. Europe is behind us. Gone. The old world. Freeways like an art installation. Freeways that have nothing to do with freedom. Never-ending. All the way into the lightless desert, wherever that is. All I can see is light. Lights. Neon. Will the lights ever go out here? Never. Impossible. The lights represent people's fear. The terror utopia. Strong, individual and violent. Or strange, lost and psychotic. Can you see the buildings? Like forgeries of histories that never existed in the first place. Inside a car. Safe. Air-conditioning. No conversation. No polite imperialism. Everything is dangerous. Everything is new. This is the city of the smile. The joyless smile. But these are snapshots. You need more than that. I'm trying to describe something that is real but is in fact a simulation. This is how reality imitates reality. The conduit. The codes. The movement. The connections. But it's all a hologram. We mustn't get out of this car. Inside this car is real. Outside is imagined. In that direction is the movie industry and in the other direction is the missile industry. Creativity and destruction next door to one another. But which is which – do the missiles create and the movies destroy? It's a catastrophe. And now that we're here we must never leave the car. But it's the lights. The lights. Lights. Everywhere. Terror of the darkness. Luminescent.

Burning. Yellows. Reds. Greens. White. Mostly white light. Eye-singeing white light. Star-gazing white. Eternal. White. White. White. White heat. Sunshine for darkness. This is the land of freedom. But for whom? Who? Me? The liberated? Is it the 1%? This is not a paradise.

What do people share here? Emptiness? Indifference? Ennui? What would Huxley think of his New Age dream space now? How would his meta-narrative divulge the cruel truths, the social viciousness of a city in the midst of a civil war that nobody seems to want to talk about?

Is this the brave new world?

Think of what you left behind – Europe. Old Europe, and here you are in the promised land. How can you make sense of it – all this modernity, this forgery. It's all perfectly fake.

'Maybe you should learn to love it. Not me. I prefer to imagine it. Fake the faker, and all that. Do you normally get so close as this when you enter people's dreams? I mean physically. I'm not complaining. I like my erotic dreams as much as the next man or woman. But this? The three of us. It's very Bowie.'

'In what way?'

'Well, theatrical erotica, talking in absurdities in this sandwich. Don't misunderstand me: I'm willing to have dream sex with you both as we travel through and over LA together – it's a wonderful way to start a new year but maybe the anonymous part is just too suburban. Maybe I need to know something about you other than your love of Bowie.'

'We're not from here.'

'But neither am I.'

'Oh, we don't mean that, we mean we are not from this planet.'

'That would have been acceptable in the 1970s. But not now. We're all from somewhere now. That's the true legacy of neo-liberalism: nationalism. It's made us all come from somewhere. And that's here.'

'But not us. We're not from here. We're from somewhere. But not here. Look up there. Into the hills, beyond the lights. Up into the sky. The darkness. We're from there.'

'Jim Ballard would have loved to hear about this dream. Me. Fucked by aliens on Sunset Boulevard as they searched for the Thin White Duke. Sucked and sodomised outside Book Soup in a bizarre floating taxi or limousine or boat or plane or even missile. Where were we? Are we? I need love. It's a beautiful quality. I'm human.'

'You are.'

'I was afraid I might not be.'

'No. You are. A beautiful human.'

The Writer looked at his new lovers, knowing that his erotic LA dream was coming to an end. He had wanted to warn them about the world they were entering but couldn't recall if he had mentioned the dangers they faced.

'Be careful of this place,' he whispered. 'Be very careful. It's the home of fear. Twenty-four hours a day. Terror. Angst. Violence. It sells joy and pleasure but feels none. Someone called it the home of narcissistic refraction.'

'Yes.'

'A perfect home for the Thin White Duke.'

'We sent you some questions. But I don't think we need any of the answers. Not today, which in your time is 1 January 2016. Happy New Year. The party downstairs is waking you up and we're losing you. We will remain in LA won't we?'

'Yes. We'll take a taxi to Bowie.'

'You're a nice man, much nicer in your dreams than on the television.'

'Yes. You're a nice man and you're surrounded with love.'

'And you helped us understand more about Bowie and this terrible place Los Angeles.'

The Writer woke in his South London home and listened to the songs being sung downstairs by his children and their friends celebrating the arrival of 2016. They sang 'Starman' by Bowie. He couldn't recall having ever heard them sing it before but it sounded good. The perfect way to celebrate the New Year. Next to him his wife slept peacefully. He kissed her cheek and thought about what his two friends had told him about being surrounded by love. He smiled as he started to hum the tune to 'Starman'.

I hope they'll be OK out there in the home of fear. I hope they find Bowie. I hope LA doesn't kill them. I hope I told them to wish Bowie happy birthday. Why am I thinking like this? Hoping. I'm not a hoper. Why am I hoping so much? I remember listening to Bowie under the bedsheets – my own private teenage decadence. My first music hall hero. My first brush with cool. David Bowie. The Man Who Fell to Earth. And now alien Bowie-loving twins who kissed me and then… and then… and then… it's all slipping away but I don't understand why I feel so sad. Why do I feel like crying? Is it the surrounded-by-love thing or does it have something to do with the soundtrack of Bowie bashing my life into shape? Childhood, nostalgia, optimism, hope.

There I go again with the hoping shit. I need to wake up. It's 2016.

Cars were floating down Sunset Boulevard with their roofs down, people were honking horns and bawling Happy New Year messages to one another from car to car. Neon spilled over the warm pavements, creating a spider's web of shadows and graphic images. The cars were all shiny and new – everything looked new in the blue and yellow light. Blue and Green fell from the edge of the Writer's dream and stood outside Book Soup. From inside they could hear music, the gentle drift of Arvo Pärt's 'Fur Alina'.

Inside the bookstore was a world away from the teenage kicks being celebrated on the Strip. Couples whispered through their favourite pages of classic American writing and book-loving loners hid in corners murmuring agreement with the chilling and apocryphal warnings of newly released crime fiction. There was order and calm in a city that had made its money and reputation on being antagonistic and pernicious.

A car stopped in front of the store. A man with sunglasses on and a zipped-up leather bomber jacket looked at Blue and Green standing inside the store.

'She Sells Sanctuary' by The Cult vibrated against the windscreen and leather seats of his black Maserati Ghibli. They recognised him from one of the fun but silly sci-fi films they had watched in their home in London. He was a famous actor, and he was on his own, standing outside Book Soup as the sound of people celebrating New Year sped past him. They wondered for a moment if he might be in a film and if this was a scene being played out in front of them, and maybe they were even in it. They looked around for cameras but there were only cars, speeding in both directions. They caught a glimpse of the actor's thoughts as words fell from his mouth inside bubbles in slow motion. The actor thought, 'I'm going to a party, do you want to come?' But instead of asking this he said, 'Is the store open?' The words floated above him inside the bubbles. Shaped words. Disappearing into the night sky. Blue and Green nodded.

'Strange,' he said, 'that it's open, you know what I mean?' But they could only shake their heads, not knowing what was strange about the store being open.

They considered that these words bubbling from his mouth might be scripted, the camera hidden, and the whole sequence a special effect. They waited for the actor to ask something else but he just sat in the car looking at them. 'Beautiful freaks,' he thought, as The Cult's anthem punched and soared into LA's invisible starlight.

'We've come to meet David Bowie,' said Blue.

'Good luck,' said the actor. 'Tell him hello from me.'

'Do you know him?'

The actor smiled at the two beautiful Bowie fans standing outside Book Soup.

Did I know him? Have I met him? On the circuit, at a party, a premiere, a dinner, a charity event? Did we laugh together? Was he with his beautiful wife? I think we met. I should remember. It's David Bowie. Iman. How come I can't find a woman like her? Someone who might love me. I should get over to New York to see his musical... *Lazarus*? That's it. *Lazarus*. Those two twin alien things are still standing there looking at me. They know who I am. They'll come with me tonight, if I ask them. Maybe they'll love me like they love Bowie. Are they listening to what I'm thinking? Why would I think that? But they're smiling at me. The two of them. I can't even tell if they're male or female. Does it matter? Maybe I'm gay. Damn, I've never really considered it but actually I might be. Maybe that would explain everything. It's 2016 and I'm sitting in my car trying to pick up identical male or female twins. Is that what the year ahead holds for me? This. Why is my life not more like that Terence Malick movie I was in? Profound. Poetic. Deep. I had substance in that story.

People said it was spiritual. But no. No. No, it was a movie. With a Star. Me. But I liked it, especially all that looking out to sea and touching. I did a lot of touching in that movie.

Spiritual touching. Maybe that's what it meant. I was a healer. I was healed. I'm a heel. Jeez, how long have I been sitting here? I don't know. They're still looking at me. How long have I been here? Shall I ask them to come with me? They look naive. Sweet. Innocent. If I don't, someone else will, a monster maybe. I'm not a monster. I've been called one. My agent. My ex-agent thinks that I'm a monster. I'm a star. Stars are whatever people want them to be, so maybe to some people I am a monster. I was listening to music but nothing is coming out of the speakers. Maybe I should go into the bookstore and buy some books. People still do that. They actually go into shops and buy stuff rather than ordering it online. Why? Maybe shopping has something to do with being lonely. Am I lonely? I think I might be. Maybe I'm gay and lonely – or lonely because I'm gay. Maybe I'm terrified of coming out. Do gay leads get to play sci-fi heroes? I need to think that one through. Has Hugh Grant ever made a sci-fi movie? I don't think so. I mean, he's gay – right? I mean he's posh English, they all dabble I was told. Who cares? But I don't think Hugh Grant has ever done sci-fi. I met him at a party, over dinner, maybe a premiere or charity event. I met him or was it David Bowie? Bowie's not gay. I mean his wife is wow. That's no smokescreen. That's love. Not like movie-love but love-love. Bowie's done sci-fi. Not like cowboy sci-fi, more of a smart, thoughtful kind of thing. He's good. I liked him in that vampire flick with the French actress and Susan Sarandon – classy lesbian scenes. If I was a woman I would be a lesbian for sure. That would be nice. Why can't I find someone like Susan Sarandon? Am I losing my looks? No, I don't think so. Women want me. I think men want me too. But I'm not interested in the people who want me. I want to know the people who don't want me. For me, that's more important. The twins are still there, watching me. It's creeping me out now. They know who I am. They want me. Sorry kids, not interested. I gotta go. I mean fuck this place, and fuck bookstores. This is LA. And I'm a star. A movie star.

He gunned his Maserati, recycled 'She Sells Sanctuary' and waved goodbye to the two strangers. In his mind they represented everything he loved about LA: disconnection, dislocation, animation. It all meant something and nothing and he was at the heart of it all.

That's why he loved it. That's why he lived here. This was his reality.

Everything he did was a movie scene. And he was in it, every one, every scene. He was the star. Maybe he should have offered them a part in his film. This film where the camera never stopped turning. They would have liked that. Being in his film. His life. Alongside him. With him. Next to him. 'Maybe I'll go back later and see if they're still hanging around the bookstore. But for the moment – this is my car. My night. My city. My world. My movie.'

As the car pulled away it revealed a giant digital billboard on the other side of the road that displayed the image of an actor in a spacesuit holding his helmet and looking worried. Looking afraid. It was the same actor as the man in the car – the famous actor in the Maserati, who had now disappeared into the night's celebrations. He had been with them for a brief moment but they understood he might be better than the teeth actors; he might have had more to offer before he came to this city. But now it was only shiny cars and perfect teeth. His Englishness was gone forever.

An LA chill ran through the air, pushing palm leaves and forcing cars to close their roofs. Blue and Green were beginning to feel the early bite of the Writer's warning. But it was too late now. They were here for a reason and they knew they had no choice, they had to see it through.

They entered Book Soup to the sound of 'Spiegel im Spiegel' by Arvo Pärt, which washed the room with anticipatory sadness, a need for nothing to happen, but a greater need for everything to stay the same. Untouched. Apart from the euphonious beauty of the cello and piano, the store felt silent, although people sat around looking at books of photography or reading extracts from magazines and making choices of what to buy and what to leave behind. For all the warmth of the music, the illusion of interconnectivity was absent. The room, like the music, was passive but that's not how the readers were thinking. Something muddy and sticky like contaminated water lay just beneath the surface of their thoughts. Was it violence? The people in the store obviously chose creativity rather than the garrulous scrum of celebration; this was their way to bring in the New Year. But there was something else going on. Something terrifying and nihilistic. Blue and Green listened to a young heavily bearded man read to his female friend a review of a movie. The review was cruel and personal and would maybe destroy the career of the writer and director. The man whispered the lines through a perpetual smile and the words seemed to arouse a beatific defence in the woman – the man's pleasure in the creative suffocation of the movie failed to connect with her. She told the man that he was simply jealous, full of envy, dismayed by an exercise in hurt, afraid to admit empathy. The man coughed a laugh born in LA that would forever be unable to travel and hustled a wind-strewn 'fuck you' into the night.

A woman stood alone at the end of a passageway, wearing black jeans and a black St Pauli T-shirt. Her black hair was cut short in a bob and her thick lips were painted shiny black, framing her snow-white teeth. She flicked through a book on LA architecture: dream homes in Brentwood, townhouses in Santa Monica, space ships in Malibu, glass towers in Century City, condominiums in Venice. The pages moved on to the Towell Library in Westwood, Rodeo Drive in Beverly Hills, Aloha in Wilshire, a Hollywood duplex, Loyola Law School. She closed the book and tried to remember all of the buildings she had noted but nothing came. She couldn't remember any of them, not even that last page she had looked at. All of the names of the architects had disappeared. Nothing. She put the book down and looked at a list handwritten on a board of the top ten choices of the week from the Book Soup staff. She whispered the names of each book then closed her eyes. She did the same again and then tried to read the list back to herself with her eyes still closed, but nothing came. Blue and Green listened to her frustration. She wanted to sound intelligent. She wanted to have something to say. To talk about. To be part of contemporary culture. To have knowledge. But her attempts were futile. It wasn't working. What will I say?

What will I talk about? Who will want to listen to me? What do I know about? I need to know things. Lists of things. I want people to like me. To be impressed by me. The young woman looked out onto Sunset and at the billboard across the street. The actor in the space suit seemed to be looking straight back at her. She wanted to know him. To talk to him. She wanted to impress him with her knowledge of things. The things she knows.

What is this music that's playing? Maybe I can buy it as a gift for the actor – maybe that will be the key that changes everything. Yes. This music. This piece of music. As the actor in the space suit looked back at her from the billboard, she smiled, thinking that the music was a sign. I'm being told, she thought, that this is a sign. I need to call my agent. Tell them the good news. About the sign. It's good. I need to get a manager. Someone who understands me. Realises my potential. I need billboards. They're coming. I can feel it. Billboards. They're coming. I've got to get out of here. All of these books. Words. How am I supposed to remember all of this? It's not about the books, it's about the music. That sounds good. I'll use that again. How did it go? It's not the music – it's books. No. I need to go. As she turned to leave, she faced Blue and Green. They smiled at her, the girl looking for a sign, who couldn't remember the lists. Meaningless lists.

'Hello,' said Green.

'Hi,' the girl replied. 'Nice work.'

'What do you mean?' asked Blue.

'Your face. Both of you. Lips. Eyes. Cheeks. It's great. Really great. Who did it? But you need to get some tits. They love tits here. You're from New York, right? Nobody has tits in New York but here you need tits. Anyway, you look great. Amazing job. My agent would love you. But hey, Happy New Year and all that shit, right... Hey, you know what this music is?'

'Arvo Pärt.'

'What?'

'It's called "Spiegel im Spiegel".'

'Whatever, it's a sign.'

'A sign?'

'You know. That this year... Well, you know, this year's going to be a good year.'

'Was last year not so good?'

'You haven't been here long, have you?'

'No.'

'Be careful. This is a nasty place. Full of nasty people but if you want to be a star – you know, make it – then it's the only place. Arvo Pärt, you say?'

'Yes,' they answered together.

'You're like... kind of odd, cute though, I think you can make it here. I can feel it. Anyway, thank you.'

They watched the young woman leave Book Soup in search of the music that would fulfil her hopes of becoming a star in the nasty city. Loud bangs from the street slipped into the store as the door opened. Fireworks or gunfire. Was this, the first day of 2016, a day of civil unrest – vengeance – gang warfare – militia groups – the army taking control – LAPD face to face with unhappy disenfranchised black men and women? These were some of the fast-flowing comments piercing through the store from the crime department as students from Chapman discussed their lecturer Ryan Gattis's new novel *All Involved*. They chose to read random sections to one another, but Blue and Green could pick up the storyline of anarchy and revenge as LA fell into a nihilistic explosion of rioting and looting.

Characters Ernesto Vera, L'il Creeper, Termite, Gloria Rubio and Anthony Smiljanic all smashed into the same orbit over a six-day period of hysteria and ultra-violence. The students tried to hook into the vernacular bit of the language employed by Gattis but they were way out of their depth and bristled with discomfort as they realised that Blue and Green were listening. This was their private 2016 entry-point party – and these fashionistas were not invited. What were they? European? Russian? New York, maybe? They were paying homage to their teacher and these two oddballs were not welcome – they were getting in the way of their cellphone filming of each reading, each performance.

Blue and Green moved to another aisle but continued to listen to a stream-of-consciousness violence that felt painfully real. Heavy armour. Sadistic savagery. A delineation of fearlessness and terror erupting like volcanoes in parking lots and back streets. The dream.

The sign. God. Vendettas and loveless children playing with death. Gattis's apocalyptic view of LA was mesmerising and left Blue and Green experiencing new sensations. Was this fear? Was this foreboding? Outside, the digital billboard had changed from the actor in the space suit to an illuminated graphic which read: DISAPPEAR HERE.

Behind Blue and Green a young man in a Kalifornia T-shirt sat on his skateboard reading extracts from *Imperial Bedrooms* by Brett Easton Ellis. Music spilled from his headphones: London Grammar's 'Hey Now' pulled them closer to the young man's thoughts. He was crashing through this elliptical LA noir with a mixture of amazement and glee.

Who are these people in this book? Are they different bits of the writer? It's so violent… shit. The people are so violent. All of them alone. Disconnected. Isolated. Alienated. Asking questions nobody ever answers. Looking for punishment as a way to feel real. Everyone on their cellphones – the illusion of connectivity. A night-time city – when the sun has gone down – they come out to play. All their voices. All saying nothing. Nothing. Nothing much. Getting stoned.

Fucking. They're all so sick and dysfunctional. And rich. So rich. Nobody is interested in anything apart from themselves. Valium. Coke. Heroin. DISAPPEAR HERE. I think I know some of these people. I think I know where they live. How they live. Vapid. Empty. Vacant. People who are not really alive. Only pretending to be. This is LA. It's so violent. People are having their hands chopped off – their skin is being pulled back from their faces. They're being dipped in acid. I know all of them. All these people live here. The brutality. The commerce. Sex. It's scary. No. No, it's not. It's here. He must be getting older. The writer. This is like a documentary about LA. This is how it is. Where's the fun of his book *The Informers*? Where's the Betamax tapes, Culture Club, Jane Fonda workouts, MTV, Duran Duran, *Flashdance*, Kajagoogoo T-shirts, Librium, swimming pools, air conditioning, dope-smoking children, vampires and real-estate executives? And AIDS. It's about AIDS. That's not fun. But it reads like fun. The 1980s. This new one is definitely not fun, it's too real. I know AIDS is real. I know. I know. But the book was fun. All that blood. This is like screenwriters, movie execs, agents, actors, parties and nihilistic violence. Where's the stupidity?

The pre-AIDS stupidity. What happened to LA? Did everyone become serious? Or were they always serious? And shit... look at this, the screenwriter dick called Clay is doing a rewrite of *The Man Who Fell to Earth*. And he lives in Doheny Plaza, practically on top of where Bowie lived in LA. Crazy shit. The Bowie years... man that must have been fun...

Blue and Green shivered together when the connection was made. They stopped listening to the jumbled, stoned book review and nostalgia for stupidity. They were both reminded of why they were here and where they needed to go. Out on the street the billboard had changed to ALIEN ZONE as the young man's music changed to New Order's version of 'Ceremony'. The boy closed the book and watched Blue and Green leave the store. 'Why does nothing ever happen to me?' he thought, as he decided to buy the book. 'Maybe I can make a movie out of this story. Maybe I can be the star, or do the music, or the sets or write the script or maybe...'

'Why had Bowie come to this place?' thought Blue and Green as their arms entwined against the honks and horns of 2016's celebrations along the Strip. Even the fireworks were more demanding than London's as they sprinkled the night sky with a never-ending fizz of gunpowder. 'These people,' shared Green, 'have a built-in neurosis; a cocktail of violence and messianic selfishness. Nothing feels real. We were warned by the Writer. He told us it would be like this.'

'Yes,' Blue replied, 'he did, but we need to know how it helped Bowie. *Young Americans. Station to Station.* How could something so beautiful come out of this horror? It's like they are all in a movie, their own movie. But was Bowie not in his movie when he became of this cityscape?'

'Yes,' agreed Green, 'that's it. This is where Bowie lost his famous sense of humour. This is where he took everything too seriously, even himself. Especially himself.'

Green held Blue's arm even tighter as more explosions wrecked the starlight above them and framed the buildings with a sharp and sinister backlight. Faces swung out of bars and side streets as LA's young and privileged embraced the night with the cold-hearted glee of sated vampires.

'I don't understand how I'm feeling at this moment. It's new. A new sensation. New to me. To us. Should we be concerned?'

Blue touched Green's face gently as the vampires pushed past them.

'Let's not worry. I'm sure it will pass. This is where we have to be to travel back to Bowie's time here. Maybe it was different then. Maybe it was more sophisticated. More generous. Less of them seeking pain. Or corruption.'

'Was it like this? I mean, so exhibitionist?'

'Maybe not. Maybe Bowie was here when things were better.'

Green's head shook slowly as the digital billboard that lit up Sunset and could be seen for many miles changed again. This time it read:

ARE YOU LONELY – we have people who can take you for a walk.
ARE YOU LONELY – we have people you can hire for a chat.

ARE YOU LONELY – we can supply mourners or wedding guests.

Blue looked at Green with a new concern. The world they had entered was not a place Green seemed able to deal with. Why? Why not both of us?

'I can hear your thoughts but I don't understand either. I thought we were exactly the same. But this strange city is having a much worse effect on me than you. Why?'

'Shall we find a way to return home?'

'No. No, we must carry on. Bowie found something in this terrible place, the inspiration and expressive force to create. To make beauty. We need to understand but we also need to be quick.'

Traffic sat still along the wide boulevards. Occasionally they would edge forward with a grudging limp in a taxi where the music blared thin, tinny sharpness against the waterfall-sounding air conditioning. Los Angeles was many things to many different people but in transit all were equal and each separate vehicle held a stubborn refusal to be silent.

Radio shows hawked and hacked away at their favourite victims. Celebrities endorsed charity in one breath and nail varnish in another. It was a city lost in its sense of now. The past here was pointless and the future was too complicated to think about. It was a city of per-petual flatness with a terror of darkness. Lights shone in every direc-tion. Lights lit up buildings, boulevards and advertising hoardings, and helicopters shone spotlights on the lights of the gridlocked cars. The colours were primary and sodium soaked, neon and jagged – they were invasive and all consuming. There was no escape from the light – day or night.

And the noise of the voices on telephones bellowed a singular ennui – a bloodless disconnection with body and soul. Conversations were being held where there was possibly nobody on the other end. It all felt like the set of a pop video where director and artist had found a two-dollar narrative that wrapped itself in divorced remoteness – a lonely splurge of unplugged existential valour. Everything in the city at night could be ludicrous, in fact it was absurdity at its best, as nothing needed to make any sense as long as it had atmosphere and was touched by sensation – the currency of the senseless.

Blue and Green sat in the back of the yellow LA cab struggling with the big freeze of the air conditioning and the rasping, hissing chainsaw of opinions coming from the radio. They listened and tried to decipher live crime reports coming from the outlying areas of the city alongside sportsmen selling energy drinks and wishing everyone a Happy New Year. The hosts of the show laughed, mocked then gurgled their way through topics that meant nothing to the confused travellers. The driver watched them in his mirror, intrigued but not surprised; after all, this was Los Angeles.

'You have friends in Doheny Drive?' he asked over the air-conditioning wheeze and the now near-violent tone of the radio show.

'You visit family?'

Should they answer? Should they ask him to turn the radio down? Should they ask him to turn the air conditioning down? Should they tell him that they're not from here? Should they tell him that they were beginning to feel sick because of his combination of cold air and maniacal radio? Should they tell him that they were being followed? No. They smiled back at him, hoping that the traffic would start moving soon.

'You not speak English?' he asked.

They nodded, knowing that it wasn't enough but it was all they could do in the commotion that swirled around them. They shared a thought of their house in London and how peaceful it had become once they had settled there. Was coming to this city a mistake? They understood that in Bowie's history and memory this period was fragmented and vague.

But the music was dramatic and intoxicating. This city had been the start of another phase – the Thin White Duke, The Man Who Fell to Earth. No, although they knew they had less time, they knew they had to feel this moment in his life.

Thomas Jerome Newton came to Earth looking for water to save his family and planet. Blue and Green had loved his simplicity and elegance when they first saw the movie. The film as a story was a messy affair but they concentrated on Bowie as Newton and were compelled by his beautiful innocence and style. The story made them laugh but only when Newton wasn't on the screen, which was seldom. They had understood a human condition: fans don't laugh at the things they love.

The cab slowly pulled away in the evening light, sparkling with human substitutes which could be read as a welcome, a theatrical archway of opportunity for the new and the brave. But somehow, Blue and Green understood that this was another kind of fakery that had nothing to do with storytelling, characters or even fun. This was a place that had never understood morality, compassion or kindness. This was a place where even success made people unhappy.

They tried to understand what all of these new sentiments and small pieces of knowledge meant to their quest. How had this culture affected Bowie? They knew what it had done to Newton, but what about Bowie? This was the birthplace of *Station to Station* – the first part in what would become Bowie's next phase in Berlin. This was Bowie as a musical experiment rather than a character or was it? What about the Thin White Duke?

The cab dropped them on Doheny Drive outside a house with two stone sphinxes on either side of the front door. The street was dimly lit. There were no people wandering around and the only sound was the call and response of crickets clicking their mating patterns amongst the manicured lawns of a private neighbourhood closed off from public view.

This was the house Bowie had lived in during his time in Los Angeles. From the outside, nothing looked particularly special. It was a Hollywood bungalow, expensive but anonymous, apart from the watching sphinxes.

'Do you want to me to wait?' asked the cab driver. They looked at one another.

How long would this take?

'I can come back in an hour.'

They nodded without knowing whether an hour would be enough to do what they needed to do here.

'OK, an hour, right here... OK?'

They watched the cab drive off into the sodium fog of the LA streets. The house was in complete darkness. They wandered around the pathway towards the back but the gateway was locked. In the distance, a dog barked a threatening repeated chorus of unhappiness and malice. Everything, they thought, in this city had some kind of tangible violence – even the mating war of the crickets all around them. They did not understand fear but they could feel its movement around them. It was in the air, maybe it was the fog that lay a few centimetres above the ground, maybe it emanated from the homes and the gardens of these invisible people who had obviously detached themselves from any formal connection with one another.

London had been odd but fun, but this was tense and joyless. They shared thoughts that this might have something to do with the other person at the Hammersmith Odeon who had caught Bowie's attention and was not part of the audience. Someone from their home had come looking for them. It couldn't be anything else. Had this new change in the narrative caught them unawares and had it now introduced a human complexity making them suffer simple overtures of paranoia and terror – purely human and for the most part impulsive and illogical?

They reminded one another that this was when Bowie fell deeper into his perverse interest in the occult and various manifestations of evil – they understood exactly why he would have come to LA. This was the perfect home for these kinds of thoughts and ideas. This was the perfect home for the Thin White Duke to throw darts in lovers' eyes, to scramble words and cut them up and stick them back together again – words that somehow managed to retain their meaning. This was the perfect place to practice his interest in psychic self-defence; a place where fear and oppression were part of the natural oxygen, a clear sign of an occult attack.

The seething guitar, thumping drum and sonic riff captured an insanity they had never understood until now. In the silence of Doheny Drive, where there seemed to be no people, the sound of *Sta-*

tion to Station rattled their position at the end of the pathway to the house. What did it all mean?

The European man was here. Here am I…

They held hands and concentrated on the doorway. Nothing much had changed since 1976. The crushing feedback of Earl Slick's guitar pierced their ears and concentrated the mind. It was a soundtrack for the hunted. The fog slipped around them with an icy touch but failed to pull them back from the measure of time. They were stronger this time. They knew what had gone wrong the last time and had made sure they were stronger and better equipped to deal with the strange unwillingness of this new environment to allow them to bend back the timeline.

The light became mustard-gas yellow. The crickets were still there but were less authoritative and confident with their metallic love songs. The doorway was there but this time small splinters of light came from the windows with slatted blinds pulled closed to the bottom. Music seeped out from under the doorway and danced around the fog, blowing it in different directions before it quickly reconnected like water or, worse, thick oil. The music did not break up or slow down or even speed up, it remained as it was written. The sound of Germany brashly brought order to the night air of LA – Neu!, or was it Can? – and sharpened its smartness against the restricted fear and terror of a city at war with itself and with anybody who dared to enter its enormous spread of anonymity and horror.

They knew the world of 1976 was moving as it should. They held it tight, concentrating on every aspect of the house but realising this time that they could not venture further into the night. The night would have to come to them like it had done with the fog and the beautiful German music for travellers. They watched themselves walk up to the door and listen to the other sounds, of which there were many. Inside the house was a party to celebrate Bowie's twenty-ninth birthday.

People were talking and snorting and drinking and fucking and lecturing and arguing and dreaming and playing and presenting and failing and winning and near-death and nearly alive and sick and willing and not-so-willing and in need and in love and out of love and dressed and undressed and loving their reflection and looking away and being somebody and being better than somebody and nobody was nobody and, most importantly, nobody was listening. This was LA theatre, where everyone performed and bought into the idea that they were part of an important moment that allowed them the freedom to explore everything they ever wanted to discover about themselves apart from the truth. That was what what they heard just by placing their ears to the door.

They stood back as a silver Mercedes pulled up outside the house. A man and two women got out of the car and stumbled towards the door. There were no frozen frames or juddering images, this was all done in real time. The women laughed and the man was vicious in his response. They stood next to Blue and Green unaware that the strangest thing that could possibly ever happen in their lives was happening right in front of them. The man banged on the door. But nobody responded to his fury so again he spoke to the women like they had done something irredeemable rather than simply accompany him to a party. He hit the door again and this time it creaked open and after much discussion about having 'something for the man' the door was opened further to allow them in. Blue and Green quickly followed them into the darkness of a hallway lit by candles and reduced to long shadows and the grumble of the lost.

The low tone of fast, subdued voices came from the rooms leading off the hallway. This was not a house to be loud in: nobody was competing with the German music, nobody was competing with anything other than themselves. They could have been standing alone talking to themselves, unaware that anyone else was there. They all talked at the same time. Layers of compressed anxiety filled the space with only a slight touch of nuanced psychosis grading the difference between them all.

It was a montage of self-delusion and personal horror and hatred. The music made no difference. It was wallpaper to an evening of verbal provocation to which there was no response. The room captured something truly of its time – an expression of freedom: they could do as they pleased, but the problem was that they didn't know what to do. Nonetheless, they were all pleased to be there, to be in the room, with 'The Man'.

They were part of an inner circle – the ones who knew. They were touched – involved – part of the scene. But the scene was dereliction, suicide, defeat and self-destruction. This was not a salon of enlighten-ment. There was no Hume here, but the other one was – Nietzsche. He was here on the black glass tabletops where the late guest unloaded a bag of white powder that made him a dear friend for a moment. They loved him but didn't know his name: the cruel man with two women who were hypnotised by his power to enter such a world as this. Such a world. Everyone in the room marvelled at the magic of the heap of powder on the table as they continued to talk and talk and talk and talk and talk without ever actually saying anything.

Nobody knew what might happen next because they had lost the ability to rationalise anything other than the moment they were cur-rently in. Blue and Green felt the sickness in the room both in terms of a physical manifestation – a smell – and psychological torture – a numbness.

They all had a beauty, but it was scarred by a knowingness that their beauty was all they had, and that even though it had got them this far, to this moment, there was nothing else. Was there nothing else? They had all stuck with the moment and tried to forget what else there might be on offer in their lives. They knew deep down that this was not the important stuff, but they had developed an echo cham-ber into which they could drop all the permutations of life apart from the single moment. This single moment. They could hear the screams of their other lives but after a while they were no longer affected by them.

Blue and Green could also hear the screams and felt the different lives drowning together without any hope of survival. They had all sacri-ficed life for fantasy. They had failed to grasp the distinction between illusion and reality. They didn't understand the beauty and theatrical-ity of fakery. This was a room of condemned men and women who in their own minds were within touching distance of success. They saw themselves as Apostles near the Messiah but this was distortion and poison where cocaine was the traitor, the Judas, the giver of illusion. This was a death cult who thought they believed in life but had lost sight of its sanctity and beauty. Daylight had begun to crease these people, it had damaged their idea of the exterior world: it was too bright, too many people, too many nobodies.

They were now dependent on the night light to protect them, but it didn't, it crushed them.

There were drawings on the wall, expressionistic, stark and removed from anything they had understood. Reversed pentagrams convulsed historical and future dates in meaningless equations. The information on the walls and lying on the floor was convoluted, a mixed bag of everything that had happened in the 20th century. Germany was at the heart of everything: Otto Dix, George Grosz, Max Beckmann, John Heartfield, Bauhaus, Bertolt Brecht, Erwin Piscator, Joseph Beuys – all presented from open books, all ignored by the party guests.

On television, images from *The Cabinet of Dr Caligari* crept from frame to frame – this though was expressionistic cool in comparison with the occult poetry of Aleister Crowley and his many devotees which was stuck to the walls like instructions for profound rituals. Blue and Green struggled to make sense of the various connections. What did it all mean? The images were impressive – the words, though, were dark and beyond light.

What had drawn Bowie to this confused palette?

The people continued to talk and talk and talk in a mood of self-congratulation. There seemed no end to their peculiar self-serving optimism. Blue and Green marvelled at their energy and ability to talk so much about so little. They listened to a cacophony of conversations that were happening simultaneously, looping and layering the room.

A man dressed in a white T-shirt and jeans sprung open his Zippo lighter then closed it, repeating the process continually with a percussive click as he revealed his idea of what LA should mean to his audience, who were all already engaged in their own one-way conversations. This didn't stop him. He wasn't interested in their collusion, only the platform mattered and, as far as he was concerned, it was his.

'Like, this is LA. This is where it's at. Know what I mean? Like, this is LA. You know – where it's at. You know. I mean, where else is there? Like, you know, like LA man. Where else, you know what I mean? Where else would you go? Like LA man, it's here, right here, in front of you – you know what I mean? You can't hide from it. It's right here. In here. Out there. All around us. Like, you know what I'm saying? Like LA man is all around us and some of us don't understand how important that is.'

A young, beautiful woman sat in the middle of a sofa surrounded by people who all looked at her with a longing but were obviously not listening to what she was saying.

'What do people want from me? More me. I'm giving them everything, like all of me, but that's not enough. They want more of me but I'm not sure I have anything more to give, you know, like, this is it. This is me. You know what I'm saying? Like, this is it.'

A small man in spectacles poured himself a glass of milk then scooped up some of the cocaine in a long nail on the edge of his smallest finger and inhaled it deeply through his nose. He contained himself for a moment as he looked down at the young woman on the sofa who was still talking and started to talk over her.

'My acts are reflections of me. Like, I only manage acts that in some way are about me. You know what I mean? Like, if they don't touch my life then I won't get involved. No way. Goodbye. Farewell, kiddo. They have to understand it's not about them. It has to, in some way, be about me.'

Next to him, a woman with short, tight blond hair and a black polo neck jumper rubbed some of the cocaine onto her gums beneath her pearl-white teeth. Her voice had a whispered, cigarette-stained roughness but her eyes glowed in the darkness of the room.

'Like, where are we going with this? Like, nowhere. Like, what's supposed to be happening? Like, that's the question. Like, they think I don't know but… Like, I do, you know, I do. Like, what are they thinking, yeah? Like, what's going on? Like, where are we going with this?'

A man in his late twenties with bulging neck muscles and eyes that were so open the eyeballs looked in danger of falling out was sucking deeply on a cigarette. He had his arm around a young woman who was looking around at the room as if it were a movie happening right in front of her. The man licked some cocaine from the edge of her nose and spoke to the people surrounding the breakfast bar area.

'I told them. It's me. It's my part. There is no-one else suitable for that part. It has me all over it, you agree, right? I mean, who else could do that… de Niro? Hackman? Hoffman? No. Me. I told them. The assholes. Did they listen? No. They went with Pacino. Can you imagine? Him and Me. What would you do? Well I know what I would have done. But that's the way they think it is. Like, him, at that moment – not me, but it doesn't make any sense. Does it? How can it? Did you see it? Yeah, really, like they think it's that way but they were wrong, man. With me – they would have got me, you know, like totally original. But that's the way they think it is. Assholes. You know what I'm saying? Like, that's just the way it is.'

The young woman with the actor's arm around her was speaking to the same gathering of people at the breakfast bar as he was. Her voice had a rich, expensive certainty. A small bead of blood had gathered at the end of her nose. Nobody drew any attention to it. She spoke quickly without breathing.

'You know I got a new apartment but I miss my old place so I made the new place look just like the old place same furniture same art same everything why did I do that because the old place was more about me than the new place and my therapist thought I needed to find the old me because that is what was missing and he was right as soon as I put my old stuff in the new place like everything made sense for the first time like suddenly it was clear to me that the old me had gone missing and by finding the old me again I had found the real me you should speak to my therapist he is amazing look what he has done for me.'

The bead of blood dripped from her nose in slow motion and exploded onto and into the heap of cocaine on the table. The conversations stopped for a second, but only a second, as the party guests tried to fathom what that might have meant. The overlapping noises picked up again as if nothing had happened, led by a shaky bug-eyed twentysomething in a white leather jacket with long blond hair. All around him were pieces of paper with written or printed words that had been cut up and stuck back together in no obvious order.

Drawings on the walls had words stuck over them. He didn't address anyone in particular when he spoke but continued to look at the various collages.

'Like, here we are in Bowie's place. Like, he's here but he's not here. Get it. I mean. Wow. Like c'mon man is this it or is this it? We are in the man's place and like can you feel the vibes, man? We're here to celebrate his birthday. Us. Fuck. Yeah. The music is everywhere. Can you feel it? Fuck yeah. It's amazing and we're here, like the man said, waiting for the man. Yeah, fucking dig it yeah. And the thing is he's coming. Can you feel it? I can. The vibes man. C'mon this is fucking crazy. Crazy. We're all here. In the mix. In the moment. Waiting. Like we're important, you know – like, we're the ones who have been chosen.'

In the darkest part of the room a man sat in black leather trousers and jacket wearing sunglasses. On the floor all around him young men had their arms around one another. They shared joints and small phials of amyl nitrate.

'Who said we had to be good? Tell me. Like some redundant ideology. Theosophy. Controlling bullshit. What's with the morality crap? Who said we had to go down that route? Think about it. Think about it. Who said we would be rewarded for our pious goodness? Our philanthropy. Our decency. Who said that? You know, I don't have to tell you. You know. Don't you want to be bad? Discover something about yourself? Like who says evil is the wrong route? Think about it. Think about it. Would you not love a little taste of evil? Screw the Devil shit. I mean temptation. I mean seeing it through. I mean getting in touch with what's going on inside your head. That's all that matters. Think about it. Think about it. Are you going to leave this planet having done nothing other than being a good person? Someone who did the right thing – a dull, anonymous nobody who toed the party line or are you going to challenge yourself and dig deeper in search of who you really are? Think about it. Think about it. It's our time. Look around you. Us. All of these people are engaged in the same endgame – looking for the meaning of the innocent – pure sensation. And it's not sainthood. No way. It's dark. Delicious and very very bad. Now. Think about it. Think about it.'

The room had a lazy, slightly out-of-focus feel. It was as if the fog had made its way inside and enveloped the party, adding to the tension.

Books by Crowley lay in piles alongside poetry anthologies by W.B. Yeats and studies of the Golden Dawn, Hitler's war machine and Himmler's search for the Spear of Destiny. Books on Sanskrit, the Kabballah and European history lay alongside essays on the occult. Biographies of Charles Manson, Kenneth Anger, Himmler and the Masonic brotherhood lay next to a book of Goya's violent drawings which lay open on the floor – the culture of the room was laced with a sense of where the world had turned against itself. The history of a people through violence prosecuted by fear on the many.

The conversations dripped with a vacuous nihilism and the people in the room shared a sense of glory that nobody really understood. 'Was this the environment he needed to be creative?' Blue and Green thought as they watched the delirious fools climb their personal mountains. Why these people? Is this normal for him? Is this the way he works? Or was it reflective of where he had been and what had happened along the way? Was this what they meant by context? It was a bruise of an experience for the two of them, an introduction to personal deceit and mockery of what they had thought was brave and beautiful. This was ugly.

An acoustic guitar stood against the wall next to a large mirror which was covered with a black sheet obscuring any reflection. It looked familiar. Had they seen it in photographs? Had someone being playing it at the Hammersmith Odeon? It was the one thing in the room that resonated with their story and why they had come here.

Nobody paid any attention to the guitar other than Blue and Green. They understood that the force that had driven them to visit this strange little planet lay in the noise and melody that were born from that very guitar. They both touched it with fan-like hope and desire. It was an object of great beauty and complexity to them. The charged turbulence of the room diminished like the last wave of an aftershock.

Blue strummed the six strings, which had been openly tuned and a gentleness eased back into their lives – something that had been suffocated earlier. Green followed Blue and strummed the guitar again. They shared their perfect smile – they were really here in the house on Doheny Drive. They really were touching Bowie's acoustic guitar creating a small cascading sound that delighted them in a way only a fan would understand.

The voices in the room faded into their own whispering self-glory. The collective fevered discomfort continued in a sweat but the fog from the street diffused the shapes into a muggy smog as they faded and eventually disappeared. Blue and Green were in the room alone with the guitar, which they quickly understood and played with a new knowledge.

Their medley moved from the groaning poetry of *Hunky Dory* to the juddering majesty of *Ziggy Stardust* and *Diamond Dogs*. They found the riffs and soul of *Young Americans* before smashing *Station to Station* with a calculated abruptness. It was only when they sang 'Sound and Vision' that they became aware that someone was watching and listening to them.

The room had all but disappeared apart from one door. And it was from there that an emaciated male figure stood looking at them. He held an elegance and dignity in silhouette.

The figure was unmistakably Bowie. He was listening to their version of his song. A song he had yet to write. They stopped playing. The silence was as thick as the fog that moved around them. Bowie moved backwards into the fog and closed the door which then started to fade away. Only Blue and Green were left in what remained of the interior of the house.

'It was him,' Blue shared.

'It was Bowie.'

Their thoughts were interrupted by a new voice that slipped through the fog.

'What are you doing?'

They both turned, shocked that they had been seen by a party guest. But it wasn't what they had thought. They could see no guests. The voice asked again, 'What are you doing?' A shape shimmered in the fog. The room was fading fast.

'Who are you?' Blue asked.

'I've been looking for you. You need to go back.'

'Why?'

'You're meddling with their timeline. You're creating instability in a vulnerable place.'

'No.'

The room was fading into a grey emptiness.

'You need to go back.'

They looked into the greyness and saw a shape that moved in and out of the grey mass.

'If you don't come back now, you might never be able to return. It will be too late. You are acting like children chasing a man who is behaving like a child. This is regressive and stupid. You need to come back with me. This is not a good place for either of you. For any of us. Come back.'

The figure shimmered and disappeared into the grey. Green coughed into the wet fog that surrounded them.

'Who was he? Do you know him? No? What will happen to us? Are we interfering with their timeline? We played a song to Bowie that he hasn't written yet.'

Blue held Green tightly.

'No, that's not what happened. The song was already with him.'

'But how do we know? How do we know that's how creativity works? Don't reduce the power of it to some kind of predestination. That's what we are. That's why we don't understand it. Reduction is their biggest problem. Everything has to be explained.'

'Is that not what we're doing?'

'No. We are trying to feel it. Not understand it.'

'Yes. That's true. Are we children? Like he said? And Bowie?'

'Everything here is about spectacle. Is that not what children love? And wonderment. They love wonderment. We want to feel that,' whispered Green, who looked pale and drawn.

'We need to get out now,' Blue said.

'Yes. We do,' agreed Green.

Blue touched Green's face. 'You need to rest.'

'Yes.'

Blue and Green stood outside the house on Doheny Drive. The crickets continued to sing but otherwise the street remained silent. They opened their eyes. Blue held Green tightly.

'What should we do?'

'Rest.'

'No. We don't have time.'

'You need to rest.'

'He saw us again. Bowie was watching and listening to us.'

'Yes.'

'The house was strange.'

'Sickness.'

'Yes.'

'It affected you.'

'I didn't like it.'

'No.'

They heard the sound of a car slowly moving along the street. The crickets seemed to groan rather than croak and the night sky was yellow and grey: poisoned. The house was quiet again. The party was locked into the past, confined to memory and myth.

'Everything has changed.'

'Yes.'

'We need to move quicker.'

'Maybe it's too late.'

'What do you mean?'

'I can feel something. Something bad.'

'What. Tell me. What is it?'

'I don't know. It's not here. It's... when did we come here?'

'December 2015.'

'I can't explain it. But we need to find him soon.'

'We will. We will. I promise.'

They watched as the car came closer and stopped across the street from them. It was the cab that had brought them to the house. The driver leaned out of his window.

'Where you wanna go now?'

They looked at one another. Blue touched Green's face with a gentle, almost breeze-like touch.

'Albuquerque.'

'Albuquerque. That's nearly a thousand miles from here. You wanna go to the airport?'

'No. You can take us there,' Blue replied, still looking into Green's eyes.

'No. You don't understand. Albuquerque. I mean. That's a long journey.'

'We have the money.'

'Maybe 14 hours.'

'Lots of money.'

'You looking for UFOs?'

'No.'

'It's the home of UFOs. You know, people from up there, somewhere.'

'We're looking for someone from down here.'

'Albuquerque? It gonna cost a lot of money.'

The cab drove through the night into the epic landscapes of California, Arizona and New Mexico. Long and endless roads, silver from moonshine, with a star-gazed loneliness that smothered the world in silence. The cab driver had been paid his fee in advance; startled at how easy it had been to name a preposterously high figure, he sat in silence as he rolled the car along a road so strange it seemed to mock nature. His thoughts remained so taken up with his new-found wealth and what he might do with it that he had turned off his radio;

the Californian hubris and love of confrontation were nowhere to be heard in the emptiness of the night.

Green, with eyes closed and heavy breath, lay tightly against Blue's arm in the back of the cab. Blue thought about what Green had said about feeling something bad coming.

Was it the strangeness and sickness of LA? Green couldn't explain what it was but there was a sense of disappointment, that something was about to end, a sense of foreboding. LA was tainted with death, suicide, a city of extirpated souls.

It was as if there was a terror of being disconnected and being left alone on a planet that had lost some of its beauty since the trip to Doheny Drive. Blue watched the road, entranced by the childlike symmetry of the cab moving along a straight road in the light of the argent moon. Their hands were pressed together in such a way that it would not be possible to define which one belonged to either of them. The shape looked like a carved, luminous sculpture – a signature of their belonging together – as Blue's fluids moved through the membrane into Green.

Blue listened to the irregularity of Green's breathing pattern. The fluids were slowly calming what had become a panic. The introduction of new sensations such as fear had not been good for either of them but it had had an even more destructive, deleterious effect on Green. Rest was the answer, they hoped.

Blue considered their experience in LA – it had not been entirely negative. The sight of the Thin White Duke watching them from the doorway as they had played his music on the acoustic guitar was worth all of the rigours of their long journey. He had been there, right in front of them for the third time but on this occasion he was interested in who they were and what they were doing.

Would they ever have another opportunity to speak to Bowie, thought Blue. What would they say? Could they tell him that they had travelled an incredible distance to try and understand the effect his words and music had had on them or would that be another run-of-the-mill narrative he had heard a thousand times before? Would he understand that they really were from another planet and that their colossal journey was by Earth's standards truly amazing? But why would Bowie be interested in their journey? It would probably be irrelevant to him. He seemed to already understand that there were other life forms out and up there, somewhere. Would the reality of their journey destroy the mystery? His mystery.

Blue felt that they would have to explain to Bowie that the sensation they had experienced when they first heard his music from the crashed satellite had awoken something in both of them they had not understood. Blue wanted to explain that the sensation was so deep and profound that they felt they had no choice but to follow it and, by following it, they might get closer to its meaning. The effect of the music and the words had no history or context in their home, and therefore their lives. They did not disallow violence – it just didn't exist. They had no need for messiahs or meaning to their existence. But the effect of hearing the rush and irreverent glory had ignited a curiosity that had been buried in millions of their years of evolution and personality precision. There were no individuals in their home – they were a technical collective who had survived the burning genocide of the Mercury Sun.

They had no illogical impulse to be creative like this anarchic, shaman-like fakery; they had no word for creativity. Yet, here, creativity was part of how these people conducted themselves. Creativity was part of them – it kept them alive or took them to the edge of despair. Even the superficial presented their lives with a creative flair. Creativity was used to show how beautiful these people were but, at the same time as they had just witnessed, it showed their fear and horror and stumbling idiocy about who they really were – their identity.

LA had introduced Blue and Green to the latter experience. Green had been poisoned by the near-death-cult nihilism of LA fakery. It had soaked into and through their thin membrane – the fog had caused the acrimony, leaving them no choice but to inhale its toxic waste. And Blue had been transfixed by an intangible divination. But that was not possible. They couldn't move into events that had yet to happen, they could only go back and then from there into the real-time world they had arrived in. Moving into the future was something they couldn't do.

And now they were faced with not only a sickness but someone had followed their unconscious travel-lines and time-shifting narrative to this small planet to bring them back or leave them here with no way back. The impertinence of creativity would never work in their home and would undoubtedly be removed before it had a chance to make an impression. The satellite had been left to melt in the Sun. Most of the citizens showed little interest; only Blue and Green had been captivated to the degree that they felt the need to understand more.

The music and words had made the thought of danger a secondary consideration in the beginning. But now, it had become clear that they were both in a dangerous position that would not have an outcome they could have foreseen. Their search for the meaning of creativity had left them with the possibility of never going home.

Blue also considered the thought that the effect of Bowie's creativity on them might be something so raw and atavistic that it could be from a time of pre-meaning. These were a people addicted to sensation. Is that what this is – pure sensation? Was it meaningless? A primordial flux of atoms bouncing in the wrong direction?

To be a fan, Blue thought, was a declaration of love. An approximate identity – the human desire for heat, warmth, togetherness – a tribal pleasure shared by like-minded people.

But, it was more than that, otherwise they would have uncoupled from their fandom in their post-adolescent years – but they didn't. With Bowie, Blue thought, the love continues – through all the confusion and exhaustion and fragments and crisis – Bowie remains in their hearts, deeply loved by fans who have tried to explain it but couldn't.

'But these people are primitive,' Blue shared with the stars, briefly hoping for an answer from somewhere. Does this love come from a primal gene that remains underdeveloped in their evolution, or is it in fact an overdeveloped gene that has been too quick for their centuries of slow progress?

Blue could feel Green's tight grip loosening. The fluid exchange continued but now not so rapidly. The road ahead was an eternity of straightness. In the distance a car's headlights dropped from full beam as it hurtled along a similar line in the opposite direction. The vast sprawl of California had spilled over into the enormity of Arizona's dry land. Signposts for the Mojave National Preserve were intriguing to Blue and if time had not become so invasive and potentially destructive, it might have been a place to stop and contemplate – but such diversions were now impossible.

This was the final thread of the Thin White Duke before his return to Europe and rehabilitation in Berlin. They were heading into the still dark night looking for a connection to Bowie's finest onscreen presence as The Man Who Fell to Earth. Blue was aware that the cab driver was looking at him in the driver's mirror. Blue smiled. The cab driver scratched his head and lightly slapped his cheeks.

'All this silence is making me tired.'

'The road never seems to change,' Blue answered.

'That's America, you know, everything is big. The country. The roads. The history. The debt. Your friend is he, sorry, is she, going to be OK?'

'Just needs to rest.'

'No radio?'

'If that's OK?'

'Hey, this is your cab, you paid for it.' Blue smiled at him again. 'Can I ask you something? You know, are you, are you like... brother and sister?'

'No.'

'Really?' Blue nodded.

'You look, like you look, really similar, you know, like alike, like twins maybe.'

'Where we come from, everyone looks like this.'

'Really. Wow. That's cool. Is that like Sweden or somewhere?'

'No. A bit further than that.'

'You're Russians. Right?' Blue laughed.

'I knew it. I knew it. What are you, like spies or something?'

'No. Nothing like that.'

'Maybe you're looking for the UFOs? Aliens? Huh? Am I right? C'mon, I'm loving this.'

'No. We're visiting a movie set.'

'No shit. Like a movie movie?'

'Yes, I think so.'

'Who's the star? Tom Cruise?'

'No. David Bowie.'

'David Bowie? The singer guy?'

'That's him.'

'Cool. You sure you're not twins?'

'I'm sure.'

'9/11. He sang for the firefighters in New York. "Heroes". It was very cool.'

'You like that song?'

'Yeah, you know. Not bad for a skinny white guy. No offence.'

'None taken.'

The cab driver continued to speak but his voice faded away as Blue watched a satellite circling the planet move directly above them. It was watching and listening to people's lives from above. It recorded their every action. This was like being in a non-stop movie. Is this how life is here? Are they all performing their lives knowing that every frame is being captured by someone or something up there? Blue wondered if other peoples had visited Earth and if they were still here. What conclusions will they have reached? Why had they not made themselves more evident? Would they recognise each other?

Blue had encountered other life forms closer to their home but none of them had made much of an impression, although they were all in so many ways more sophisticated than the people on this planet. But sophistication they were beginning to realise might be irrelevant when it came to natural creativity. Sophistication was only a shaping tool to distinguish levels of achievement – there was nothing natural about that. Were they beginning to envy the very thing that made the people of Earth so worthless and irrelevant to their own planet?

Blue smiled. All of the knowledge and understanding meant very little when it drowned the instincts and impulses that made beauty happen from anywhere at any time.

Green's breathing continued to slow down as Blue shared fluids to try and to push it back into a regular pace. They needed to share thoughts on the new circumstance they found themselves in, but first they would visit the set of the movie in 1975 and watch how the director Nicolas Roeg worked with Bowie to create Thomas Jerome Newton. They had already watched the finished movie and had responded to all of the human questions that arose from the story – all of which made sense as a tale of an outsider trying to conform to a world that would never understand him. The dislocation and distance in Bowie's performance worked beautifully, they had thought, but the rest of the actors seemed to be in a different movie and were allowed an erratic edge that never quite worked with Bowie's mix of helplessness and paranoia. But then, if they were to truly reveal themselves to these people, how would they react? Violently and destructively, no doubt. Blue felt they needed to see how Bowie became the Thin White Duke and presented such a delicate, finely woven performance.

The name of the next city shone on a billboard: Albuquerque. In the distance the colour of the sky was changing as the sun began to rise and push light and warmth back into their lives. Blue imagined that the party people in LA in the house on Doheny Drive would be trying to get home before the sun came up. They were people of the night who had lost touch with the planet's beauty. Blue wondered if that's what happened to Bowie when he moved to LA.

Murmurs of distant cosmic echoes whispered from Green as the fluids battled to control a pulse exhausted by the poisons of LA. Blue had hoped the quiet night and soothing single road might have helped Green find a calm to re-engage a protective shield against the scale of cynicism and sickness that had trapped them in the house on Doheny Drive. The person who had followed them had warned them that their interference would lead to a situation that could mean they would never return home. The follower had foreseen the possibility of one or both of them becoming sick through a blended assimilation of culture and physical contact.

Blue wondered if this was the moment where they should stop, right here in the New Mexico desert. Is this the place where their epic journey should end? Was this the moment where their pragmatic rational programming should kick in and they should abandon this search to understand human sentiment? There was maybe still time to leave this behind and go home. Go home. To yield or to be stranded. Blue could feel the fluids moving too quickly from one body to another. It happened with such speed that the sound of a sharp wind bellowed through the cab.

The conversation had never stopped with the driver but Blue had not been participating, allowing a separation to continue automatically. The driver was unaware that he was no longer talking to someone who wasn't listening but he stopped talking when he heard the sound of something rushing through the cab.

'What was that?'

'I think you have a storm coming,' answered Blue.

'Was it lightning? Did lightning just hit the car?'

Up ahead the blue and green neon sign of a gas station flickered against a daylight that was increasingly darkening.

'Look at those clouds. Shit. They say it's weird around here. You know. Roswell. That kind of thing. You know anything about that?'

'No.'

'You wanna stop here for a bit until this passes?'

'OK.'

The black clouds thickened and snarled around each other, swirling into a rage above the New Mexico desert. The cab stood motionless in the parking lot of the gas station framed ominously by the clouds. Blue and the cab driver carried Green on their shoulders towards the rest room.

'Your friend. He's so light. He gonna be OK?'

'I'm sure. Just tired. Maybe you should get yourself a coffee. Watch the storm. I'll stay here until it's over.'

'OK. If you need me give me a call, I'll sit in the window area so you can see me.'

Blue smiled a thousand years of kindness at the driver who nearly stumbled backwards from the power of its purity.

'What's your name?' Blue asked the driver.

'Miguel.'

'Thank you, Miguel.'

Blue sat against the door with Green's head placed tightly against

Blue's legs and chest in a near-foetal position. Green's eyes opened and looked directly into Blue's.

'What happened?'

'You reacted badly to LA.'

'How badly?'

'You're weak.'

'I've never felt like this before.'

'There's so much we've never felt before. We'll be OK.'

'I'm not so sure.'

'No. Don't think like that.'

'I can hear your thoughts. I could hear you in the cab. I could hear your hope. Your excitement. Your knowledge. Your kindness. Your love. I could hear your love.'

'If we have found love, then I love you.'

'We have found love. And I love you.'

They lay silently together, their faces so close their profiles were a perfect mirror of each other.

'What was it you thought was coming? Was it the storm? Was it the effect of the person following us? What was it, Green?'

Green looked into Blue's eyes again, gently touching lips and cheeks. 'It's not good.'

'I know. But I can't hear you thinking. Are you blocking me? You've never done that before.'

'Will you promise me something? Something important to both of us?'

'Yes.'

'Will you promise to not give up the search? After what happens?'

'But what will happen?'

'Something we will never understand.'

'We can understand. That's why we're here.'

'How close are we?'

'Us? I don't know how we could be any closer than we are.'

'I agree… here, on Earth, they think that it is possible to lose something of yourself when someone you love dies.'

'What does that mean?'

'I think it means that part of you also dies.'

'How sad.'

'No... no it mustn't be sad. It must be...'

'Reassuring.'

'Yes... yes, that the connection was so powerful and strong. Like us. Like how we are like one person.'

'Together.'

'Yes.'

'Kiss me.'

They kissed as a sudden breeze pulled the desert dust into a swirling musical note around their feet.

'I need you to promise. Promise to not give up the search for Bowie,' Green said weakly.

'But we're here. Together.'

'Please... promise.'

'I promise.'

Blue helped Green up with a delicate sweep of the arms and legs like a dance move. A defiant tango against the coming storm. Behind the station was a small hill, which Blue carefully navigated, with Green now almost unable to walk. The black clouds had spread, leaving no cracks of light other than from the occasional shift of lightning that joined both sides of the horizon like a cinema screen. They sat together at the top of the hill watching Earth's weather disrupt and lay waste to the land and people. A tornado could be seen hovering like a giant umbilical cord from ground to sky. It bent, curled then pounced – it was silent then erupted into a gory nonchalance as it swept up everything in front of it.

Blue and Green had closed their eyes to the coming turbulence. The Earth shook below them appearing to breathe deeply in dark collusion with the scything architecture of the tornado. Their mouths met and they kissed with a new understanding of why they had made the journey. They began to travel backwards through time as they sat clenched in the fragile significance of their devotion and kindness. Lovers travelling through time in search of Bowie, the man who had given them a new reason to live and be together forever.

Nic Roeg called 'action' in the heat of the New Mexico desert. The camera pointed to the hill from where Blue and Green sat watching. There were people and vehicles everywhere; a small army had invaded a space that had up until that point been left alone to nature. Thomas Jerome Newton or David Bowie or the Thin White Duke stood alongside Blue and Green on the hill as the sun sparkled behind them.

His skin was pale. He looked dehydrated. He needed water and he had found it. He was The Man Who Fell to Earth. He stumbled past them down the hill and fell upon the edges of a lake and drank deep gulps of fresh water. Blue and Green followed every moment of this live theatre. The director called 'cut' and the people watching suddenly sprang into action, moving like an army of red ants. Newton was surrounded by make-up, costume, assistants, more assistants and assistant-assistants. There were so many people that Blue and Green found it difficult to understand what they were all doing.

Bowie as Newton drank milk rather than water and stood in the light breeze like a linen flag barely able to stand upright through exhaustion. He looked back up at the silhouettes: two figures sitting on the hillside. He pointed to them but nobody else could see them.

But they were there, he could see them, he knew they were there. The Strangers. Blue and Green.

Roeg and Newton spoke quietly together as the camera was reset in a different position. This was the silent and desperate arrival at the beginning of the film – Icarus landing in the desert. Newton seemed numb, trapped like Bowie in character, terrified of the coming fall. The army of people stopped moving around as everything was set for the same action to happen again. Newton was escorted to the top of the hill where they left him standing next to Blue and Green, who watched in awe. His leg was so close it was possible for them to touch it. They did. Newton didn't seem to notice. They both looked at his sad alien face, wrapped in a human condition transported for the sake of the story across galaxies – a shared sentiment.

Could aliens feel sad? Blue shared the thought with Green but Green was fading and slipping back from the setting. 'Yes,' Green said, 'yes, yes, yes, yes…' and fell back into the time-frame of a crumbling Earth and storm that wrecked the ground around them. Blue pulled Green back into the calm of the desert sun at the top of the hill where they held on to Newton's leg as he stood tall above them. Green struggled to continue but Blue gave more fluids than they had ever been programmed to share and momentarily it kept them together. To Bowie's eye the Strangers had disappeared and he again concentrated on Newton, The Man Who Fell to Earth.

In the distance Roeg called 'action' and Newton was about to repeat the previous drama of stumbling down the hill but, with paranoid terror, fell out of character back to being Bowie. He suddenly became aware of Blue and Green desperately holding fast to his leg. He could see and feel the turmoil, the ground shifting, a tornado coming towards him and the two people who seemed to be glowing blue and green as they held his leg. They both smiled with an uncontrollable joy and shared with Bowie, as the eye of the storm approached them, the true beauty of happiness.

'Who are you?' Bowie asked.

Green's fluid intake had suddenly stopped. Blue pulled open the closed eyelids but the eyes were gone. There was no breath from Green. No movement. Green started to fade from his arms.

'No!' Blue screamed and looked back up to Bowie but he too had gone. Blue was sitting at the top of the hill as the tornado pulled and pushed and destroyed. Blue was alone and had returned to a world that had gone black. There was no light in the dense whirlpool of clouds that swung, whipped and grabbed with ferocious stealth.

The sound was ancient and deep: a crumbling, explosive ripping apart of the air. Although everything moved, nothing seemed to have direction. Blue was in the middle of the tornado, which hung around the hill gasping in some fresher air before continuing an apocalyptic charge across the landscape.

Blue held the earth, the ground, the soil, the field, the hill and the stones as legs and body were scooped into the air. Amidst this anarchy Blue looked down to the ground in hope of seeing Green, but the ground was only a shape to be held onto – it couldn't be seen. The landscape of New Mexico had vanished – this was a pre-Earth experience, a near-cosmic storm that lived only to live and had no other reason to exist.

The tornado pulled at Blue's arms with a violent surge. The only alternative was to release the grip and allow the tornado to take control. Although weakened from sharing so much fluid, Blue gripped even harder with a determination that was beyond simple strength. Blue became a rigid spike piercing the ground, allowing the helter-skelter of the tornado's waves to push and pull but never leverage the tightness of the grip.

In what was the briefest of moments, the tornado turned one way and then another as it decimated fields of corn and churned lakes of fine fresh water. And then it was over. Blue watched as the tornado danced its uneven twists through the landscape until its ultimate exhaustion and end. The gas station was destroyed, the people had been sucked into the vortex and the cab was destroyed. All that remained were a few pieces of yellow painted metal.

The neon sign, an unlikely survivor, lay on the ground flickering its welcome to the grey, dust-filled sky. Nature had punished this small rest-stop for weary travellers; its history was now a neon sign and a few pieces of wood. All evidence that life had existed here had been erased.

As the dust fell, Blue scampered around the area of the hill where they had penetrated time and watched the filming of *The Man Who Fell to Earth*. The dust was thick: it contained hard earth, including small rocks which bounced off Blue throughout the desperate search for Green. Eventually, light pierced through as the sun took back control. Large shafts of angled rays split the dust open as if it were a wall sliced open with a sharp knife. Blue followed the patterns created by these splits in the grey curtain of clouds and used them to navigate to the position where they had sat together before the storm.

On the crest of the hill were two small indents. It was the place. Green wasn't there or anywhere nearby. The truth of the situation hit Blue with a thud so enormous the ground shook and the fallen dust rose again. What the tornado had failed to do was now done with such simplicity and ease. Blue fell to the ground.

The dust and stones continued to fall all around and even when they bounced off Blue there was no reaction. The spot where they had sat together had oddly been untouched by the zigzagging mayhem of the tornado.

'What did this mean?' Blue thought. They had always been together. Forever. They did everything together. Studied. Worked. Invented. Smiled. And loved. The beautiful simplicity of their lives had brought them closer together. They had shared everything. They had repaired one another but this time Blue had been unable to save Green.

The poison of LA had had a negative, toxic effect on Green. The nihilism, the stupidity, the madness and the evil had penetrated the sensory membrane of Green's skin and had left a disease on the tissue; it was melancholy, and the skin had sent out a distress beacon asking for help but there was no help for melancholy on this planet.

Blue knew they should have gone back at that point but their new love had driven them on. They felt they needed to get closer; almost as if another meeting with Bowie would relieve them of the bruise and hurt Green had suffered in LA. Blue turned the sensory composer off and allowed the combination of breathing and pulse to decide how to react to this series of events.

It was complicated, as turning the sensory composer off could have unknown ramifications for other parts of the body, especially the brain, which was 60% artificial intelligence and 40% real brain tissue. But Blue knew that everything now was unknown and becoming more real. As the dust eventually settled, Blue breathed deeply without the help of the sensory composer. It was overwhelming.

Blue screamed. The sound rose over the landscape and echoed across the universe. It was a scream born from love and its deathly collision with loneliness. It pushed the dust off the ground into a heap that became a new hill and the beginning of a mountain. It showered the Earth with stardust and pulsed the ocean into a perfect storm.

The scream connected to starbursts and red dwarfs that were recorded by physicists before David Bowie had even been born. It was here in the New Mexico desert but it soared through the streets of St Petersburg, Tokyo, Shanghai and Sydney. It interrupted the processions and rituals and compositions of a people lost in their own existential dreams.

It awoke David Bowie in his New York apartment to a new day and a new challenge. It was his birthday, 8 January. He kissed his wife and told her like he did every day that he loved her and then in his mind he wrote songs, beautiful, wondrous songs that told stories of lost love and alienation; stories of the hopeful, the helpless and the damned. The scream vibrated and strummed the console table in Hansa by the Wall Studios in Berlin as Iggy Pop and David Bowie laughed as only friends knew how to laugh: together. It tore the pages on Bowie's notebook as he wrote the words to 'Quicksand' in London. The scream connected all the parts of the journey that Blue and Green had hoped to make together. It ran backwards and forwards through time with a disdain for chronology and the physics of the cosmos.

The scream became a wind: a song, the door closing, a gentle kiss between new and old lovers. It became a sonic cry for help that remained with those who were touched by it, forever. For this was the cry of love. Its tune was a medley of human frailty and melancholy. It was followed by an albatross out into the vast oceans of the Earth and awoke the legions of the mythical sea-dead. It was the cry, the heartbeat and the story of everyone: the terror of loss, the pain of love, the whisper of the lonely. No-one who heard it could not have been moved by the pain that became the soundtrack of the universe: the hope for life, for existence. Blue wept human tears and knew that whatever might happen, going back was now not possible. This was a new home. With a handful of dusty, dry soil Blue felt the ancient history of Earth welcome a foreign body to its humble planet. The neon sign continued to blink its message.

For Blue it read: 'We know what's happened to you and we care, we really care about you.'

Blue stumbled down the hill and fell by the edge of the lake and drank the water of Earth. A new fluid for a new life. In the distance he heard Nic Roeg shout 'cut'.

Blue was alone. The starkness and absurdity clashed and whirled a dance around the terrible fact of what this actually meant. They had always been together. They had been chosen for cancer tissue repair and replacement at the same time. They had met as they were being saved.

The miracle of their resurrection was never lost on them. They constantly shared the thought of how they felt when they first listened to one another. The feeling was raw and without the assistance of the sensory composer which had not been installed at that point. It was a small tremor of vulnerability that had overcome them. How would the changes affect them – how would they respond to having cancer tissues removed and artificial intelligence become part of their everyday lives?

Before the changes their lifespan would have been short, probably months rather than years, but now they would have a long, sheltered life together. They knew they would be together from the first moment they lay next to one another as they were about to be slid into the deep silence of the tissue-repair operation. They had lain side by side as fully mechanised artificial intelligence made the necessary changes, ensuring their future survival.

Blue had looked at Green and shared a thought that everything was going to be alright and that afterwards they might spend some time together. Green had agreed, responding to Blue's friendship offer without the help of the sensory composer for the last time. It was the last natural reaction either of them would have until the moment they heard the music of David Bowie.

Green had whispered 'Is this love at first sight?' and Blue had blinked a beautiful surrender to a beautiful idea. They disappeared into a dreamscape as their bodies and minds were altered. There was no pain, only landscapes and colour and a prescribed memory bank of sonoluminescent beauty and images that became their new story. The old story was finished and they had been chosen to begin again in a new world that was both startling and hypnotic.

The sound of war was over. The new sound was of communication through thought patterns rich in knowledge and information. The silence had a pulse – a breathing hush undulating like a newly formed wind with no designated route. It just lay there amongst the people, the shapes – the sheer theatricality of a new world faked and perfect. Everything was new, especially nature. The trees were higher and thinner yet light shone through without any interruption. The light had a pastel-blue flourish with floating cotton-ball clouds of perfect white.

The Sun was the strangest component as its liquid fluidity spilled out in silver sheets of what looked like unstable patterns and rhythms but nobody seemed particularly concerned. Liquid temperature gauges hung from every tree with a warning line which indicated the ferocity of the heat of the Sun, with another gauge below which indicated when the sheer calefaction of the planet had ceased. Their renewed imagination accepted the unfamiliar and strange combinations as their memory banks distilled an idea and identity from this furnace. This was their home and they could no longer remember a world they had been part of that was different from this. This was their home.

Their job was to teach, to assist with the new knowledge, help people understand how to use their memory banks to better effect. They were allowed to be together, originally through luck, but then it became obvious that as a couple they were part of the great new success story.

They personified all the memory bank traditions of kindness, self-lessness and sensuality. They were the new people born from the ashes of a terrible war that people had now been programmed to forget. Disease had been marginalised through tissue repair and replacement with artificial intelligence. The risk of memory erasure had been the last act of a desperate people broken by the struggle for supremacy that had left them in a perpetual conflict.

They had been made aware of the planet Earth but its distance, primitive inhabitants and need for violence had made any prospect of travelling to meet and share thoughts hopeless and beyond any rational intelligence. The humans were regarded as an atavistic, barbaric race with nothing to offer the evolving efficiency of the new society. They were allowed to watch the newsreels and visual essays that fell from the sky in metal boxes but after some initial interest they were regarded as disposable or recycled into something useful.

Everything that was good on Earth, they already had here in much more rewarding interactive relationships: the songs of the birds, the gentle breeze, the seductiveness of nature and water that flowed in many different colours at different temperatures. There were no everyday certainties on Earth but here on this planet banality had been banished in a flourish of different incalculable days of indeterminate lengths. The need to measure by rising and falling suns had little meaning here – the only measurement was heat.

The new Sun burned with a silver shine. It felt close enough to touch but radiated unmanageable volumes of heat that could penetrate the souls and melt the memory banks of the new people. They all diligently worked on a solution to regulate the supply but to date all attempts had failed. The Mercury Sun was the legacy of the war that nobody could remember. It was indestructible and beautiful but held the power to subvert the need for light. The people were inspired into a subterranean existence where they themselves became the light that provoked the sharing of thoughts and productive ideas. They all knew that they would eventually find a solution.

The sound of the Mercury Sun could still be heard in the underground cities. It rumbled and groaned and creaked a syrupy flow of liquid. It slipped metal against metal in a sparking feud. The fuel, the silver liquid, was reborn with every wisp of particles losing life from its inner core, which maintained a sound only heard from within. The Mercury Sun had a supra-heated queen bee protected by her army of workers; they were sent to create the Sun but now could not stop its venomous sting as the planet overheated.

It was in the end all a fabrication, everything was fake. The world that they had created was only able to look at itself when the Sun cooled down in one of its many cycles: trees, plants, rivers and animals were all a beautiful illusion. The bees kept the sun alive through a strange mix of mercury pollen and a demented psychosis that drove them on to finish a job that had no end.

Blue and Green taught new people about their Sun and how slowly their planet revolved around it. They inspired them to consider solutions to the problem of heat. Their pupils were alert and willing to consider mathematics, exhausting possibilities as part of the dampening process and the eventual suffocation of the queen bee. Each memory bank was different and when combined with the remnants of human-like intuition anything was possible in the search for a breakthrough to the problem they now had with heat conductivity.

Blue and Green shared their frustrations from a benign, hopeful and supportive position, making them figureheads, nearing parent status. For their pupils had become their children by default. Their faked world had provided them with a planet where the relationship between people and landscapes was harmonious – it was all one body: theirs.

They understood that their destiny was to repair the Sun and, beyond that, return their world to something natural. The word 'natural' became less and less relevant to the people who had fought and lived by their self-made sun. They never considered the question: are we real? It was something beyond their understanding of who and what they were.

They had no word for 'real' and their introduction to the people of Earth and their history was a series of vicissitudes that seemed irrevocably fake and full of plasticity and untruths.

They had lain together since their repair and new memory banks had replaced their failing organs. They had been in the same position, the same space and had never moved. They had and would always be in the same physical place. Information and knowledge were fed through fluids that joined their bodies with a homogenous mountain of people beneath the surface of the planet. Layer after layer of working organisms repaired with artificial intelligence lay breathing together as they sought the solution to the burning sun.

It was only when they had heard the music of David Bowie from a crashed satellite box that the beautiful effortless rhythm of their lives had been changed forever. To link into the planet Earth and create a path to the story they wanted to follow was not something available to them. They would have to discover how it could be done: how they could transport themselves into a story that would give them access to the strangest fruit – the thing that made these primitive people creative and able to make other people have an emotionally unstable reaction that projected a melancholy joy of love and happiness and tragic sadness.

Blue had marvelled at Green's insouciance to the people around them. A decision had been made when they first met and that could never change. They would be together for as long as their repairs would allow them. This was the irreducible tenet of their existence together.

When they had decided to enter the unknown time-frames and changing ecologies of Earth they had known there might be a danger. The plastic truths of how Earth worked had been fed to them through the crashed satellites but the physical world was completely unknown. It had never been discussed during memory bank procedures as no-one had any inclination to visit there. They thought they were the first from their planet to visit Earth's timelines. The first to be caught by the intuitable nature of their creativity – a world less defined by logic than pure, raw emotion. When it happened they had both been shocked and were almost unwilling to share any thoughts on what it all might mean. It was not something their sensory composer could have prepared them for, it was not something they could ever teach their attentive students.

It was beyond enlightenment and more fevered than any process for living they had learned and taught. It had reminded them most closely of the feeling during sex, their own version of coupling and entanglement to receive and give one another pleasure. But that was a programmed response; this was unabashed and caught them in the world of the senses. It caught them in a place they never knew existed. The repair and replacement tissue operation had left something of their former selves behind, something that had lain dormant until that moment. But, now, here in front of them had been a reawakening, a new type of response that wasn't pre-programmed, but held the same rush and heartbeat they shared during their intimate time together. It was a position that held no meaning, there were no words to describe and no knowledge to understand where it might take them.

Blue now realised that they had always been different. The very thing that had drawn them together so quickly and easily was the catalyst that drove them to discover more about David Bowie and the art of creativity. The memory bank had not completely worked because the tissue replacement had left samples of DNA that had helped make them who they now were, as opposed to who they were supposed to be.

They had been warned about spending too much time learning about Earth. It wasn't worth the effort, they had been told. But the words and music had driven them on. They had become secretive with their research, knowing it was difficult to stop other people from listening to their shared thoughts. Only in their most private moments did they use the sensory composer to explore Earth's strange history. They had immediately decided to focus on Bowie as he was the person responsible for capturing their interest and engaging them with a new sensation.

They had been told Earth was a dying planet. There had been a war between continents and cultures that had resulted in utter destruction when vast arrays of nuclear arsenals were unleashed on city after city until there was nothing left but dust. The collision had been so effective that nothing had been untouched by the lethal poisons which spilled into the lives of every inhabitant and killed nature with a terrible venom.

Continental shifts and arctic meltdowns soon followed with the residue of the Earth soon covered in fine threads of dust that blocked out their sun; they no longer received the very thing that kept them alive. The planet was finished. All that was left of the former inhabitants was the data from the fallen satellites. Nobody and nothing had survived. It had been a tragic end to a tragic people who were destroyed by the very thing that they thought would spare them – belief.

The telling of the story of the end of Earth had meant nothing to the people listening, but it had gripped Green and Blue's senses and ripped into their supposedly controlled souls. This was a place that had had mystery and a wonderful celebration of creativity that was not predetermined.

Creativity, they began to understand, was always a surprise to those who participated either as the maker or the receiver. It was an adventure that didn't seem to matter when it failed – it was the journey that was the heart of the matter. But it was over. Earth, as they had seen it on the newsreels from the satellites, was finished. It was now just another dead planet surrounded by radioactive dust which would conceal it from its sun forever. Blue and Green understood the death of stars but found it difficult to comprehend the death of all a planet's inhabitants through their own calamitous stupidity.

They wondered together where Bowie had been when the end came. How had he dealt with the existential knowledge that all of the beauty, the great beauty of Earth was coming to an end because of a human fanaticism based on death and hate? They shared their thoughts about the warning they had been given about spending too much time assessing Earth's attributes.

Who had told them Earth had no attributes? Who had warned them? It wasn't clear as it had come as a shared thought and smashed into their conversation from no-one in particular. They now assumed it had in fact come from the memory banks. This made sense to them but also made their position more difficult as anything they shared was stored there.

It brought them closer together, their secret life – it wasn't something they could share with anyone else because they didn't know what it was. But they had found new words that they had to give meaning to such as Love, Melancholy, Hope. They told one another that they now loved each other and tried desperately to determine the alchemy of the word 'love' – its poetry and complexity. They decided it was Earth's most powerful word.

Green would share a thought during their private moments that read: I Love You. Blue would answer: I Love You. They repeated the words many times like a mantra hoping that this might help give meaning to something they understood to be the most important thing to the dead people of Earth who had never embraced their hateful war.

Again, they wondered where Bowie had been at the end. Had his songs in some way predicted this kind of apocalypse? Had he envisaged a world gone mad and capable of turning in on itself and prosecuting the ultimate crime of complete destruction? Again they traced the songs in their memory banks and decided that until they had found a way to visit the planet before it was destroyed, they would only share thoughts about what had existed and dwell on what had gone, rather than participate and see and feel the reality of Earth. There was also the problem of the memory bank understanding and digesting their thoughts and presenting warning signals when they strayed beyond their understanding.

They would have to find a way to limit the memory bank's access to their togetherness and use of the word love. The memory bank had deciphered the word for them but it had not given them its true sensation – its application, its reality. It was only a word to the machine but in the part of them that had defied their machine-controlled rebirth, they knew they needed to know more.

Green spoke again: 'Love, love, love, love, love, love' and Blue joined in and said the word in unison like the chorus of a song: 'Love, love, love, love, love.' They touched and brought themselves closer together, with a new understanding that deep within them lay a mystery they needed to solve and the only way it would ever be explained would be if they travelled to Earth and sought Bowie.

But their memory banks shook their togetherness with a sudden randomly placed thought which read: 'Maybe we should be separated.' It was greeted with a gasp. What could have provoked this thought? Did it come from either of them? Why would they have done that? It wasn't possible. The memory banks were working against them. It was suggesting they should separate. It was time to make a move.

They couldn't wait any longer. Their preparation was not complete, nowhere near, but they couldn't consider the possibility of arriving in the wrong year. Now, they would have to go and work it all out once they had arrived. Their world was changing faster than they had ever known but they felt they needed to respond or the mystery would be taken away from them and, more importantly, they might be separated. They held each other close.

Green shared a thought with Blue in the knowledge that the memory bank was recording everything.

'We must always be together.'

'Do the others know?'

'Do you care?'

'No. But I don't want them to be part of us.'

'No.'

'Do we behave like there is only us?'

'Probably.'

'Is that what is called selfish?'

'Maybe. But the others are not like us.'

'Are you sure? Maybe they're more...'

'Private, like us?'

'Yes.'

'We sound alike. You and I.'

'Yes.'

'We use the same words.'

'Share the same thoughts.'

'That must mean something.'

'Is it normal?'

'We chose to be together.'

'Did we?'

'Before we were repaired.'

'You can remember that?'

'Can't you?'

'No. But I can imagine it.'

'Imagine. Where did that come from?'

'I don't know.'

'What does it mean?'

'I'm not sure but I think I can picture us before we were repaired.'

'Can you?'

'You blinked.'

'Yes.'

'That was the signal.'

'Yes.'

'I remember.'

'Or can you imagine rather than remember?'
'I know that you are here and that we will always be together.'
'Forever.'
'We need to prepare to leave.'
'Before the memory bank stops us.'
'Yes.'
'Are you ready?'
'Now?'
'We don't have a choice.'
'We do. We can stay.'
'Do you believe that?'
'No.'
'We are like one person. You and I. Together. Forever.'

They lay together, holding each other tight. The remarkable silence of their world encouraged a tranquillity and concentration. Blue and Green shared their body fibres, sinews and fluids as they drifted beyond their utopia in search of Earth. The soundtrack was deep-space emptiness but the spark that had ignited their new search for knowledge was born from an imagination that had not been destroyed but had been asleep and was now being wrenched from the arms of Morpheus to live again.

Time was now immeasurable as the two somnambulists lay together, sharing everything they had to share on their journey into time. They gave their adventure a physical shape as they were transported on a burning ship through galaxies unseen by the naked eye that radiated beauty so vibrant and real that their new fresh power of imagination was overwhelmed with narratives that stretched through a billion years of light. And then the first storm started as they listened to the slow fog of 'Subterraneans' from David Bowie's Berlin hymn *Low* as their ship crashed and burned through a myriad of timelines.

In Berlin it rained, windswept from the east over old Prussian battle-fields, over the plains of Upper Silesia, from the ancient Baltic port once known as Koenigsberg, engulfing the heart of Europe with thin needles of icy-angled water that cut into the face with contemptible precision. Down it came through Lake Tegel and into Moabit, across the Tiergarten, and then viscously penetrated the clean sweep of Potsdamer Platz and a Berlin history that had been reimagined and rebuilt as a temple to Western democracy and its 'wonderful' international success. Potsdamer Platz was now a threading of tall glass buildings with metal dividing lines that supported the vision for the new Berlin from the base to the bold open roofing that allowed the light to penetrate the thoughts of the people sitting below by the fountains, drinking their franchised coffees and eating plastic-world food.

But on and on, the rain attacked the city, like nature's revenge on a human outpost that had learned how to deal with the anarchy of carnal brutality, but never with the surprise precision of the elements. Everything was exposed – nothing was sacred. Nothing. Not the Holocaust Memorial. Not the Topography of Terror. Not Checkpoint Charlie. Not the Brandenburg Gate, which was eroded with jet-washed rigour as the wind pushed on into Mitte and swirled around Alexanderplatz.

The large square emptied of hurrying commuters and lost tourists. The ongoing reclamation from the former East German Communist zone's functional-style architecture was a work in progress that had stalled and looked stubbornly confused. Alexanderplatz felt flat by comparison with what was happening in the rest of the city, but the elegant TV Tower which once looked over the Wall from East to West still stood erect and told its own story amidst the cemented banality of the badly imagined nondescript stores and memento shops.

Blue stood below the tower looking up at the bubble at the top with its rotunda views of the old East and West. This was no longer the Berlin of Bowie. This was the reunited German capital of politics and commerce. Bohemia had been replaced with Bonn – the other Germany – the country that functions, looks after its people and is less concerned with imagination than general well-being. The new Germany made sense but lovers of Bowie's Berlin would, as he had, find it a city of ghosts. It wasn't shiny and grotesque like the reinvented London but the art that had been its heart had gone. Blue enjoyed the empty wet streets. The light was plum grey and the vast expanse of the square gave an impression of water being close by, which of course it was as the river Spree kicked and spat its way around the bends and tight corners of the central Mitte district.

The top of the tower blinked a red light warning to low-flying aircraft. This had once been a deeply disturbing nightly memorandum to the people of the then East and West that they were being watched. Now of course, as Blue understood, the peoples of all countries and cities were randomly watched and listened to for no apparent reason. This had become a habit. For a moment in the rain, Blue turned up the sensory composer and listened to the conversations of a thousand different inhabitants of Berlin as they talked, munched, drank, argued, whispered, shouted, acted, sold and bought, embraced and loved one another. This was still Bowie's city and the people knew it, and were proud that he too was one of them.

Blue's soundtrack was the wistful hymn to Berlin 'Where are We Now?' from the album *The Next Day*. Although now living in New York, Bowie had looked back on his time in Berlin and reminisced about the bars and clubs and trains and hopes of millions of people. The song was without any mawkish sentimentality as it engaged Bowie's sense of romance and sad realisation that many of his friends from that era were now ghosts. It had a frightening mortality at its heart but David Bowie was immortal, thought Blue: he would never die.

Blue pushed the end lines of the song out into the crowded side streets and main square of 'The Alex' and the anthem caught the wind, gently feeding into the Berlin frazzle, lifting the dissonant gloom with a spontaneous whispering and singalong of soulful harmony.

Blue watched the changing mood with a heavy heart. If only Green could have been here to see the power of the man's music lift a city. They might have danced. They might have kissed. They might have made love. They definitely would have sung along.

Alexanderplatz had a rush – a sense of people needing to get somewhere quickly – so Blue infiltrated another district north of Mitte, the gentrified streets of Prenzlauer Berg. The rain had stopped as quickly as it had started and in true Berlin fashion people were pulled by social gravity out of their homes back onto the streets. The conversations of coffee-drinking mothers, children coming home from school, street cleaners, parking attendants and beer-drinking musicians clamoured into a city symphony – a cacophony of friendship and communication, an ancient language reinvented by another generation.

Blue listened to a young Scottish couple standing in Kollwitzplatz in front of a sculpture of a seated woman. They were talking about a great artist called Käthe Kollwitz. She had lived and worked in this district alongside her doctor husband, who had treated the poor with the same grace and dignity as she had in her woodcuts, drawings and sculptures.

The young couple looked at the large sculpture of Kollwitz in the middle of the small park where children ran and laughed and splashed in puddles of water left from the rain. They loved her saintly sorrow and, from all angles, the beatific harmony of a gentle but strong woman in a period of great hardship during the Weimar Republic era. She was indeed a great woman, Blue agreed, considering the majesty of human bravery. This was a perfect example of their humility and beauty.

Blue thought of how Green would have loved to listen to the young couple talking on this wet Berlin day, in a changing neighbourhood, in a transformed country. Blue was gripped by a Berlin melancholy. Losing a friend, a fellow traveller, a confidant and a lover brought a lonely, doleful air into the park as the conversation about Käthe Kollwitz continued. Had Bowie stood here in front of this sculpture or was it too difficult then, as this would have been part of the East? Blue felt empty. In comparison to LA, this Berlin, however much changed, was a city of great beauty and compassion, through its people and their need to revive hope. But Blue was also gripped by the city's sad history, evoking deep tragedy and loss. The people here understood that bad memories cannot and should not be erased, but at the same time they needed to re-engage with the possibilities of who they could and might be: dreamers, lovers. The sanguine and the determined.

It was at this point that Blue decided this city could be a home for someone sad and lost. Like Bowie had felt, this could be a city where solace and inspiration would supplant sorrow that lay deep and hurt badly. Blue could feel the turmoil of the memory bank as it fought to try and stay relevant while its power slowly drained away.

'This is my new home,' Blue said aloud. And the words drove through the afternoon light as the rain stopped and the wind lost its reason. The young couple standing in front of the beautiful Käthe Kollwitz sculpture looked at one another and said, 'Did you hear that?'

'Yes.'

'Was it you?'

'No. You?'

'No.'

'Shall we?'

'Live here?'

'Yes.'

'Yes... yes... yes... let's live here.'

And they kissed and clasped each other with a new-found sense of adventure as the children ran around the sculpture, which seemed to smile in the changing light. People heard Blue's statement of intent, 'This is my new home.' Berlin had an electric pulse that vibrated through its districts and people. It shot through the U–Bahn and connected people's downcast eyes, all the different versions of being German for a brief moment connected: the young and the old, the black and the white, and the gay and the straight. It engaged the Turk and the Armenian, and the newly arrived Syrian, it disrupted old meanings and grafted the opportunity for new ideas. It favoured no-one and everyone. It lasted for only a moment, but it would be remembered forever.

Blue had needed a reason to continue and it had been found standing in the rain in Kollwitzplatz listening to young Scots lovers talking about the amazing humility of great art and how Berlin would become their new home.

Berlin had been the home of David Bowie in the mid-1970s and was the true, pure moment where his creativity outshone his personality, Blue considered whilst walking through the grounds of Humboldt

University. *Low* was the recording that they had both responded to most acutely.

This was where he had found himself, regained his sense of self-worth, and Blue must do the same. The technology that was layered beneath the skin was going to be needed, before it failed and became obsolete, to take the journey deep into Bowie's Berlin. It would be the last occasion where this time-shifting precision would be possible. Blue knew that Bowie's New York years – which had been loved by both of them, especially *Heathen* and *The Next Day* – might be impossible to visit through a different timeline. Blue's only chance of meeting Bowie in the real-time world would be in New York, where he was celebrating the release of a new record, *Blackstar*, and a stage production, *Lazarus*. But for now, Berlin was maybe the last chance to breathe the same air of truth and meaning and meet and share time with Bowie before Blue started to fade. The fissures caused by *Blackstar* were all around Blue: syncopatic expressionism, 'Todesfuge', Die letzte Fahne, 'The Sound of Love', 'Liebeslied', 'Wir waren tot und konnten atmen', *Night Will Fall*, *Lazarus*, *Lazarus*, *Lazarus*... But Blue decided to concentrate on Berlin. *Blackstar* must wait. This was the city where Bowie had reclaimed his life from certain death. This was the city of his reawakening, a rebirth, a new beginning. This was his city of hope. Blue turned to look for Green, awaiting a response to this train of thought, but Blue was alone. A ghost wind born in Siberia whistled across the flowing river as if to emphasise how a city could quickly turn against the sentimental nature of lone-liness. Blue shuddered.

They had both consumed information from Bowie interviews about Berlin. He had described it as a city made up of bars for sad people to get drunk in.

Was Bowie ever alone? His Green was Iggy Pop – his protégé and friend. They shared their experiences together: 'The Bewlay Brothers', 'Dum Dum Boys'. Blue now understood that humans needed friendship more than any of their selfish desires – they needed to communicate. They needed to share (though maybe not in LA).

'Would it be possible for me to communicate with someone from here in a deeper way?' Blue whispered, watching the university students laugh and enjoy each other's company.

'How would they respond to being told the story of our journey, or should that remain a secret? My secret.'

The sun pierced through the clouds. The Siberian wind had gone as quickly as it had arrived. There was now a vapid, breezeless momentum as the city approached the hour when the Humboldt students would pour out of the university buildings and onto the grass plains along the side of the river Spree. They sat opposite the Altes Museum drinking cheap fresh wheat beers and were soon joined by office workers and tourists, all of whom were in states of exhaustion – work and leisure had taken their toll. They shared the sight of the water pushing and pulling with the slightest of sparkles reflecting the low sun's grace back onto the banks and into their eyes.

Blue watched an outdoor tango lesson entertain Berlin's tribes. A beautiful man locked eyes with his female partner, who held her head modestly low and followed his body's slippery movement with ease and elegance. They glided along the pebbled ground as if on ice and when her head rose it shone against the now silver Spree. Her hair was pulled back tight to her head and into a small bun like a ballerina's. Her black dress skimmed and skipped as she navigated the moves in her high-heeled sandals. But never once did they break eye contact, even when the movement accelerated and they were all but thrown apart, only to be pulled back together again.

The crowd was enchanted but the dancers were beyond public performance. This was private and personal in every detail. The dancers swam around one another as the violin slid and juddered chords and notes then tunes that spoke a language neither of them would ever have to speak about – their bodies were talking to one another.

They too shared thoughts through movement, considered Blue. It was primal and majestic, erotic and savage and in so many ways the dance held the key to the secret life of these people – agony and ecstasy, sensation and belief. They were quite extraordinary, Blue thought. The loneliness that had so gripped and burdened Blue's arrival in this new city lifted as the dancers went face to face in the final entanglement of the tango.

'This will be my home,' Blue repeated and the words followed the flow of the Spree's bubbling fauna. The people on the banks clapped joyously as the dance ended. They had heard the words 'This will be my home', but thought they themselves had said it as they had responded to the beautiful dancers from their hearts. Blue smiled with the sun. A new career in a new town. In this new, energising city it was time to look for Bowie. A Bowie who was trying to feel his way back into the world.

Schöneberg glimmered as the emerging sun reflected the wet ground against the racing clouds. This was a Berlin moment: rain, sun, heat and a refreshing visceral yellow and white light. Cleansed again, the city calmed and people reappeared on foot and bicycle crossing from street to street and district to district without a glance in each other's direction, with an unwritten language flowing between them: 'No time, in a hurry, must get there before the rain comes again, hello, goodbye, speak soon.' Berlin inhabitants seldom apologised for their directness – they were what they were or are what they are – unlike Blue's observation of the English who seemed to apologise for everything and anything: 'Sorry, pardon me, excuse me, sorry, sorry, sorry, sorry.' This was manners as a formality rather than culture. The differences were slight between the North Europeans but Blue understood why the Berlin way was preferable to the English. Bowie had come in search of inspiration and anonymity and had found both. Although the people of Berlin were not impressed by the English rock star in their midst, neither were they unimpressed: this was the Berlin way. Bowie had cut his hair, grown a moustache and dressed like a man who had a job – becoming another Berliner in a hurry with no need to apologise for the fact that he would rather keep going, keep moving on, keep on looking, keep on changing and at the same time keep on pretending to be the same. The 'keep on' element was the important part of his day: 'I've got to keep on doing things – got to keep on looking and seeing and writing and creating.' It was a hello-goodbye culture that had suited his mindset – a man in search of a private rehabilitation. Bowie's story of a man in the city had inevitably become about the city itself. Berlin's nonchalance became Bowie's psychic quarantine. He had projected an image of Berlin onto the city and had searched for its remnants – the delirium that came from the financial ruin and hyperinflation of the 1920s. The names fell from his thin lips: Nabokov, Grosz, Veidt, Heckel, Dietrich. Blue could sense Bowie's longing for history to help him find his creative pulse. To renew him, make his life and his story more candid; to help him escape from his natural ambiguity.

The project which would become *Low* was not the biography of a new character. It was the story of David Bowie.

Schöneberg had retained its reputation as a district where gay people were welcomed in bars, clubs, cafés and the many small, uber-cool boutique hotels. This is where the English writer Christopher Isherwood realised Sally Bowles and the camp delights of Weimar-period cabaret clubs. This is where he found delight in working-class rent boys and extravagant transvestites. It was his home during the best and worst of Berlin excess. This free expression of sexuality was brutally brought to a halt by the new politics of Germany in the 1930s, when being gay was a death sentence.

Heading south on the U-Bahn, Blue spun the history of Schöneberg. It was a district easily accepted in the new Germany in much the same way as it had been at the time of Isherwood's first step off the train into a world of opportunity. But the period in-between shocked Blue when following the chronology of events into the realm of the putrid death cult that had waved their mythic Bismarck-emboldened storm of steel into race, subcultures and the sick and disabled. They had transformed the beautiful into the damned.

This was why Bowie came here, thought Blue, wasn't it? To recreate some of that period, to follow in the footsteps of Isherwood, to feel the hub of expressionism, to be part of the fun, to understand the fear, the desolation and the terror. But Green was no longer there to share these ideas, and the absence again plunged Blue into a solemn mood.

'There is so much to share but no-one to share it with; so much to see and hear but who can I talk to? Where are you? Are you here? Where are you? Green…'

The memory bank tried to instigate a pulse – a warning – that Blue should go home. Leave now. But the signal was so weak that Blue understood that it would only be a matter of time before it was finished. Once the memory bank failed there would be no return and they would never find traces of the journey that eventually ended here in Berlin. But there was still time for someone to arrive with the dangerous message that this must end now, whatever it takes. Blue was beyond fearing their presence. Since the loss of Green there was nothing to go back to.

'This is my home,' Blue said again, but this time with less delight and more sadness. The sensory composer stumbled through a stream of instructions but like the memory bank seemed doomed to ultimately fail the resetting of its original purpose.

Blue left the U-Bahn and felt closer to the people moving into the light. There was a sudden realisation that the sensory composer had been used less and less since the horrors of LA. Blue felt it was no longer something that was required to understand emotion: it was happening naturally. Everything here had an emotional value but to gauge the values meant it had to be treated instinctively – that was not the purpose of the sensory composer. It was finished. The incubating of innocence and management of a route to the heart had created simulated emotions that could be regulated and understood. They had not been vulnerable. But something had changed from the beginning of the trip. New thoughts. New results. New confusion. Blue knew that everything ahead was no longer predestined, it was becoming real or an ongoing simulation of what was real. It was new.

Blue stood in the central reservation of Hauptstrasse in front of No 155. The building held a mucky-yellow glaze that defied any signs of a previous glamour; it was a dull building. On either side of the road, cars and bicycles moved past at various stages of fast and very fast. The south of Schöneberg was no different from the rest of the city, identifying the Berliner in a hurry – the perpetual rush from one moment to another. Blue felt deeply their need to beat time.

On either side of the entrance to the building were an assortment of

shops, cafés and physiotherapist surgeries alongside dentists and doc-
tors. Schöneberg was a place where people came to get fixed, it would
seem. Turkish women in traditional dress pushed pram-loaded children up the slight hill, passing the door of 155 without a second look.
There was no sound and vision in their soundtrack for life – only family, food and water and the sound of a country far away but still in
them, with them and always beside them. They, thought Blue, were
the beginning of Bowie's exploration of a new sound on *Lodger*: the
sound of Eurasia. But Blue was here for another sound – the sound of
Low and *'Heroes'* – and for Hauptstrasse 155, the home of Bowie and
Iggy Pop at the beginning of their Berlin adventure.

The apartment building exuded a miasma of lights onto the street,
different glows, different lamps, different lives. Blue could see the
apartment windows where Bowie and Iggy had lived but there were
no lights on. The seven-room space was now used as a surgery to fix
people's problems with medicine and technical knowledge. It was no
longer a place to dream. No-one lived there at night.

A few doors away a café called 70's spilled bright neon onto the pave-
ment. In the window a man sat alone nursing a beer watching the
traffic zip past towards Kruezberg. Blue caught his eye but the man
was transfixed by the delightful whizz of the traffic as he listened to
his music through his earphones. Blue decided to listen with him. The
music was lush and electronic, a bold narrative playing alongside the
passing traffic. It was Edgar Froese's *Tangerine Dream* – German elec-
tronica with a hint of cinema that cemented a clear story: a man lost
in a busy city, destination unknown.

Blue enjoyed the man's singularity, as in the distance planes circled
high above the streets awaiting their permission to land at Schönefeld
airport. The afternoon had become a brisk, active evening where people were left with their thoughts in the darkening twilight. Further
along the street a bookshop sold editions of artists' exhibition cata-
logues, both contemporary and ancient. The proprietor pushed her
grey bob away from her face and watched the same scene as the man
in the café, but this time the movie mood music was Schumann.

Blue crossed over and stood outside the bookshop. Next to a lime

tree by the roadside someone had planted a few small herbal plants at
its base and there was a poem, laminated and pushed into the ground:
'Vorfruhling', by the German poet Rilke that read:

Härte schwand. Auf einmal legt sich Schonung
  an der Wiesen aufgedecktes Grau.
  Kleine Wasser ändern die Betonung.
  Zartlichkeiten, ungenau,

greifen nach der Erde aus dem Raum.
  Wege gehen weit ins Land und zeigens.
  Unvermutet siehst du seines Steigens
  Ausdruck in dem leeren Baum.

And somewhere in the beauty of the poet's understanding of the Earth
and universe, Blue had found words that matched the story, encircling
this strange journey that continued to unfold surprises: a small piece
of laminated paper at the bottom of a tree: 'Tendernesses, hesitantly,
reach toward the earth from space'.

'Can you hear me Green?' thought Blue, 'Can you hear me? Did
you hear these words? It's us. You and Me. Härte schwand, it's safer
here. This is not LA. These people are civilised. They know love. If
we had come here then, then you would still be with me.'

Along the street, Blue watched a female couple both wearing the
same style of black-framed glasses affectionately hold hands as they
entered a café, Neues Ufer. Outside the door of 155 were a number of
apartment buttons. The doorway was framed in faded old dark wood
that needed some attention, as did the metal caging that formed a
dull shapelessness against the glass. Blue continued to think of Green.
Being alone. Alone. Gone. Green was gone.

An old lady opened the door of 155. Her hair was pulled up onto
her head and her face was heavily made up. She pulled the collar of her
dark grey tiger-striped fur coat up around her neck and held a crimson leather bag with gold buckles tight to her chest as she looked at
Blue standing in front of the doorway. Her eyes wandered over Blue's

face taking in the lack of lines, the near-moulded plastic curves and the occasional flash of blue pulse close to the sparkle of the eyes.

'Schön,' she whispered.

'Thank you.'

She touched Blue's hand and gently held it in hers before lifting it up to her chest and close to her heart as if looking for a key to youth, another opportunity to live a life: to be young again. They shared a small conspiratorial smile. She knew why Blue was standing in the doorway. There had been others, many others but this one was different. She kissed Blue's hand. 'Es ist nicht hier, nur die Geister.'

'Ich weiss.'

She left the door open for Blue and wandered into the fading light of Schöneberg. Blue watched her move heavily with a slight awkward lean to the left as if burdened with a thousand stories to tell but with nobody to tell them to. Maybe she was off into the night looking for an audience.

'Only the ghosts,' Blue repeated and whistled the words towards her, which gave her a gentle push and new lightness on her feet. She waved back to the entrance of Hauptstrasse 155 knowing the source of the miracle without turning around – this was not a night to be turned into a pillar of salt, she thought. This was a night of memories, memories reawakened by the beautiful creature in her doorway.

Blue entered the hallway which was gloomy and dark, but there was enough light to see a number of doors and a stairwell. There was no need to go any further. This was now a place where Blue could concentrate on connecting with their home – Bowie and Iggy in Berlin. Blue's eyes closed and, searching for the Berlin of 1976, whispered again, 'Only the ghosts.'

There was movement in the apartment. Drawers were opened and closed against the sound of soft voices laughing together, male and female. Clothes were pulled from cupboards and dropped to the floor, belts were taken off and then re-buckled. The traffic from the street was barely audible but it was still difficult to hear what was being said, although it felt gentle and affectionate. Blue had expected to hear music but there was none. The corridor between the rooms was in near-complete darkness, only a sliver of light slipped out from underneath a bedroom door and spilled across the dark wooden floorboards.

More drawers were opened and closed and more clothes were thrown around the room as the laughter became more hysterical. Rain suddenly started to fall in the inner courtyard of the building and echoed all through the apartment. The laughter stopped and a window was quickly pulled closed and the rain could be heard clattering and splashing against the glass. The mood in the apartment seemed to change as swiftly as the Berlin weather. The bedroom was silent other than the occasional creak of the floor. Blue pushed back against the wall in the corridor, disappearing into the darkness. The rain started to fall even harder. Blue considered the dramatic effect nature had on their moods and relationships.

It seemed to scare them with its ability to surprise and envelope them, as if they were no longer in control. The Rilke poem spoke of how 'little rivulets of water changed their singing accents'. Why was the rain on the building different? Why was the cleansing of the air not a beautiful thing? They seemed not to understand how their own world worked so beautifully for them.

Blue's thoughts were brought back to the corridor when the doorbell rang twice in quick succession, a rasping, tight and tuneless sound that vibrated through the apartment.

The bedroom door opened but nobody came out. The doorbell rang again, this time with an angry acceleration of two and three and then four presses of the outdoor button. Whoever it was, they were getting wet and were already impatient. A female voice could be heard in the room. She spoke in English. 'We'd better go. You know what they're like. They won't wait.'

And then, there they were, standing in the dark corridor with the light from the room catching the edge of their clothes but not their faces. Blue froze against the wall and stopped breathing. This time the motion was not interrupted and everything moved and sounded as it should in the apartment Hauptstrasse 155, Berlin in 1976. The man turned the woman towards him and kissed her lightly.

'You look beautiful.'

'Do I?'

'You know you do.'

'Do I?'

He laughed and kissed her again. The doorbell shook the corridor as it rang again and again. They broke away from one another and walked fast hand in hand, passing Blue without acknowledging any other presence. When he opened the door, the light from the hallway poured into the corridor but the man and the woman were in too much of a hurry to look back. If they had turned around they would have seen Blue, a strange shadow coming out of the darkness.

Blue had only seen the back of them in the doorway but had seen enough to realise that the man was Bowie. Before Blue could do anything the door was closed and they were gone in a Berlin rush to catch their taxi. The sound of their running feet on the marble floor was soon replaced with that of hard falling rain. Blue remained in the corridor in the darkness slowly breathing again, regaining composure and wondering what was to be done next.

Blue opened the bedroom door where Bowie and his female friend had been only moments ago. Clothes lay on the floor and sprawled over furniture. Cigarette smoke hung over the lamp by the bedside table that lit the room. The bed was unmade and a half-finished bottle of champagne sat on the floor with a couple of glasses that had been knocked over. The clothes were all male and there was no sign that the woman lived there with him. Blue touched the clothes: silk, wool, cotton, linen – every season seemed to have been pulled from cupboards and drawers.

A scarf with red dots had been thrown onto the edge of the mirror but this time the mirror was available for reflection. Blue looked at the image caught in the glass as the red scarf was tied tight. It was worth a smile. Everything felt so different to what they had experienced so disastrously in LA. There was a glimmer of joy here, a mediation with exhaustion and hope.

Above the bed was a painting in a German expressionistic style of the great Japanese poet Mishima, who stared down at Blue as if warning that this was a private room and that he was its guardian. Mishima's sallow skin and bold black eyes were stirring; the heady mix of humour, eroticism and violence emanated from the painting and seemed to control the room.

Books lay everywhere: J.G. Ballard, Jean Cocteau, Bertolt Brecht, Joseph Beuys, Bill Brandt, Egon Schiele, Raymond Radiguet, Caspar David Friedrich – all open at specific pages showing text that had been underlined in a coloured pencil or images with notes alongside them.

The images and text were still tortured but the nihilism of LA had evaporated into a mixture of dazzling creativity. Blue picked up a book of Brecht's plays open at *The Threepenny Opera* and read the words of the character Mack in answer to the question, 'What keeps mankind alive?'

A pattern was emerging, Blue considered, as the rain continued to fall heavily against the window of the bedroom. A pattern was emerging, from the books, the words and the images – human exploitation, especially against the vulnerable. Blue's thoughts turned to Green. What would they have shared here in this room? What conclusions would they have reached in their search for the meaning of human creativity? Could it be this – the unbearable cruelty that lay at the heart of all of their stories and ideas?

Blue thought of the Rilke poem 'Early Spring' that lay at the bottom of the tree outside the apartment. It had offered nature as a response to a world of cruelty. Green would have seen a way to combine these thoughts, shaping them into a more controlled way of thinking. They would have shared a pattern of thought that might have resolved the puzzle.

But Blue was alone. The rain slapped the building with nature's contempt as the light in Bowie's bedroom provided Blue with an opportunity to see how Bowie was repairing himself with art: art that was beautiful but art that was unmercifully honest.

Blue wandered through the apartment. There were so many rooms it was easy to lose a sense of shape and how the place worked and didn't work. There was a flood of books: on chairs, on the floor, on tables, spilling out of bookshelves. The acoustic guitar from LA was against the wall surrounded by open notebooks, full of scribbles and fragments that would become the albums *'Heroes'* and *Lodger*.

Blue sat on the sofa in the middle of the room and patiently documented in detail the living space. The rain outside had been caught by another wind from the east that shot bullet-like strikes against the window as if the apartment was under attack. Street light lit the room with enough grunge-yellow light to lift the gloom and reveal the spasms of Bowie's creative life here in Berlin. An open English newspaper depicted an exhausted island, where everything that could go wrong was happening as a daily live event. But that was Bowie's home from a long time past and this city was his home now.

Photographs of Weimar Germany's nightlife lay arranged on the floor: the scantily clad dancing girls, Dietrich, men in drag, poets and artists all simultaneously drinking, smoking and laughing. Next to these, the daylight Weimar-period photographs told the opposite story: people fighting poverty, mass unemployment and the violence of a new sobriety that cast deep dark shadows on their lives. But somehow the nocturnal decadence danced a merry dance that seemed oblivious to the ugly realities of the world around them. Maybe, thought Blue, their attitude was a response to the reality of their lives. It was their way of escaping – to create a new world, a fake world, a fun world; but were the smiles and laughter maybe born from a deeper sadness?

Blue breathed in the volumes of local history and immediately foresaw the dangers. These people on this planet looked for leaders, needed hope, wanted love but were happy in the end with a false sense of safety. Blue could see where the social contusion was leading to but knew it was something that could never be altered. History was set and the happy, laughing faces of Berlin's nightlife of the Weimar period were about to be enveloped in a madness that would wound humanity forever. And here in Berlin, this strange city with the dividing wall, was the place at the centre of man's barbarous hymn to mutual destruction.

The rain continued to clean the air and the streets, but the gloom of Berlin could not be lifted by nature, it would have to be done by men and women who decided that a false sense of safety was not enough. They would have to decide it was a time for love. They would have to be brave. Blue was amused by their fight against fakery: the ideas, the reason and the isms were all make-believe, a desperate loop, rehashing already tired patterns and paradigms that just wouldn't leave them alone.

Since turning off the memory sensor, Blue's thoughts had become increasingly illogical and in a perverse way more human. Was it possible to become like them? Was it possible to act like them? Everything was a discovery but nothing felt new. It was almost as if the abundance of knowledge had changed Blue's understanding of who these people were.

Or was it more to do with Green's absence?

A tangible reality was all around the apartment. Christopher Isherwood's Berlin love letter was open. Bowie had been reading once again the Englishman's observations of a city that was imploding and exploding at the same time; it was a carnival of urban cannibalism that somehow retained a desperate sensuality. Blue digested Hans Fallada's *Kleiner Mann, was nun?* with its original book cover design – a painting by George Grosz. It was a story that wallowed in a mixture of charm, realism and bitter self-pity. It caught the mood of its time beautifully. There was an innocence between the lines that had clearly not envisaged the horror that was yet to come.

Blue stood next to the record player with its enormous amplifier and speakers and put on a vinyl disc of Kurt Weill recordings. Lotte Lenya crackled 'Moon of Alabama'.

Blue listed to Lotte Lenya sing one more time and turned the volume up high before leaving the apartment with its echoes of another period. The music pulled 1976 back into the undulating 1930s. The song swarmed the room like homeless bees – it buzzed and sizzled and then stopped before jerking back into life with a sultry ennui. The rain danced against the windows to a tune that was a benchmark for how art and politics could be interwoven, a time when highly original creativity never felt shame, only a wonderful usefulness that kept these people alive.

Blue understood why Bowie wanted to be here now. He needed to sample the origins of something as majestic as Weill and Lenya and Brecht and Grosz and Beckmann and Heartfield and Dix and Kollwitz and Piscator and Lorre and Dietrich, Fallada and Albers. He needed all of them but he also needed to feel the horror and its terrible aftermath: the Wall. The old Berlin was now the city of ghosts and it would never recover. Everywhere you looked was death: in doorways, in reflections, in an apartment building like this one, in street names, U-Bahn routes, bullet holes in the Reichstag building; wastelands where once the Unter den Linden was a poem to the modern liberal world – but now it was gone, gone, gone. Berlin would return but never as it once was. The new Berlin where Blue had watched people dance the tango by the Spree would become the heart of Europe but everything would become new and shiny, a place where the past was buried in concrete bunkers. The new Berlin would become the centre of the civilised world, as it always should have been.

In Bowie's apartment on Hauptstrasse 155 Blue listened to the rain slowly fade into the slash of fast-moving traffic. Blue pulled the guitar over and thought about how art had become a form of human immortality; it was the thing they left behind for the generations to come.

'The Alabama Song' was as powerful now as it had been in the 1930s. And in this world of fakery and imagination it felt honest, as if when it was written they had known the world was fake but they wanted this to feel real, like it was part of them and how they saw the world. It was what they called honesty. Blue curled the word around and around the shape of the mouth until it was eventually spat out into the night.

Blue's eyes were closed. The ability to travel into different time zones and periods was diminishing as it became more exhausting. But every time, the journey revealed another short history of these people and Blue understood even more how extraordinary they really were. When Blue's eyes opened a stranger was sitting opposite on the edge of a chair looking directly at the sofa.

'You can see me?'

'Yes,' the Stranger replied.

'Who are you?'

The Stranger walked over to the window and looked out at the passing traffic. The rain now drifted through the gloom in long, soft movements. The Stranger looked exactly the same as Blue and Green. The voice was different, it had the same rasping hiss that Blue and Green had spoken with before becoming accustomed to the rhythms of the language; and the clothes were less expressive, more uniform in a grey cotton with a high-buttoned collar.

'My name is Quangel. I've been sent to ask you to come back.'

'It's too late.'

Quangel continued to watch the cars pass by.

'Why is it too late? You still understand that this is not your natural home. I know. I can hear you thinking about how did I get here and was it me that followed you to London and LA. Yes, it was me. And yes, you must come back. This is not good what you've done. It's difficult. It could cause problems. What happened to your friend?'

'Gone.'

'How?'

'Green became ill in Los Angeles and when we reached the New Mexico desert it was too late.'

'Green?'

'And I'm Blue.'

'These names are absurd. What do you think you are doing? Why are you chasing the ghosts of David Bowie? What did you think you were going to achieve? Green and Blue. Have you become children? Is there a malfunction somewhere? Is there a rip in the repair?'

'No, the repair left some of who we once were in place. It went undetected.'

'So this is not your fault. But, look at what's happened by you making the decision to chase this improbability. Your friend, sorry, Green, got sick. A Los Angeles sickness, you say?'

'Yes.'

'All the hatred and vileness?'

'Yes.'

'And then you came here.'

'It's better.'

'Really?'

'It's my home.'

'Why won't you come back?'

'I don't know how to.'

'I do.'

'Then go back.'

'Without you?'

'Yes.'

'The same thing will happen to you.'

'I know.'

'You'll be finished just like…'

'Green… Yes, I know.'

'These people are primitive. Why are you so interested in them?'

'Why are you not?'

'Because I know what happens to them.'

'They're doomed.'

'Yes.'

A police car's siren interrupted their conversation as it sped down the street. Quangel waited until it had disappeared into the distance. Blue looked over the stranger's shoulder as the sky started to clear and the gloom lift. In the distance a star sparkled or was it an aeroplane? Quangel answered the thought.

'It's a star. A black star.'

Blue's eyes closed in concentration, emptying thoughts and questions, but it was too late. *Blackstar* was the title of Bowie's new recording in 2016. Why did he call the distant star a black star?

'Where are we from? Where are we from, Blue? Which galaxy? Which planet? Which distant universe?'

Quangel turned to look at Blue. The room had become brighter as the gloom had lifted. He looked around at the books lying everywhere detailing myriad aspects of people's lives here in Berlin. The turntable was still rotating the Kurt Weill vinyl and the needle was scratching at the end of the record an irritating loop but it didn't seem to affect either of them.

'We're from here,' Quangel replied.

'Here?'

'You were repaired but, as you say, maybe not well enough.'

'From here?' Blue asked again.

'Don't be so surprised.'

'We can't be. We travelled… We…'

'No. No you didn't. You were programmed to think you had travelled if this kind of thing ever happened.'

'I don't understand.'

'We're from here.'

'How can we be?'

'You can't change things, you know that don't you? Your ability to travel in time will soon diminish, your energy levels are low, too low to interfere. They can't hear you or see you. You don't really exist here.'

'They do. I've talked with them.'

'It's not possible.'

'It happened.'

Quangel picked up one of the books and leafed through the pages looking at the images. Bold expressionistic images from Ernst Ludwig Kirchner, Erich Heckel and Emil Nolde. 'It's all from this. Nothing is natural. They are external people who live on the inside. Your understanding of their world and history is all from this. Information. You're programmed to consume information. This is all fake. Bowie is a fake.'

Blue grasped for ideas to find some kind of reply. 'I know that they use fakery as a tool but they are not fake. They are real. He is real… His work is real. They are creative. Something we could never be.'

'Don't be ridiculous. We are so far advanced from this that we make them look like savages. Which they are.'

Blue wanted Quangel to leave. Blue didn't want to believe that what was being said could be true.

'How far ahead of this are we?'

Quangel looked at Blue sadly.

'We stopped measuring. The past didn't matter. History had died. We killed it.'

'No other planet?'

'No.'

'Am I still there?'

'Unconsciously yes. But you are here now.'

'And Green?'

'Beside you. But Green will never awake.'

'And me?'

'If you come now we can save you.'

'What will you do if I don't come?'

'Nothing. I've come to ask you, not to force you. We don't do that, remember. When we killed history we also killed violence. But here will be different.'

'But you said they can't really see me.'

'Eventually they will.'

'They already can.'

'Then it's not safe for you. You've seen the history of these peoples. Their violence.'

'I want to stay here.'

'Then you've decided… It was me that let you through.'

'Through?'

'The gateway. It was me. It was my responsibility.'

'Why did you let us through?'

'I can't explain… it was a mistake of course but…'

'But?'

'Well, here we are and look what has happened, you have lost your friend and have now discovered the truth about who you are and where you're from. And still you want to stay here in this… insanity.'

And I, the one responsible for these events, must now find the answers as to why you would want to stay.'

'Will you be in trouble?'

'I am in trouble. As you are.'

'The Mercury Sun. The Underground world. The sharing of fluids.'

'All real, but all fake.'

'What are we?'

'Survivors.'

They sat silently together. Voices could be heard coming up from the streets as people shouted across from one side to the other in Turkish. Bowie's apartment framed the two time travellers against the neon spill coming through the window. Everything Blue had believed to be true was now revealed as fake. Bowie was the last opportunity left to grasp and protect a love that made any sense to Blue.

'May I ask you something?' Quangel's voice had fallen to a whisper.

'Yes.'

'Why David Bowie?'

'He touched us. Made us feel differently. It happened at the same time. The same moment.'

'Love?'

'Yes.'

'So, what you say must be true. You were a defective repair.'

'A mistake?'

'No. Not a mistake. The repair should have eradicated the need for impulse or what you now call love but we failed to do that. You will eventually become like them. If that's what you think you want then that's what will happen. I have to go now. I'm becoming weaker. You need to understand that this will be the last time anyone comes looking for you. You do understand don't you?'

'Yes.'

'You won't be able to alter anything. Don't try. Maybe then you might live as long as they do. Which is not very long.'

'Are you a man, Quangel?'

'I'm an older repair, before the decision was made to end specific gender identity. End violence.'

Quangel looked back at Blue and smiled.

'He's not immortal, you know, your new hero.'

'His work is.'

'It doesn't exist any more.'

'Then why did I come?'

'Do you like these people? Do you admire their vanity? Stupidity, violence, hatred, sentimentality? Their pointlessness? Surely these are the qualities you have discovered in your search for Mr Bowie? Is that not what he writes about? Small visions of a near future: annihilation, dystopia, nothingness.'

Quangel got up and looked out of the window down towards the street.

'This city of all cities; can you hear the echoes? The guns, bombs, bullets, rape, death, destruction... I know you can. Is that why Mr Bowie came here? To sample the horror, the real horror of what his fellow savages are capable of? This is an outpost. A place where death is looking down on these people every day. Is that the creativity you so need? The art of death? They could destroy everything in minutes. Total destruction. Each war they fight becomes more horrific than the last one. They become more creative with their weapons of mass destruction. Can't you see, that's them, that's who they are, that's where they're going, in the same direction as before, the same direction as they always go. Only each time they become more creative in their ability to prosecute their insanity. Give up the search. You're in the wrong place. The wrong time. You're with the wrong kind of people. Come back. We're better. We're less committed to delusion.'

'No. No, Quangel. You're wrong. You don't understand. You don't understand why we need to come here. Bowie's creativity is not about nothingness. He's a romantic. It all makes sense here in Berlin, the words, the music – it makes sense. It's about what they call hope and love, not hate. I'm sure of it. You're wrong, Quangel, you're wrong.'

'And this is based on your short time here following the shadows of a...'

'An artist. A great artist.'

'Great?'

'We had something that was able to connect with his music and words. Something you don't have Quangel. The beginning of emotion. And emotion leads to love.'

'You sound like a child. Primitive, like them. You have become like them. You're regressing.'

'No. I'm growing.'

'Into what?'

'Who knows?'

'A world without certainty.'

'Maybe.'

'No. Not maybe. That's how it will be. You will go the same way as Green. It will end the same way. You are not supposed to be here. You are not designed for this. For their air. Their chaos. Their disease. Their hopelessness. Their stupid ideas about what it all means. You were repaired for better things. Truly great things. Not this fan worship, idolatry, search for connection. You don't need it. They do. They need it because they are unsophisticated, naive, foolish, childlike. They're not very good are they? They're worthless.'

'And hopeless.'

'Yes.'

'But maybe that's their beauty.'

'You were not repaired to become this.'

'This?'

'Looking for false prophets. Your hero is not immortal.'

'You have already told me that. It's the trail of his work I'm following. It's helping me.'

'In what way?'

'I feel real.'

'You are real. But not here.'

'Then neither are you. So this conversation is not happening and never happened.'

'You have their sense of fun.'

'They made us laugh. We laughed together.'

'You can laugh?'

'We laughed at their clumsiness. They also laugh at their own pomposity.'

'Laughter. Creativity. David Bowie. London. Los Angeles. And now Berlin. What and where next?

'I want to stay here. In this city.'

'But the Bowie story continues. It travels to New York.'

'I'm hoping I can get what I need from Berlin.'

'But what about the funeral?'

Quangel turned and looked at Blue. He sat down in front of the creature he had been sent to collect and take back. They looked at one another, allowing the room to fall silent. The sounds from the street had dampened and become distant and soft. Blue held Quangel's gaze trying to unlock his thoughts but he had disconnected Blue's ability to recognise what he might be thinking. Quangel could read everything going on in Blue's mind: the confusion, alarm, early signs of fear. Maybe it was too late, thought Quangel, maybe Blue has slipped too far into this period's human consciousness. Yes, maybe it was too late. 'Should I tell this sad creature more about New York and death? The end of a story. A journey. Would I be believed?'

Quangel listened to Blue contemplate the new information about their real home – a place somewhere in the future but on this same planet. And now Quangel had foretold a funeral in New York. Was it Blue's death? My end, thought Blue. That's where the story will end. Quangel considered interrupting Blue's train of thought to say what he really meant, but knew immediately that it would have been a mistake.

Blue sat in front of Quangel in David Bowie's apartment in Hauptstrasse 155 in Schöneberg, Berlin as if the fog of a coma had entered the room. Quangel considered how this beautiful creature could collapse so suddenly into being lifeless after searching so dangerously for the answers to the meaning of consciousness, emotion and therefore creativity. Blue's thoughts had shut down as a protection against

Quangel, against listening to a series of trauma-laden questions and answers.

He was aware that Blue had stopped thinking as they stared blankly at one another. It wouldn't be for long, thought Quangel; curiosity would pull Blue back from this state of listlessness and emptiness. He considered going back and confronting the ones who had sent him here. He should tell them what had happened. Maybe Blue could catch the edge of the journey and watch how it unravels and understand the consequences. Or should he go now but remain in the room? It would be dangerous. It would weaken him but it might keep Blue in the room. He liked the creature in front of him and was beginning to understand a glimmer of what might have provoked them to undertake such a precarious and unpredictable search for meaning. A meaning that would have no context in their real home. Maybe that was why they were afraid of this type of thing happening. It introduced the impulsive into a world that was designed and premeditated. Quangel closed his eyes and concentrated on the firestorm he was about to enter as Blue sat opposite looking into self-imposed oblivion. And then it happened: Quangel was sucked out of the room, although he continued to sit in front of Blue. His journey this time was different; there was no light. There was only black. The pressure of the colour invaded every part of him, leaving nothing other than a feeling of drowning and suffocation. His white hair floated as if he were in some kind of liquid and every time he opened his mouth the blackness drank him in towards a fate he could have escaped from if only he had never followed the mysterious disappearance of Blue and Green.

The room was a grey cube: metallic grey. One light bulb was suspended from the middle of the ceiling and cast light over a small square silver table and two wooden chairs, where Quangel and a woman, Blum, sat opposite one another. In front of them was a jug of water and two glasses. There were no windows, only walls, a floor and a roof, all painted the same grey. Dust particles floated in the spill from the low-wattage bulb and danced in the stillness of a room that felt detached and cast adrift from any sense of what might be the architecture of a bigger building. The grey cube could have been in a basement or high in the sky, but once inside it no longer mattered.

Quangel held his dishevelled head in his hands with his eyes closed, as if trying to hear something arise from the silence. He was wearing the same grey cotton overalls with high-buttoned collar. His white hair caught the light, which threw ageing shadows across his face. Blum sat patiently looking at him. Dressed in an immaculate light-grey suit and white collarless shirt with super-shiny black shoes, she continued to allow the silence to create an exhausted link between them. To the innocent eye they might have been brother and sister. He was hunched and tightly drawn but retained something soft and likeable around the mouth. Blum's short hair, long neck and easy elegant posture betrayed the composition of the room: she wasn't there to share familial experiences, she was there for information.

Blum continued to watch Quangel hold his head in his hands. Her black eyes showed no sense of impatience or sympathy; only the occasional blink and flicker confirmed her attention was willing and complete. Quangel's nose twitched in reaction to the microparticles of dust that floated around them. He opened his tired and lined eyes, which squeezed above bags shaded black and blue, and looked straight at her. His once blue eyes were now green but had a milky thin transparency that clouded out any brightness which might have expressed hope that Quangel was feeling his strength return. Blum watched him slowly awaken from what had been a long pause in their conversation.

Again, she gave away no emotion as to how she felt about the man sitting in front of her. Quangel rubbed his nose and then with agitation his eyes, as he coughed gently into his right hand.

'You're still here Officer Blum,' Quangel said with a gruffness that rattled with age like an old car engine. He swallowed hard, obviously thirsty, but continued to hold Blum's gaze.

'Where else would I be?' she said softly but with a slight sibilant edge to her emphasised 's'.

'I could think of better places.'

'You're still thinking. That's good.'

Again, they sat in silence. A soundless fatigue had set into Quangel's body language as Blum's casualness wrapped itself around him, and he seemed unable to muster the storm that might put paid to this hush. But her eyes held him in a remorseless gaze that fed his imagination with enough ideas to maybe keep him alive another day.

Was she listening to him think? What did she hear? What could she tell from looking so deeply through him? Maybe that he was left incapable of challenging his position, which was now weaker and fading. But Quangel held on to his ability to think, to allow his imagination to rise and help him survive Blum's gaze.

He wanted to talk but his mouth was dry and his tongue was stuck to his upper mouth. He wanted to tell her something that she wanted to hear but he could no longer remember what it was she was looking for. He wanted to tell her about his childhood and his journeys through the stars, his discoveries and realisations as well as his disappointments and failures. He wanted to talk about his life, who he had been, who he had met and talked to and worked with. His life.

His life, he thought, was worth talking about but his tongue was stuck and his mouth was so dry and his eyes were sore and he wanted to sleep again, to fall into a deep sleep. He knew that he had been falling asleep at the table. He could no longer tell how long. There was no time monitor in the room but Officer Blum always looked the same when his eyes reopened so it couldn't have been for very long. Her clothes, the suit, the shirt, the shoes – it wasn't a uniform, it was Blum's style, her way of doing things. She dressed like a man but looked like a woman and had the patience of an owl.

That's what she is, thought Quangel, she's an owl. She hardly ever blinks and those eyes, those black eyes, just keep looking at me. Can you hear me Officer Blum? Can you hear me thinking this? I think you can. Can I hear you? No. I can't hear you because you aren't thinking anything. You're waiting. Waiting for me to tell you something that you need to hear, but I don't know what that is. What is it? Help me. Help me, Blum. Please help me.

Can you hear me? Can you? Can you? Give me a signal. Anything. Nothing. Nothing. Nothing. So, then, this is it. You can't hear me.

'I'm tired. Very tired. How much longer is this going to go on?'

Blum sat in the same position and looked at Quangel with the same deep dark eyes, giving nothing away as she asked, 'Why did you come back?'

'I've told you, I can't remember.'

'You erased parts of your memory bank.'

'No. Like I said, there was a technical fault.'

Blum smiled.

'But you know that's not possible.'

'Then how did it happen?'

'That's what you need to tell me.'

'But you say you already know.'

'It's an obvious presumption.'

'Then there must be others.'

'Yes. But I always come back to you.'

Quangel shook his head and coughed.

'We're going round in circles.'

'That's not so bad.'

'You want me to give you an answer I can't give.'

'Which is?'

'That I wanted to forget something.'

'But didn't you?'

'I don't think so. Anyway, it doesn't matter, I can't remember.'

'It does matter.'

'Not to me.'

'Really? So, you're happy here?'

'Happy?'

'You want to stay here?'

'I never said that. I said it doesn't matter.'

'But surely that's the same thing?'

'How can it be? Of course I don't want to be here. But I can't tell you what I don't know.'

'You can't remember.'

Quangel seemed exasperated. His voice was becoming more distant, lower, depressed. He looked hard at Blum.

'That's correct. I'm very tired. Very thirsty. Can I have a little water, please?'

'Soon. Soon.'

Blum continued to watch over Quangel with a remarkable calm. Her posture remained unaltered but something about it felt intimidating. It was sharp and straight like a flagpole waiting for the wind. Without blinking she found the moment to continue.

'If you can't remember then tell me why you think you came back, based on the few facts that you now know.'

'But how can I?'

'You told me you can still think, so, use your powers of thinking to explain, if nothing else to yourself, why you came back.'

'I can only guess.'

'No.'

'Then what?'

'Think.'

'I can't.'

'But you said you could only a few moments ago.'

'Things have changed.'

'Nothing has changed.'

'I need time.'

'There, you see. You're thinking.'

'I need more time.'

'Then take your time.'

'Can I have some water?'

'Soon. After you tell me why you came back.'

'But that may be never.'

'I don't think so... So, take your time and start to think about why you might have come back.'

Quangel seemed to disappear again, locked into the thoughts that Blum was keen to hear, which might reveal a glimmer of his position on why he chose to come back. Blum also considered the possibility that Quangel may be so completely worn out and despondent that his mind might indeed be empty, and that these continual pauses were symptomatic of his demise; he was trying to breathe, to survive. The time Quangel so desperately needed was drifting away. Blum would have to wrap up the conversation soon, unless there was a break-through of some meaning. She needed something substantial from him, but couldn't yet tell if he was actually able to give her anything. Blum was slowly losing confidence in Quangel but had retained her impassive, easy-going attitude that always succeeded in unnerving the other person in the conversation. It was clear at this stage that he was hiding behind the failure of his memory bank. He had obviously decided that this was the best strategy, maybe the only strategy given the circumstances. Blum considered another approach as she filled a glass of water from the jug and pushed it in front of Quangel.

When he opened his eyes he was greeted with the same sense of self-possession sitting opposite him. There she was: Blum. Who? How? Where? When did this begin? Now had become soon. In front of him was a glass of water. Why had I come back, thought Quan-gel. To this. For this. Her. Nothing made sense. He knew his strength was fading but he needed to hang on, to try and recover a sense of what this represented. Could he survive? Why did I come back? He thought for a moment he knew, but then it was gone.

Where? How? The silence of the room was unchallenged by his desire to make a map out of understanding his position. I must make a map. Should I drink the water in front of me? Will she start to poi-son me? This was the clashing agglomeration of his thoughts. Blum would have been no clearer if she could have heard him thinking.

She had heard that in special cases some were able to share their thoughts and communicate without speaking words or acting sym-bolic movement. Was this really possible? She had heard of repairs that were not consistent and had left open the possibility of conversa-tions conveyed through thoughts. Blum had enquired about revision advancement learning, but had been told that if it were possible to communicate through thought, then it was because of a repair mis-take and Blum had no repairs. Blum was not a mistake. Blum was flawless.

Quangel touched the glass and looked at Blum as if trying to find some hint of what was about to happen next. His mouth and throat were so dry that he wanted to throw the water back but this was something to savour. He kept eye contact with Blum as the water trickled down his throat.

He nodded.

'Thank you.'

Blum didn't respond but waited for him to take some more small nervous sips.

'You were a communication engineer.'

'Was I?'

'Different zones.'

Quangel put the glass down and considered what this meant.

'I travelled.'

'No.'

'Then what?'

'You stopped people travelling.'

'Like police.'

'No. Like a communication engineer in charge of different zones.'

'Was I any good?'

'Were you?'

'I don't know.'

'Then the answer must be no and yes. Technically yes. But no because you allowed people through.'

'How many?'

'Two we know of.'

'I let them through.'

'And then followed them.'

'Why?'

'Of course.'

'And then you say I came back.'

'You're here.'

'I am... why do you think I followed them?'

'Maybe we need to understand why you let them through first?'

'Yes... yes... of course.'

'So...?'

'Are they still there, the two I let through?'

'One… one malfunctioned.'

'Malfunctioned?'

'Obsolete.'

'Who were they?'

'You are asking too many questions. That's my job.'

'But I want to know… I need to know what I did.'

'I just told you.'

'I allowed people through to travel. Why only two? Why these two?'

'There you go again asking me questions.'

'But you know all the answers.'

'No… it's you that knows the answers and it's this that we must start to address.'

Quangel looked around at the walls and the ceiling, taking in the polished metal-grey that reflected the light bulb splash equally around the room. Why this light bulb? Why not something more sophisticated like Blum's suit? What was the light bulb supposed to represent? Cruelty? Taking another sip of the water, Quangel tried to pull together his thoughts on the room, Blum, the questions, his job, the two people he allowed through…

'How do we proceed?' he asked.

'We continue.'

'Can we turn the memory bank back on?'

'We could but it would be very dangerous.'

'In what way… dangerous?'

'There's a real danger you could return to the period you arrived from, which was 1976, and from there you could start slipping into different time zones without any control. It's not worth the risk.'

'But if it's not worth the risk why are you asking me questions about things I cannot answer?'

'Because you failed in what you were trained to do, so it's important to understand why.'

'To stop it happening again?'

'Yes.'

'So how do we continue?'

'Your memory beyond the memory bank should still work. Let's talk about what you can remember.'

'About what?'

'Anything.'

Quangel seemed about to slip back into one of his exhausted lulls but this time Blum pulled him back.

'What can you remember?'

'Nothing.'

'Nothing? Do you remember what we just spoke about?'

'Yes.'

'Then that's not nothing.'

'No.'

'So...'

'How do I begin?'

'Just begin.'

'Anything?'

'Anything.'

Quangel gathered himself knowing that he needed to find some energy to present even what lay at the surface of his thoughts. Anything. Anything. Anything. Begin. Now. He looked for a trigger to start the process, something that would make sense of his thoughts, shape the words and help Blum understand him, Quangel the communication engineer, who had lost his ability to use his memory after shutting down his memory bank.

He started slowly and whispered his way into a glaze, an atmosphere of words and sounds that would hopefully mean something. He touched the water glass, as if for luck, and started his story:

I remember awakening and feeling exhausted. I was drained. Never before had I felt this way. The first concern was illness. Maybe I had become contaminated, but how could that be possible? And then I started to fall into a deep sleep. And when I awoke I was in front of you. Right here. In this grey room. Directly opposite you, as we are now. I know you don't believe my story of memory loss but it's true. And if all the things you say are true – the job, my responsibility, the two people, my return – then all of this makes no sense to me. I don't know who I am or who I was supposed to be. I can't answer your questions. I understand your concerns about my lack of information but as it stands I cannot help. I feel I need to rest, to sleep, to reawaken with hopefully a mind full of this missing information but as for now, there is very little for me to say. I don't even know if what I told you about waking up and feeling ill is true. Maybe my imagination has done this…

Quangel suddenly stopped and looked alarmed, and for the first time in their conversation Blum sat forward, as if at last catching the sound of something that might herald the beginning of the end of this meeting.

'Imagination,' Blum whispered.

They sat silently together both appraising the word 'imagination' and what it could mean in the circumstances in which they both found themselves. Imagination, thought Quangel, where did this come from? What does it mean? This word. Imagination. When did I learn this word? My imagination.

'What do you mean by imagination?' Blum said quietly.

'I don't know.'

'You said "Maybe my imagination has done this". What did it do, this imagination?'

'I don't know.'

'But you do. You presented the possibility that what you had told me as part of your memory might have been the creation of your imagination.'

Quangel looked lost. His attempt to help Blum and his search for memory were now beyond exhaustion. His body language was an inert slump. He whispered the word again, seemingly familiar yet somehow it sounded like another stranger in the room.

'Imagination. Imagination… what is it?'

Blum waited and watched Quangel perform his hopeless man-at-sea routine. Memory, even without the memory bank, was stronger than this. Quangel was a poor actor, no depth – only ennui and an enervated rasp of existential gloom. Blum knew most of the answers but was curious about how someone as dull and inconsequential as Quangel could have been a willing participant with the two travellers. The couple who foolishly called themselves Blue and Green were innocents in search of the folly of fandom or love and creativity – they would not survive the turmoil and disappointment of their journey into what was once called Earth.

Quangel knew something had changed in his relationship with Blum. Although she was almost impossible to read, with her black eyes giving nothing away, and her soft sibilant voice always at the same pitch, he knew something had changed. Oddly it made him want to tell her more about the information that was slowly leaking back into his memory, even if it was immaterial to her line of questioning, but she had said anything, tell me anything.

He tried to gather the memories together and make sense of them before offering them to Blum; he knew he needed to impress her with details of what had happened but at this stage he simply couldn't.

He listed the array of thoughts and memories together in the hope that they would start to take shape. It began with dark skies, strange turbulent weather, elemental schisms that threw sounds up into the air that raced back to land with a hostile roar. This was the sound of a weather he was unfamiliar with. It wasn't from here, this place, where silence was the sound of their progress. No, this was the sound of divergent pathways clashing and holding onto one another in a tumultuous swirl that pulled the air from the atmosphere and threw it back again as hard rain. Where was this place with dark skies and fierce winds? Was it the entry point to where he had been? Or maybe it was both the entry and exit doors to a world he felt he had definitely visited. He saw himself working, lying sedately amongst his fellow workers, lying like they were all asleep, but collectively assembling the world that they were part of: their world, our world. My world.

They were listening to other people. So, he was correct, people could listen to others: they were using their collective power to monitor and control people's health. They were listening to their thoughts. So, that's what my job was as a communication engineer – it was to make sure people were functioning properly. He watched himself listen and compute the information from the subjects. Everything was good, people were healthy, the new generations of repairs were working beautifully. There were no problems that Quangel and his team could see, but then what had happened to cause this conversation? What had he done when monitoring the successful repairs that had pushed him into making a mistake? After he had explained the weather, which sat alongside images of his department working together, as they monitored repairs, Blum sat quietly watching him, looking for small clues as to what his intentions were.

'You say weather...' she dragged the 's' into the vowel and continued to watch Quangel with her unblinking eyes.

'But we no longer have changing weather here... we control the weather.'

'Then what did I see?'

'Maybe it was your imagination at work again.'

'Do I have one?'

'Do you?'

'I would think not... but I don't know what it is.'

'So how do you know?'

'I don't, but you do and by the way you have been talking to me, I understand that there's no need for imagination, whatever it is.'

'No need?'

'Was it something that was removed during the repairs?'

'But I don't know what it is.'

'Neither do I.'

'But you talked about it as if you knew it meant something.'

'I made a mistake.'

'Another one.'

'What will happen to me?'

'I have no idea.'

'But surely Officer Blum, you will decide...'

'No... so, let's get back to your imagination.'

'If I could tell you where this word came from and what it actually meant, I would tell you right now so we could end this conversation but I don't know the answer.'

'Oh, I think you do... I think you understand. Let's go back to the weather and the point where your team were working together. You were monitoring health checks and then something happened... what was it? Did you hear something? Were you asked something? Did any of your team hear it? Let's try thinking about what it was that happened that took you from the health checks to the weather storms. Let's concentrate on what you heard. Who you met. What was the moment when you decided to make a mistake?'

Quangel was caught in the softness of Blum's voice and the deep black of her eyes. He was slowly being pulled into her world. He could feel it. He was at his weakest. The grey room began to fall out of focus and the walls and ceiling and floor had a wave-like feel that moved with her words. Quangel was fading and could feel a warmth run through his body... the water, the water, the water... he tried to hang on but knew he couldn't fight a sensual, delicate feeling that was now running through his blood, a purl that connected his exhaustion with something beautiful and distant.

He felt no danger although he could hear Blum's now-beautiful voice. He had never thought of her in terms of her beauty but now it was clear to him what a beautiful creature she was. Her eyes were unrelenting as they ripped him open, looking for some hidden secret. Her mouth was large but her words continued to come at him softly, almost physically pushing against him then floating away. He could see the words as they left her mouth, her beautiful mouth. He wanted to connect with Blum, be somewhere else, have another conversation, not this one, but now... the water, the water, the water... Quangel wanted to put his hand out to her, tell her how he felt at this exact moment, tell her that he loved her, would always love her. He tried to say it, to say the words... I love you... but nothing came. He tried again and again. He could see the words floating from her mouth...

'Tell me about them.'

The words were different sizes and different colours and were shaped like clouds as they drifted towards him. His hand slowly came out towards Blum, who delicately smiled back through those black eyes at Quangel. He wanted to bring her close to him, to hold her tightly, to hold the beautiful Blum in his arms and tell her everything she wanted to know. And it was then he realised what had happened.

Blum had become tired of Quangel's vagueness. The memory bank had been reignited.

This was now the world of the unknown as Quangel's erotic craving to have Blum in his arms submerged any possibility of fighting the drugged water that flowed through his blood. He was now in a story that had nothing to compare itself with, there was no context or recorded history of what might happen. It was all chance. The words still floated from her black lips but now they came faster and bounced around the room. He almost had to catch them in his hands to look and make sense of them.

'Tell... me... about...'

Why don't you kiss me Blum, thought Quangel, why don't you want to kiss me, why have you done this to me...?

'Tell... me... about...'

This time the words moved so fast that they moved through his body and then smashed against the grey walls, bouncing back, but this time they were solid and the words would punch him hard on the face, on the side of the body, on the legs. He could feel the pain of their impact but could also tell that none of the words went near Blum.

'Blue,' he said. And then the words disappeared and the room returned to its quiet formality.

Blum hadn't moved and continued to watch him.

'Yes...'

The room had changed. The walls had changed. They were no longer solid but made up of faces listening to every word between Blum and Quangel: the faces made no reference to one another but watched the conversation attentively. As Quangel looked around at the faces looking down at him, he realised they were all the same, they all looked like Blum. His erotic longing from only moments ago had been replaced by a memory in full flow. His energy had returned – he knew what had to be done.

The story had to be told. The silence had been replaced by the breathing of the new face walls. The respiratory glands moved in unison with Blum, who was now breathing harder but had retained her poise and position. He wasn't alarmed but realised that the story had to be told quickly as nobody knew what might happen now that the memory bank had been triggered and he was in danger of disappearing from the room back into the world of travel. His voice remained gruff but he spoke quickly:

When the communication officers were busy with health checks on new repairs I chose to go back to the portal environment. I realised that the portal door was open. It was then that I heard the repairs who call themselves Blue and Green deciding to travel and leave us. I was shocked. Who were they? I didn't know them. I had never met them. And there they were preparing to leave. I tried to stop them but they didn't hear me as they hurtled through space and were gone.

Blue and Green were innocent so I had no choice but to follow them with the message that they must come back. So, I followed Blue and Green but at first couldn't locate them.

They had travelled back to late 2015 and I located them in London but struggled to concentrate on surviving the atmosphere and possible physical and psychological illnesses from the very large and disparate population.

I have never seen so many people who seem to conduct their lives without much purpose and are for the most part insane. Their violence was remarkable, their cynicism and hatred were new to me and must have been to Blue and Green and I immediately became concerned about their well-being as they had no layers to accommodate such strange ideas as inflicting harm on others. They would be vulnerable in this place amongst these people. I knew that immediately. How would they survive? Where would they hide and how would they surface? Did they have a plan? Why 2015 or was that a random landing point? I felt it was my responsibility to bring them back. It was my fault the portal door had been left open.

The city was enormous and challenging in every way. The people spoke a similar language, as in they used words, but they talked without any reason to talk, it seemed as if they talked because they could. Their communications, which interested me greatly, were very simplistic and mechanically riddled with flaws and bugs and, like everything else in their culture, suffered from some kind of sickness. They traded in sickness, it was an unwritten currency. Why would Blue and Green have wanted to come to this dying world? I set up a communication base that might pick up a signal if they used any of their sensory intelligence to connect or travel from 2015.

I watched for any signs from something they call media and news but other than stories about the strange land I was now part of there was no sign of either of them. I watched and monitored London hoping that they hadn't moved and was provoked by the sheer banality of these violent peoples to try and understand what made them this way.

I wandered from street to street and travelled on their transport systems and over their bridges, through their tunnels and over their rivers. I walked for what they call miles and miles and listened to their conversations, which betrayed their terror of living. I slumped in their galleries of what they call culture and listened to talks on their history by professors and experts debating who they were and listened to politicians who appeared to be in control without having control as they tried to remain immutable and what they call optimistic.

The experience started to submerge my position into a new context I don't think I will ever understand. I started to feel something. I don't know what it was but it started with laughter and then more laughter and the absurdity of them and their world gave me an acute recognition of their dilemma – they felt they were doomed, so in a faux-primal way started to live like people who had only a limited life ahead of them. The violence, the emotions, the betrayals, the disruptions, the isms, the lamentations, the crying, the love, the lost and the dying were all there in front of them every day without order or shape. The stories they shared were exploding myths and stellar hope.

As I contemplated my now irreversible dilemma I received a signal from outside a building in Hammersmith in the west of London. A sensory device had activated an alarm and I rushed to the area understanding that Blue and Green had penetrated a veil and were attempting to re-engage a concert by an artist called David Bowie in a venue called the Hammersmith Odeon in 1973 with his music band the Spiders from Mars. I had found them, but not in a place that would be easy to communicate with them as they were between plates of time. Inside the building they struggled to maintain the structure of time and it slipped into different speeds but they somehow navigated their way to the stage area to see the performance; and it was then from listening to them that I understood why they had come.

The man David Bowie had engaged some of their DNA fragmentation which had been irreparable and had lingered quietly, only to be activated when they heard Bowie's music from a fallen satellite. I stood in the crowd behind them as they became mesmerised by their audience with an artist of whom they had now described themselves as fans. It was odd. Like a religion but with creativity and imagination mixed with love and friendship. It was new to me and although I began to understand their intentions I didn't share them. I had to try and speak to them to make them understand that these things, creativity, imagination, love and friendship, had no place in our world. This was the language of the fools, as I now called them. But their ability to hold the time-plates was waning and they were no longer able to share enough fluid to make the images real in front of them. Bowie saw them in the last few moments of their experience in the room alongside the other fans but in the distance he also saw me. As the images faded I had lost the connection with Blue and Green but knew I would find them again and that they too had noticed Bowie's eyeline concentrating on the new stranger in the distance.

I could see that their idea of following David Bowie to the 21st and 20th centuries was wracked with problems that they had not considered, and would cause great damage to them. I wanted to tell them that they couldn't get involved with any of the people that they might meet as they would be interfering with the timeline and therefore we would have to split the time-plates for our own safety, meaning that the very thing that they came to understand might be damaged in the future, that is, Bowie himself. I needed to find them and compose a conversation that they would understand was not intended to damage their journey but to make sure that the implications were clear.

They believed there might be something else. Not us. Because we are them but on a higher plane. No, they thought there were things like creation and a beginning and maybe it was then I started laughing. Laughter is their best currency – they love to laugh but for the most part their laughter is cruel, it's used as a way of hating one another. And I really could feel something happening to me and knew that I couldn't stay here for much longer for I was surely being infected by their incipient emotions which were directionless and random.

I was, as I have said, not in a position to force them but anticipated that their intelligence would make them understand what needed to be done. I had lost their signal but knew they were close. I also thought that when they had worked out someone else was part of their journey then they might feel obliged to move on. I decided to analyse the work of David Bowie and try to understand where they might next try and connect with his history and, of course, him. They had chosen the end of one of the artist's many different and somewhat oscillatory characterisations. They would think in terms of the importance of the artist as they were more than likely aware of time slippage and the sheer weight of energy required to sustain a time-shift through travel. I listened to, read and watched the Bowie library of music, words and images over and over and came to the conclusion that they would attempt to escape me by leaving London and going to Los Angeles, a city in what was once called the United States of America. I left London and found the house where Bowie once lived in a quiet neighbourhood.

I was transfixed by how terrible this place was. It was a city that had no protection from a howling nihilism for the inhabitants and they reacted with an utterly desperate emptiness which they proudly presented as their sense of how their world worked. This was a microbubble which had no connection with any other part of the world. The people were a different type of insane from those in London. The insanity of London was pitiful and gloomy and a reaction to the terrible city planning that had swamped and suffocated them. Los Angeles was a city that took pride in its madness. It dealt in madness.

It wanted more madness. It sucked in the sane and spat them out as deranged wide-eyed psychological torturers of their fellow men and women. There were no principles as such here, only a willingness to destroy souls as they called them, which is in fact a direct correlation with what they regard as spiritual freedom. I know it's laughable but that's how their minds worked. I was in the strangest place on Earth. All the things that Blue and Green had cherished in their idea of how this culture worked – and again I repeat, creativity, imagination, love and friendship – were the enemy of Los Angeles.

They would be in for a terrible shock when they arrived and I was deeply concerned for their health. They were of course both repairs but they were not perfect repairs, thus the room for them to examine such trivialities was there – a perfect repair would not be interested in creativity, love or friendship. They would acknowledge Bowie's symbol of being different not so much as the individual, more the alienated specimen who did not cherish the conservative ideas of his upbringing and felt abandoned by the simplistic idea of being either a man or a woman.

It's strange to see but somehow Bowie was a precursor to Green and Blue who now regarded themselves in a new language as lovers or non-gender-specific lovers. They arrived in Los Angeles as I had suspected, thinking they might be genuinely happy but concerned that their happiness might be under threat from the stranger who was following them. When they arrived at Doheny Drive, the home of Bowie, and began to transport themselves to 1976 when Bowie lived there, I quickly followed and watched their entrance into a world of deep unhappiness which immediately suffocated their joy. I tried to connect with them but they were powerful together and my attempts to block their movement were futile. Inside the house was a mess of people talking over one another and taking several types of drugs to enhance their awareness of themselves. The room was laced with a toxicity that had a near-material liquid reality and it was apparent that Green was becoming insular and losing any sense of the room's authenticity and, in truth, was losing fragments of the energy they required to travel through the time-plates. They played Bowie's acoustic guitar and as Bowie watched from the doorway, they started to fade out of the moment into a deep fog and it was then I again tried to connect with them. They were aware of my presence this time and departed into the night and onto a long journey towards the New Mexico desert where they might again find a connection with Bowie on the set of a movie he was filming called *The Man Who Fell to Earth*.

It was here that Green's sickness became more precarious and the hazards of Los Angeles had taken a fatal turn, leaving Green very weak. Blue tried everything to sustain Green but could do nothing as this antediluvian landscape erupted into a cosmic storm and Green was sucked back into an unconscious state and was immediately obsolete. I can't explain the effect this had on Blue, but I would say it was close to human emotion, in that there was deep anxiety and loneliness, neither of which a perfect repair would be capable of understanding or expressing. I watched from the side of the lake where Bowie's movie character was looking for water to send back to his homeland, which was dying of a drought in the story. I saw Green fade back to here and Blue stand and make the decision to continue with their journey, but this time alone. In logical terms the next phase of this story would have taken them to Berlin.

Quangel leaned forward and drank some more water and looked at the wall of faces watching and listening to his every word. They might look exactly like Blum but he felt the woman in front of him was different from them, more interested in his well-being.

'How do you feel?' she asked.

'Weak... very weak... but I have more to tell... and then... when... what will happen to me?'

'We don't know for sure but there is a possibility that you will fade into one of the timelines of the story you are telling us or you might even slip further back in time or forward. We just don't know. We took the chance, because we need to know – you understand that, don't you?'

'Yes... yes, I understand.' Quangel had slowed down and his

rhythm of speech sounded much more akin to that of the man who had started the conversation with Blum.

'Just try and let us know where Blue is, and hopefully we can do the rest, but this is all hypothetical as you might not fade.'

'I will. I can already feel it beginning to happen.'

'Would you like to stop?'

'No... no, I want to tell you about Berlin.'

'Then please... continue.'

I followed Blue to Bowie's home in the city in 1976. I decided that the only place to wait would be in the apartment and eventually Blue would turn up and I was correct. We met and talked. I asked Blue why the journey had been worth making and why David Bowie? The answers didn't mean too much to me but I could feel changes in Blue that were different, more human. I explained from my position as a communications engineer that Blue was not from another planet as they had both been pre-programmed to think, but from the same planet Earth from a future timeline. It was a difficult conversation as everything they had believed was revealed as being a falsehood and no matter the logic behind the deception Blue seemed disturbed. I said that the journey they had taken was dangerous and they must not adjust the events that had happened or will happen. Blue was heedful but had decided that the journey must continue and that going back at this point was no longer an option. It was then that I decided I must come back and, if possible without turning on the memory bank, retell this story with accuracy. Unfortunately, as I can feel now, I'm fading and will not be able to continue. I apologise for my failure and will search for Blue and somehow work out a way to communicate with you. I would like to thank you Officer Blum for showing an understanding of my position, although I'm sure you also think I'm a fool. Which I am. I have a wife and children. Please tell them that I am thinking of them. Always.

Blum came closer to Quangel's face and watched his eyes slowly fade away. She touched his hand and gripped it with a new-found anxiety.

His powers would be reduced and he had no knowledge of where he would land but he knew he was going back to the old Earth.

At that point Quangel slipped away. Blum and the wall of faces looked at one another with the same calm rationale but there could be no doubt that this was the beginning of a new consciousness and reality.

Blue sat alone in the apartment trying somehow to grasp an understanding of what had just happened. Quangel had gone and only his new version of the truth was left. There was no other planet. Memories of the Mercury Sun were theatrical backdrops to their new version of this world. They had been part of a future Earth. What were they other than humans with artificial intelligence implants replacing the parts of the body and brain that had been vulnerable to illness and disease? Their genetic order had been altered. They were no longer gender specific, they lived longer, possibly forever, and they had killed violence.

Was Blue really travelling through time or was this all a journey into the imagination? But this was Berlin, and this was 1976. It felt real. Blue touched Bowie's sofa, the guitar, the vinyl records – it all felt real. Was 1976 where Blue would be stuck on Earth in a time-warp? Is that what Quangel had meant? Or did he mean stuck on Earth now, rather than in the future? Blue listened to Lotte Lenya sing one more time and turned the volume up high as she reached the line 'Oh show me the way to the next whisky bar' before leaving the apartment with its echoes of 1930 and maybe a thousand years later swirling around the room.

New emotions overwhelmed Blue: anxiety, trepidation, excitement and confusion mixed with happiness and loneliness. The happiness of loneliness – is this possible? This was the thought that engaged every fibre of Blue's remaining energy. The Berlin street outside 155 was quieter after the rain but people continued in their rush to do things, to be together, or to just find a place to be alone. Was it better in the future, Blue considered, was it better than this, the here and now of Berlin? Was it better than listening to David Bowie and reading the books and poetry and looking at the paintings and sculpture that could motivate people to change and become better human beings, even though they had never been repaired?

All of them, all of these people, were damaged but they continued to participate in a world that had found a beautiful blend of fakery and reality. Blue could no longer tell if this was 1976 or later. The city felt empty and exhausted suddenly: Schöneberg was not shining tonight. Quangel had told Blue how it would be, but he hadn't seemed to grasp how it had been. Blue walked into a café called Anderes Ufer.

Sitting alone in the window watching the cars push through the wet streets was as good a place as any to consider the enormity of Quangel's tale of gateways and time travel. The café light was dimmed with a faint tint of red. A few people sat around the wooden tables and banquettes talking quietly. In the background a recording of the French actress Jeanne Moreau floated around the room as Blue thought about what had just happened in Bowie's apartment and whispered, 'All the ideas. All the stories. All the understanding of what I thought we were, has gone.'

The journey through space, the arrival on Earth, the memories of a planet that didn't exist, all gone, thought Blue. And now life, as it had been understood, was all a mirage. Who am I? Was the story told by Quangel true? Am I an evolved form of humanity? I had a mother? Maybe I had a family. Are they also alive? Where would they be? Why have they not tried to make contact with me? Will I be able to find them? Who are they? If they had wanted to know about me then they would have been in touch. I have a story.

Me. A story. Green, where are you? I can't understand all of this alone. I need you. I need your help. Our love. Us. Together. Our journey. Our story. Did you know any of this? Were you aware of this story – where we came from, who we were? No. Of course not. How could you have? What am I to do? Is this the end? Talk to me. Talk to me. Show me something. I'm lost. Lost in Berlin. Is that how Bowie felt when he came here? His life was not what he had thought it was. The world he came from in LA wasn't real. And he came here. Berlin.

This is where he found himself. Found a new reality. Another shore. Is this what they do in this part of our evolution: have instincts, read signs, allow space for improvisation? It's all ridiculous and at the same time offers the glance of hope.

I was born. I had a mother. I am human. Repaired. Unconscious, but human. And it was this fact that brought me here, to understand something that had been taken away from us. I can love. I am one of them. Do I stop being me? Try to be like them. Us. Us. Us.

Oh Green, what would you have thought? You would have understood. You would have wanted to stay. Yes? Yes. I can try. I will try. Blue looked around the café. A neon sign on the back wall flickered the name of the café, Anderes Ufer. Another shore, thought Blue. Is this a sign? Is this part of how it works in this part of my world? My past world. Signs.

Meaning. Contact. Thought.

Blue picked up a magazine which lay amongst many others on the window shelf. Bianca Jagger smiled a sultry sensuality from the front cover, which was in perfect harmony with Moreau's cigarette-layered voice in the background. Blue touched Jagger's face thinking about the natural beauty people had – people who were no longer any different from those where Blue and Green had come from. Them had become Us. Jagger's lips pouted from her face, but it was her actor's eyes that captured Blue's attention.

A soft female German voice interrupted the mood.

'Wunderbar.'

'Yes,' Blue replied and looked up at a woman of around twenty-five with slicked deep-black hair in a side parting, wearing wire glasses that framed large brown eyes.

'She might be the most beautiful woman in the world,' she said in broken English.

Blue smiled at the young woman.

'Yes, she might be.'

'You have come here from England?'

'No. From the New Mexico desert.'

'You're American?'

'No. I'm from here now. I'm from Berlin.'

The young woman smiled back at Blue.

'Good. That's good. We're all from somewhere. Can I get you something? A beer? A coffee?

'Maybe water.'

The young woman continued to stand in front of Blue, looking at the magazine and then back at Blue's face.

'Is everything OK?' Blue held the young woman's stare, hearing distant echoes of her thoughts.

She wanted to know if Blue was a man or a woman. She couldn't tell. She wanted to know more about this beautiful creature who was sitting in the window of the café watching the traffic speed past, looking at a photograph of the most beautiful woman in the world. She wanted to sit down and talk about Bianca Jagger, beautiful women, different countries, the East, Jeanne Moreau's movies, how David Bowie has breakfast here most mornings and sometimes a beer in the evening with Iggy Pop, she wanted to talk about the Wall and wall sickness, she wanted to show Blue her favourite Schöneberg clubs and wanted to tell Blue how she liked to make love.

And it was then that Blue interrupted her explosion of thoughts.

'Bowie and Iggy Pop come here?'

'Yes, often... how... did you...?'

Blue looked at the top of the magazine at the date. It was 1976.

'This is 1976?'

The young woman couldn't be sure if that was a statement or a question lost in translation, but the coincidence stayed with her.

'Yes, 1976. A good year or a bad year I don't know. Everything stays the same here in Berlin even when everything changes.'

'Nothing moves on?'

'Nothing.'

'It will.'

'You think so. This is too opti... mistic. Yes? This is correct?'

Blue nodded and continued to smile at the young woman.

'I'm Blue.'

'Blue? That's nice. I'm Jena.'

'Jena.'

'Blue.'

'Shall we go to a Schöneberg club tonight, together?' Blue asked.

'Tonight?'

'One of your favourites.'

'Are you asking me where to go?'

'To go with you, yes.'

'Together?'

'I would like that. I... I don't want to be alone tonight.'

They continued to look at one another as Moreau sang the theme to the Marguerite Duras movie *India Song*. Odd things had happened to Jena in her life but this was the strangest. A sad song, a sad beautiful creature and a sad night pulled her into the world of human fantasy... could this be... could this be...?

'I'll have to close the café,' Jena whispered.

'Is that OK?'

'Why not?'

'You see? You've just changed something.'

Jena laughed softly and touched Blue's shoulder as Moreau sang a ballad of infernal love and loss.

'I have to get dressed. I won't be long.'

Blue watched the young Berliner walk to the back of the café and up some stairs. This was not a night to be alone. This was a night that needed contact. This was a night to try and understand Quangel's revelation and allow the flood of new emotions to enrich Blue's new-found soul. *I am one of them. Just like the beautiful Jena – I need to find love – could this be... could this be... could this be...?*

After the rain the air was clean and fresh. Blue and Jena walked through Schöneberg as people re-emerged from apartment buildings and coffee bars. They passed a derelict corner still damaged from an aerial bombardment thirty-six years previously; even in West Berlin progress was slow. Blue was intrigued by how people took the relic for granted, not knowing that in a few years' time this would be a new development greedily sought after by new Berlin residents coming from all over Europe. It was clear to Blue that this Berlin, in 1976, was a place where people were not concerned by the future, as they never thought they had one. This was a city engulfed by another country that spoke the same language but served a very different ideology. Blue had wanted to see the eastern sector of the city, knowing that it was locked in a time capsule, but for the moment it was all about the West.

Jena had decided to take Blue to the opening of an art gallery and cocktail bar that was celebrating the life of the artist Jeanne Mammen, who had recently died. The artist had been born in Berlin and captured women in beautiful drawings and paintings from the Weimar period. The exhibition would be an array of her finest work and the gallery bar would become an exclusive women-only cabaret club for this one special night. Blue heard small echoes of Jena's thoughts as she tried to find a way to ask if Blue was a young woman or a young man. She thought that there might be a response when she told Blue that the exhibition party was a women-only event, but Blue had only asked more questions about Mammen's work.

'I don't think I should tell you any more about the work until you see it but there are no men in the paintings, only women in love.'

Blue's response gave Jena a little more reassurance.

'How beautiful.'

'Where are you staying here in Berlin?'

'I'll find an apartment, maybe a hotel.'

'It's not so easy as people think. In West Berlin there is a housing shortage. Too many people, not enough homes. Hotels are expensive.'

'I'll find somewhere.'

'Can I make a suggestion please?' Jena said softly.

They continued to walk into the labyrinth of Schöneberg streets heading north towards the brightly lit Kurfürstendamm. As the rain clouds moved deeper into the west, slivers of grey and deep blue emerged from the east. The light cast a sullen spill on the streets creating tough angular shadows with sharp decisive edges.

'The suggestion I make is that I have a spare room in my apartment. I can offer you this, if you would like.'

Blue stopped on the street corner and turned to face her. Jena found the intensity of the stare overwhelming and blushed. Blue touched her face and leaned forward and kissed her on the cheek. They stood silently in front of one another. Eventually Blue broke the strange sensuality of their nearness – their faces practically touching.

'I decided that this city would be my new home. And you, Jena, are everything that tells me I have made the right decision. You know nothing about me but you show such kindness and love. You can't decide if I am a man or a woman, yet you will take me to see the work of Jeanne Mammen, where only women are invited tonight. Thank you... thank you, Jena.'

'Will you stay?' Jena held Blue's hand and tried to maintain eye contact but had to look away as Blue's eyes pulsed and pulled her towards the small iris dot that led Jena somewhere beyond her understanding of people and places and random meetings and clichés of love at first sight. The eyes rolled like water, spraying and casting her reflection in different directions.

'I will stay. But only if I can contribute.'

'Contribute?'

Blue took out a large bundle of euros and put them in her hand. Jena looked at the notes with the European symbol.

'What are these?'

'This is the future. If I could make money then, then I can now. Money will not be a problem.'

'But I don't want your money.'

'But I must contribute. If this is my home, I must contribute.'

Blue took the thousands of euro notes and threw them up into the air. The wind pulled them high above the Schöneberg apartments in the direction of the East and over the Wall.

'Everything that passes is only a riddle,' Blue whispered into the night as they watched Europe's future flutter and fall along and over the Wall.

'You read Goethe?' asked Jena as she slipped her arm through Blue's, who smiled and nodded, listening to her confused and bewildered thoughts.

'Can you hear that?'

'What?' Jena replied.

'From somewhere, someone is playing Beethoven sonatas. I think it's Artur Schnabel. He is playing all thirty-two. Together.'

'Schnabel? No. It can't be. He died many many years ago. It must be someone else.'

'No. It's him. It's in the echoes of the city. The history. The Volks-bühne performance. Käthe Kollwitz is in the audience. She's crying.'

'I see what you are doing. You are a writer. No? This is how you imagine the city. Then and now and maybe even the future we do not have.'

'There are moments here Jena, when I see the unseen, hear the unheard, know the unknown. It all wraps itself around me. You call it history. I call it sensation and feeling. It's all so new that I try to calm it down but it keeps coming.'

'But this is normal in a new city. A new home. The imagination takes control. Everything is possible.'

'You think that maybe I have an imagination?'

'For sure. Yes. Yes. Fantasievoll. It's wonderful. In this grey city we need people like you who can hear the echoes as you call them.'

'People like me?' Blue smiled.

'Yes, you, Blue. Just like Bowie, you came here to live. To create. To be part of something. Sometimes we who are from here cannot see.'

'Do you think the echoes I hear are nostalgia?'

'But what are we if we have no past? Our recent past here in Germany is …'

'Gehet alle zur Hölle.'

'Yes. I look back with fear and terror. We pretend to no longer see or hear. We leave it alone.'

'But that was an identity neurosis which must not condemn all the wonderful years of joy and creativity.'

'They tried to destroy it.'

'Yes, but they failed.'

'Blue, you are full of… good feelings. Thank you. And tonight. The party. It's a party of nostalgia. So you see, everything is in place. The stars are aligned. Can you still hear Schnabel playing the sonatas?'

'I can.'

'And does Käthe continue to cry?'

'With happiness.'

'I know how she feels,' said Jena as they approached a tall building where the entrance was lit with the glamour of a Berlin party from the 1930s. Flames and spotlights created a magical combination of expressionist shadows and intrigue, leaving no-one in any doubt that something remarkable was happening behind the closed doors.

The exhibition party was Berlin-full: no room for anyone else, strictly insiders only. The dress code was Weimar-period cabaret; women of all ages dressed in men's evening wear or silk gowns draped in pearls with long velvet gloves; in addition, stocking-revealing dancing-girls' skirts and breast-enhancing bras, feather boas and long ivory cigarette holders decorated the room with an historic decadence. Plumes of cigarette and cigar smoke created a haze through which rasping jazz music bounced off the walls as the women drank cocktails of every colour.

Jena took off her long black coat to reveal a short black silk dress. She proceeded to push a hairband across her forehead and placed a peacock feather on the right-hand side before putting her glasses into her jacket pocket. Jena looked at Blue, who was watching her transition with a curious delight, and pointed at Blue's coat: 'Take it off.'

Underneath was a white shirt underneath a black jacket and matching trousers. Jena lent forwards and touched the shirt collar and ran her hand along Blue's hip.

'I really like it.'

'And you. You look... perfect.'

'Thank you,' Jena gushed as she took some lipstick from her coat pocket and applied deep blood-red to her mouth and then did the same to Blue. The mirror in the doorway of the gallery shone their reflections back to them as they both smiled like children.

'Come, let's drink.'

And amidst the laughter, the now vibrating jazz and capricious joy of people feeling energised and young, there was a magnificent sense of fun in the air. This was Berlin's idea of a wake for an artist they loved, and who through history had loved them and made their lives honourable, sensual and fearless. This was a room full of love. Blue stood in the middle with Jena, realising that Jena was also a mystery as she stood shimmering in her black dress and red lips and beautiful eyes. And then they danced.

The room swayed with people who loved being together. The music continued to swirl around the dancing feet as the Fasanenstrasse gallery duped time into believing that it had landed back in the 1930s. The walls of the gallery spread the iconic work of Mammen all around the dancers, drinkers and lovers who openly touched, groped and kissed, almost replicating the action in the paintings. The paintings were extraordinary: women crucified in billowing gowns, graceful and naked, eyes covered. The eyes, the eyes, the eyes, thought Blue – why are they covered, why the sacrifice? Woman as redemption, woman as saviour – a world without men.

The paintings were full of pink-fleshed young women with curly jangling hair and deep breasts with red-tipped nipples staying close together as if they were a social group awaiting selection. An older woman with hands on hip awash in sensual yellows and greys threw a get-out-of-my-face leer to a threatening vamp as her young girl-friend entered the room in heavy mascara, dangling earrings and dynamic bobbed hair – she was so exquisite that her protective older lover knew she had to keep her close.

The shadows and colours and body angles were repeated in the reality of the room by the women of 1976. They kissed, caressed, watched, touched, licked and whispered words of drunken longing, friendship and love in a mass of moving flesh that seemed invisibly linked by the threads of their floating clothes.

Blue stood in front of the painting 'Jalousie', where a woman on her knees wrapped her arms around her lover's waist as she stood in front of a table mirror. Both wore silk slips, one was black haired, the other blonde. One looked up desperately as the other dismissively looked away. It was a rich little story that was bold and sad and deeply moving.

'Am I becoming like them?' thought Blue. 'Since Green has gone why do I no longer need to share fluid? Will I be able to travel again? Do I begin to forget who I came with and who I was... am?

What will happen to me now?' Blue's thoughts were interrupted by a woman standing looking at the same painting. She was wrapped in a transparent black silk gown. Underneath she was naked.

Blue spoke first.

'What is Jalousie?'

'Jealousy,' she said, 'is when somebody you love doesn't love you back and shows their attention or love to someone else.'

'It must be painful.'

'Oh yes... in moments it makes you feel hot then it makes you feel cold... you've never felt it?'

'No.'

The woman turned to look at Blue. She took off her sunglasses and looked at Blue's hands and fingers and neck and face and got caught by the shine of the eyes.

'You came with Jena.'

'Yes. Do you know her?'

'I'll wager she is watching us right now and is feeling maybe a little hot and cold.'

'We're friends.'

'Not lovers?'

Blue's eyes flicked, changing shape and colour so subtly that the woman could feel it but couldn't see it. It was too much and she had to turn away and look out into the crowd and put her glasses back on.

'You are an alien.'

The question caught Blue off guard. 'An alien?'

'You're not from here.'

'No. No, I'm not from here.'

'Not a Prussian.'

'What is that?'

'They say you are a Prussian first and a German second.'

'I don't know what that means.'

'Nor does anyone any more. Our ancestors would be shocked to see what has happened to their beloved Berlin.'

'Even Jeanne Mammen?'

'Maybe not her.'

The woman took Blue's hand and held it between hers, gently rubbing Blue's palms and wrist. The woman felt brave enough behind her sunglasses to hold Blue's stare.

'Would you like to come home with me?'

'Why?'

'You can touch me if you want.'

'We are touching.'

'Do you like it?'

'You have soft skin.'

'And so do you.'

'Shall we dance?'

'That would be nice but I came with Jena, who has invited me to stay and I agreed.'

'Lucky Jena.'

'No... lucky me.' Blue kissed the woman. Only the slightest of pecks that lasted the briefest of moments but Blue transferred a minor tremor to the woman who felt it enter and shake her.

The gentle fun of the room, its music and mood changed to a solid silence. The woman could only hear her own breathing.

'I don't want you to go. Not yet.'

Blue touched her face.

'Kiss me again,' she whispered, as she closed her eyes behind her sunglasses. But when she opened them again Blue was gone and the room had returned to its jazz cacophony and theatrical erotica. The woman looked desperately around the room for Blue but could only see women recreating dancing girls with flapping hands and feet. The art on the wall had come alive with an energy that caught the freedom of those living on the edge of civilisation against an external world that promised total annihilation; if you were about to die then you must die dancing.

Blue walked down a shabby street arm in arm with Jena. Thirty-one years earlier, these same streets had been pulverised by nightly bombing raids and daily swipes of Russian Katyusha rockets. The people of the city had been abandoned to the revenge of Red Army soldiers, drunk on looted booty and hell-bent on rape. Berlin had been physically destroyed with no compassion for the civilians; the women and children had paid the price for the insanity of their masters. Blue could hear the echoes of the lost, the distraught and the broken. The eternal screams of women, gang-raped by an insatiable conquerer, who prized light bulbs higher than the mothers and their daughters aged from eight to eighty who they brutalised with their conflict-machismo and an indoctrinated super-Soviet pride.

'Is everything OK?' Jena asked. 'You look worried.'

'These streets, these alleyways, the squares. They all have terrible secrets. If you listen closely, if you really concentrate, it's possible to hear the echoes.'

'Which echoes?'

'Of the people who lived here during the recent past. During the horror.'

'Oh... I... I told you, like everyone else I try to close my mind to this past.'

'Of course. But it is there. It will always be there.'

'Forever.'

'Yes... yes, I think so.'

'So, nothing good will ever come of this place. It will always be like this.'

'No. It will change. It will change in a good way.'

'In what way good?'

'Many ways, but most importantly through the imagination, being creative, repairing one another.'

'Do I need to be repaired?'

'Everyone does.'

They continued to walk through the dimly lit backstreets. Blue listened to Jena search for the words that might help her understand all of the many things that confused her about Blue.

'How do you know everything will become better?'

'Because people want it to be better.'

'But Berlin is a place of sadness and, as you say, echoes.'

'The party wasn't sad.'

'But that's what people do to hide the sadness. They make parties and get drunk.'

'And create. They make things. Art. Words. Music. Ideas.'

'Yes. Maybe this is true, but creating things does not necessarily make you happy, in fact, it could be the opposite. It could be the reason for the sadness.'

'Does Bowie look happy when he sits in your café?'

'He's very quiet. He reads. A book or a magazine. The English newspapers. Drinks coffee or a beer. He's like all the others, although of course he is David Bowie. I think he wants to be alone, or maybe anon...'

'Anonymous.'

'Yes. Thank you. No-one disturbs him. They leave him alone. Sometimes he is with friends and they talk quietly. They all smoke a lot. Everyone in Berlin smokes too much. He's polite in a very English way, which I like very much. People in Berlin can be very...'

'Rude?'

'Yes. Rude. But not for any reason. It's just their way. I prefer the English way.'

'Have you spoken to him?'

'Only about small things. You know, the weather, or sometimes he asks if there is anything interesting happening. Like tonight's exhibition and party. He wants to know about that kind of thing. Sometimes I hear about events from other customers. But this is Schöneberg and this is where gay people tend to live because of the bars and clubs and cafés.'

'Like yours.'

'Yes, like mine.'

'Is Bowie gay?'

'Maybe. Sometimes. I don't know. I think he likes gay people. They certainly like him.'

'Does it matter?'

'No... no, I guess not.'

'Are you gay?'

Jena stopped and looked at Blue. Her thoughts ricocheted, colliding and melting and reappearing in a mixture of hurt anxiousness.

'Is something wrong?' Blue asked softly.

'No... nothing. I... thought maybe that you... yes, in answer to your question. I am gay. I am a lesbian.'

'So you know who you are in a city that accepts you for who you are. And is that not the case for all the people at the party tonight? So why would they be sad? Why are they not happy?'

'Are you happy, Blue?'

In the distance the TV Tower near Alexanderplatz blinked its red ever-watching eye from across the Wall. U-Bahn trains rattled and scratched their way through Berlin's vaults, passing ghost stations where death greeted trespass. The wind from the East slipped through the streets drying the pavements and roads, stemming the reflections and the swish of fast-moving cars.

Berlin's ability to move at pace and then suddenly stop was unique to this bedraggled outpost. The noise of the West and the silence of the East was at the heart of the city's unbalanced psychotic stance, at once indefatigable and upright but then melancholic and suffering etiolation, as confidence waned on the fringe of the apocalypse. Blue considered the millennial smog's influence on the sinking feeling of the inhabitants of both sides of the divide.

'This is my home,' Blue repeated. 'If I have a home, then I am happy.'

'Are you alone?'

'I'm with you.'

'Before this. Before me.'

'I had a friend.'

'And then?'

'And then… this friend was gone.'

'Forever?'

'Forever.'

'I'm sorry.'

Jena found Blue's stare overwhelming. The eyes shone and sparkled and then clouded with grey moisture, telling enough of a story for Jena to look away, releasing a small gasp of an understanding that ridiculed sentiment. She felt something, a connection, an urgency to protect Blue from the loss, from the echoes of Berlin, from a near-rampant hedonism, from a city suffocating as it sank deeper into the tragedy of its own history. She stepped forward and held Blue tightly, hugging cheek to cheek, breathing together. They were lit by the beam of a spotlight, which spread out into an area the size of a football pitch next to the Wall.

Scrambled graffiti, automatic insignia, philosophical aphorism and primitive semiotics sunk into the grey blocks, whose height was staggering. No-one of course chose to go from this side to the other: the expression would be met within a pit of crippling death. The other side remained silent.

Were Jena and Blue watched? Almost certainly; could they be heard through hidden microphones? Definitely. Were they regarded as a potential threat? Possibly, but only in the same way that every other citizen of West Berlin was seen as a threat.

Blue listened to the guards on the other side trying to keep awake, thinking of food, of a bigger and warmer apartment, of their families, especially their children. And the wind from the East spared them nothing as it found its way through their uniforms and attacked their trigger fingers. Blue listened with Jena's skin pressed against an ear that still retained a waning power capable of listening to people's hopes and desires. Jena pulled her hand back when the sound of a gunshot (or was it a car backfiring?) sprung over the Wall searching for an audience and found one.

'What was that?' Jena asked, holding Blue close.

'The guard's finger was so cold he pulled the trigger by mistake,' said Blue, looking up along the Wall and into the night following the wave of searchlights that now looked for the cause of the disturbing crack and echo.

'How do you know that?'

'It's possible, is it not?'

'Yes... but...'

She leaned forward and kissed Blue on the lips. It was a soft, nervous kiss, born from fear and sadness and a new but deep affection for this strange creature who had entered her life. Blue accepted the kiss and wet Jena's lips with a tongue that felt like water and air; a gentle ethereal glance that held them together as the sound of the guard's gunshot continued to vibrate against the Wall and the nearby buildings. Jena pulled back, and gasped the cold wind through her body in a desperate rush for oxygen. Blue held her hand as she fought to bring herself back to some kind of normality.

'Just like the song,' Blue said.

'The song?'

'The Bowie song.'

'Which one?'

'"Heroes".'

'I haven't heard of this song.'

No, thought Blue, but you will. In the distance, Hansa Studios stood proud against the night's cold winds. A man stood at the window of one of the studios, looking down at the Wall and the kissing couple. Blue smiled. Is this the moment where we cross paths and you can see me and hear me? Is this the moment where the future inspires the past or at least sows the seeds for new provocative ideas? Blue remembered the warning from Quangel of not becoming involved with events – but that would no longer be possible.

'That is the famous Hansa Studios,' said Jena.

'Yes,' replied Blue.

'Who do you think is looking down at us?'

'Bowie? I think it might be.'

'Is he lonely?'

'Why do you ask?'

'Sometimes, like I said before, when he comes into the café I think he looks sad. Alone. Maybe in his position he doesn't have so many friends. Maybe he has to be careful. Being so famous can be a problem, no? Who do you trust?'

'But what makes him so different from us?'

'We're not famous. Or artists. Well, maybe you are.' Jena looked from the man at the window back to Blue. 'Maybe that's why you have come to Berlin – that's why so many people come here – to be free.'

'In the least free city in Europe.'

'But are you an artist: a painter, a writer, a musician, a poet?'

thought Jena, as she watched Blue continue to stare at the studio building.

'I'm a fan of what they do. The process. The idea that becomes something real, that they want to share with us. That's why I came here, to try and understand what it means. Or at least, what it means to me.'

Jena looked confused. Had she spoken her thoughts aloud?

'But you chose Bowie.'

'Yes. Does that surprise you?'

'No. Not at all. I think you have made a wonderful choice. Being a fan is like being in love. No?'

'Love is part of the process I need to understand even more.'

'The most important part.'

'Yes.'

Blue heard the wind swirl and shift, slamming against the Wall as it battered the abandoned streets into submission. Streets that had witnessed an apocalyptic violence against the young, the old and the innocent. Everything felt like near-history. A history of hate. Jena wanted to know more about Blue, but felt obliged to find no lace-fragility, no pools of sadness, no hurt. But her way was honest and truthful and, however soft, the questions felt like daggers.

'Were you in love with your friend who has gone?'

Blue pushed Jena's hair back from her face.

'We never thought about our friendship in that way, probably because we had no need to. I think it was similar to what you call love.'

'Does it have another name?'

'Maybe another context.'

'Love is love.'

'Yes.'

'Green. You said your friend's name was Green. Blue and Green.'

'Yes.'

'From birth.'

'From when we were repaired. That's when we met and that's what we decided to call one another for obvious reasons.'

'Repaired. Obvious. You talk in riddles. Did you have problems? Psychological? Maybe dependency... drugs? Alcohol?'

'No. None of that. We were both sick and we were fixed.'

'Simple as that?'

Blue touched Jena's face, moving a finger around her eyes and then along her jawline and neck then slowly upwards to her mouth. Jena kissed Blue's fingers. They stayed close together with the Wall only a few metres away. Jena held Blue tightly, no longer sheltering from the snap of the wind but holding onto an idea that her world was changing in a way that she didn't recognise; the routine and fidelity of her life were being questioned not by the arrival of her new friend but by the painful realisation that Berlin had become an excuse, an exhausted comfort zone that no longer gave her any comfort. The perilous conflict that lay at her feet was sucking the life from her and her only sense of adventure had come through a leisurely theatricality and role play. Who was she?

Blue listened to Jena's moment of understanding, a timeless loop of realisation and new hope or was it despair? She looked at the Wall as she held Blue tightly and whispered.

'The other side of this wall is a place where there is no creativity. There are no David Bowies who would risk their lives for their art. Over there, there are no opportunities to be different. Everything is the same. Young people have no inspiration, only ideology which controls their lives, it controls everything they do. They went from the Nazis to Communism, two different types of terror that were both anti all the reasons why you have come to this city. Their ideology is anti-love. It's a very sad place even in comparison to how much of a mess Berlin is in the West. In the East it's a disaster. There is nothing there to love – there's only survival, and its repetition and banality are not worth living for.'

Blue held her face and kissed her eyes. 'It will end one day.'

'When the next war comes.'

'No. Not war. People will decide. People will say we have had enough. People will want beauty again. People will want to be loved. That's what human beings live for. So, this wall will come down without war. People will do it.'

'That's so romantic. But you have never been to the East. The people have no power. They are like androids. Automatons. Robots. They are as if someone decided to take the human parts of them away and replace them with mechanical parts. It's like science fiction. Imagine. And it's just over there. They lobotomised a generation of free-thinking people. Maybe one day they can be repaired as you say, like you and Green. Maybe one day they will live again, but I don't think so.'

Blue took Jena's hand as they walked back towards Potsdamer Platz. The streets near the Wall remained empty. A thin drizzle of rain reappeared and in the sodium street lights and glaring white spotlights the rain took the shape of a veil floating and bending with the wind. Jena was aware of Blue looking back at the Hansa building. It was obvious that Blue now intended to visit the studio.

'I don't think they would allow both of us in,' Jena said softly.

Blue listened to her wrestle with the disappointment of them possibly going separate ways. Would she ever see Blue again? She squeezed their hands tightly together, awaiting a response, but nothing came.

'You're here now. Bowie may be inside. You should try. Do whatever you need to do, to go and look and listen. I live above the café. It would be an honour to have you stay at my apartment.'

Blue stopped walking and watched as the moving spotlights shone on her beautiful face. Jena smiled and hugged Blue. Fate had brought them together, she thought, and now fate was taking them in different directions. A small tear rolled down her cheek.

'I will come back there. I promise.'

'Well then, that's good enough for me,' she said with a note of distant hope as she leaned forward and kissed Blue on the lips. Again the oxygen seemed to be sucked out of her but she couldn't pull away. Blue's mouth softly pulled her in as she was becoming increasingly light-headed and faint. She tried to speak, but the words were consumed in the turmoil of what was happening to her. It was as if her whole body was free of gravity and was being drawn through Blue's mouth. She could see Blue looking back at her but not through what could be described as eyes, the colour was cloudy and grey and moved like clouds. There was no obvious iris and no descending eyelid, no blinking, just a floating foam-like aura that seemed three dimensional as it connected their intimacy with a touch. Jena could feel something imperceptible and slight cling to her cheek then move around her neck and down her spine. It tingled and shivered its way around her body like a mild seizure and part of her wanted to scream and the other part wanted to suffocate and die at this moment of happiness. And no sooner had she succumbed to the sensation than Blue's lips pulled back from hers and blew warm air into her mouth, which rushed through her body, alerting every cell to its exhaustion and need to replenish the blood's oxygen. For a moment she was startled, afraid, and then confused and embarrassed. Blue wiped the tears from her cheek as Jena tried to gather herself.

'It's important that we meet again, for me at least, it's important,' she whispered. Blue nodded and whispered, 'And for me, and for me.'

The words seemed to find their own space. 'And for me.' A delicate musical sound that belonged to the night, to the drizzling veil-like rain and to this moment where they made a pact to meet again. Blue stood watching Jena walk out of the spotlights and into the shadows as she eventually disappeared into the night. Did she turn and wave? Was she still there? Blue waited. But she was gone. There was now only the sound of a lighter wind that lacked any ferocity but, through the vast empty spaces close to the Wall, volleyed and thundered a false aggression. Blue listened for the sound of human voices and thoughts but nobody was close enough. Here by the Berlin Wall, next to Hansa Studios, Blue was alone. The studio looked tall with a faded importance that ran through many of the city's remaining buildings that had survived the flattening bomber attacks of 1945. Like a sunflower in this smashed and cremated pocket, Hansa had survived and was a beacon in a city short on hope.

Blue stood outside the entrance to the studio. The entrance had 1920s Art Deco swirls and lines cut deep into the granite and marble but only a small light shone onto the steps. Berlin seemed to be constantly hiding in the shadows. Only the Wall was treated as a spectacle: somewhere dangerous and forbidden. A street lamp gave no cover from the rain but Blue had had enough of shadow-play and concealment.

Like Jena had so openly and honestly said, this was why the journey to Berlin made sense; to be here right now, at this exact moment.

The building's neoclassical pillars would have been lit with a sense of fun and occasion in the 1920s and lit again but with less fun in the 1930s as a reminder of state power under a new regime. Blue knew that eventually the 'Meistersaal' would be restored as one of the iconic buildings in the new Berlin but, right now, it was exhausted like the rest of the city. However, it still managed to retain the undercurrent of a decadent narrative that played out thrillingly to the new Anglo-American visitors inside.

The studio's Kreuzberg location should have ensured the doors would have been locked but, when Blue turned the handle, the door opened. The entrance was in darkness, and in a building famous for recording sound it was strangely silent. Blue walked up the stairs.

The clicking and clacking and squeaking of rubber soles on the marble floors provided an eerie soundtrack to the stairway and beyond onto the corridors that spread out from each floor. Standing still, and concentrating on the echoes floating up and down the building, Blue momentarily connected with the triumphs of orchestras, singers, solo musicians, painters, celebrations and speeches, but somehow nothing was ever very far away from the horror. Beethoven sonatas met with the apocalyptic crush of Allied bombs or Katyusha rockets; and then the single ringing shot of an East German guard shooting a figure in the back as they sought freedom from another tyranny.

The building swelled in counterpoint: changing times, new ideologies, new ideas, new music, old solutions – there was a frenzy and collision on the various floors of myth-makers and artists, producers and dreamers, alchemists and failures. It was all here, and Blue could feel the reverberations of the 20th century refuse to apologise for making music that was unashamedly art. And here, right here, amongst the confusion was David Bowie, who was now part of the building's bleeding anxiety as he put the finishing touches to his new recording *Low* and was already thinking about the next, *'Heroes'*.

A door opened on the fourth floor and someone started walking downstairs. Blue stood back and waited, pressed hard against the wall. A telephone rang loudly in the reception area, and the echoes of the past were gone as a new history began. The person coming down the stairs was coming ever closer and Blue now knew there was no place to hide and that they would meet. Blue waited until the last moment before pretending to come out of a closed doorway and bumped into the person coming down the stairs.

'I'm sorry,' said Blue, looking forward and up as if knowing where to go by being part of the fabric of the building and knowing how it worked.

'No problem pal. No problem.' The American accent was lush and jumpy. Standing in front of Blue was Iggy Pop. Blue beamed and caught the vernacular like a leather-skinned sailor chasing an Atlantic whale.

'How's it going?'

'Oh buddy… it's going, big-time going, know what I mean? Like exciting. Right?'

'Right.'

'Love this place. Love it. Love it. Like look at this. Look around you. It's fucking wow. Right? And over there. It's a one-off. This city. I love it pal. Love it. It makes me wanna do stuff. You got me?'

'I think so.'

'You Berliners. You're cool man. Like proper cool.'

Iggy leaned forward and gave Blue a hug and Blue held Iggy tight, cheek to cheek. Iggy smelled of cigarettes and alcohol, a thin human layer above an animal scent that was part wolf and part puma. You could almost hear the wolf pack calling him across the tundra. Iggy vibrated with energy, a body warmth radiated from his leather jacket and thin T-shirt. Blue pulled back and looked closely at Iggy's face: it was a story. Long thin lines creased his forehead, hidden behind long strands of blonde hair. His eyes were electric pulses, throbbing a blue-grey with milky-white eyelids, fighting to close as Iggy refused to blink.

'Hey pal. You're something. I can't even tell if you're a he or a she. Who cares? But I gotta tell ya… I'm curious.'

Blue smiled. 'Who cares?'

Iggy pulled Blue closer so their lips touched then melted into a kiss. They broke away and laughed together.

'Now pal. That was good. That was the best kiss I've had in Europe. I'm going for a drink. Are you coming?'

'Not tonight. I need to be here.'

'OK, you're doing the work thing. Right?'

'I'm here.'

'You are pal. And I like you. And I like your city. And the people. All of them, old and young. Even the ones who think I'm an asshole. We'll meet again you and I.'

'I hope so.'

'What's your name?'

'Blue.'

'Nice. Real nice. I like it.'

Iggy pushed on down the stairs, moving at speed.

'It's a real nice name. Blue.' He sang as he jumped off the last few stairs and landed laughing at the bottom as he shouted back up the stairs.

'Blue. He's looking for inspiration. Go see him. Tell him I sent you from deep space or Mount Olympus. You got that Blue?' And then he was gone, slamming the door, running into the wet Berlin night.

Blue sniffed the air. Iggy's space. Like a dog, the American punk had left his scent as a warning or maybe a musky message of lust and dereliction. Iggy had scared the horror out of the building. His bleeding chorus of optimism and hopefulness was a crazed songbird of peace. Blue smiled. The encounters with Jena and now Iggy made it clear that Blue was part of this world, and no matter how profound Quangel's warnings, it was exhilarating.

What was this new feeling reverberating around the body? It wasn't unlike the sensuality of Jena's kiss. Was it nerves, thought Blue? These people, no, we, we suffer from nerves.

Nervous emotion is not curable. There was no repair required. I'm close, thought Blue. Close. No longer they or them but we. We. Bowie was upstairs. We. Jena was waiting above the café. We. Quangel had returned to the future. We. The dangers are obvious. We.

This is dangerous. We. I need to move up the stairs. But Blue was frozen to the spot on the stairs. Had the excitement, the nervous reaction, had it all become terror? Blue listened for echoes but there were none, only the silence and scent of Iggy Pop reminding Blue to go to the studio. Help. Inspire. Participate. Be there. Be part of it. Creativity. Blue moved on up the stairs.

There were two entrances. One for the studio control room and the other a small overdub recording space which Blue pushed open. The lights were dimmed and a few musical instruments lay around, including some small pieces of paper with various scribbled notes and lyrics. In the corner was a window where the glare from the Wall's spotlights created a glowing frame.

David Bowie stood with his back to Blue looking out over the Wall into the Eastern sector of Berlin. Blue carefully closed the door but it clicked shut. Bowie didn't turn around. A large, dark window of glass separated the recording space from the control room. Blue could see Brian Eno talking quietly with Tony Visconti, neither of whom was aware of Blue's presence.

'Is that you again?' asked Bowie in a soft mix of London and transatlantic stretched vowels.

Blue looked around the small space for someone else but they were alone together.

'You know who I am?'

'You've been following me since Brixton. I remember you clearly at Hammersmith. There was somebody else. Another. I think you came to LA, but I'm not sure. Are they here too?'

'No. No, I'm alone. Green's gone.'

'Where?'

'Gone forever. LA was too much. The toxicity.'

'I'm sorry to hear that. Were you very close?'

'Yes.'

'Green?'

'And I'm Blue.'

'Why?'

'It was the colour of our blood after we were repaired.'

'What do you mean by repaired?'

'We were rebuilt.'

'A bit like me, a bit like Frankenstein's creature?'

'No bolts. No scars. No anger. No gender.'

'No sadness.'

'Sometimes I think I'm beginning to feel lonely now that I'm stuck here.'

'Stuck?'

'This is my home now.'

'It's a good home, especially for the lonely.'

They were quiet for a moment. Bowie continued to look out of the window. Blue watched how the light drew a line around the edge of the profile of his face. There he was in all his beauty: thin and sad, downbeat but no longer broken like he was in LA.

'You said no gender.'

'Not specific.'

'Both?'

'Yes.'

'How does that feel?'

'Peaceful.'

'And then you visited LA.'

'You remembered us.'

'I don't remember much but I heard you play something. Is that right?'

'We played something of yours.'

'Really. What was it?'

Blue looked back into the control room where Visconti and Eno were listening to overdubs and adding small synthetic lines that were only evident through the sound of Bowie's headphones which lay on the ground.

'What you are doing here will become your masterpiece.'

'How do you know that?'

'I know.'

'It's a mess. A random mess. I think people might be shocked.'

'They will.'

Bowie looked up into Berlin's night sky as the rain started to fall heavily.

'Do you love this city?'

'I do.'

'Me too. Do you know why?'

'No.'

'Me neither.'

'Maybe that's what we love. The not knowing why.'

'Maybe... will they forgive me?'

'Forgive what?'

'The indulgence.'

'It will change how people see you. You are a serious artist who has begun to take his art seriously.'

'That sounds boring. Pretentious.'

'The artists you like, don't they take their art seriously? He does. Eno. He's serious about it.'

'I'm English. We're not good at taking ourselves seriously.'

'But you're in Berlin. Everything is serious here.'

'Yes... that's true... maybe that's why I'm here... Blue.'

Bowie turned away from the window to face his unexpected guest. They took in each other's faces. Bowie watched a blue vein pulse and then disappear under Blue's chin and along the neck. The skin was tight and had a shine like new ice but the eyes defended the face and Bowie had never seen anything like those eyes before.

Blue listened to his thoughts.

Who is this? Where did he... or she come from? Am I imagining this? What's happening? Don't panic. Don't panic. Don't panic. Hold on. Blue.

Blue. The room had become blue. Electric blue. Are you an oracle? Am I going mad? Am I mad? Blue. Blue. And your friend died in LA because of the toxicity of that culture: those people, my home in Doheny Drive. I caused your friend, maybe your lover, to die. And here you are, telling me that everything is going to be alright. That I'm OK. That I might survive. Here in Berlin. Can you hear the echoes? I can. Blue. Blue. And all the shit I'm in. Wife. Manager.

Debt. And my son who I love. Blue. Blue. And your friend died in LA. And you gave me love and I gave you poison and fear. And here you are. A beautiful creature. Why are you here? Have you come to kill me? Is it because I killed your friend? No. No, you said you were peaceful. You look full of love. Did I see you standing by the Wall kissing someone? Did I hear a gunshot? Am I imagining a world that doesn't exist? They want me to sing tonight. Tonight. But what? Blue. Blue. But what?

Blue. Blue. Tell me what. What shall I sing? Here I am. Stuck here like you. Waiting for the gift of sound and vision. Do you understand? Could you understand? Can you help me? Have you been sent to help me? Protect me. Find me. Find myself. Blue. Blue.

Can you hear me? I think you can. You look like you are listening. You are. I know you are. Blue. Blue. I'm waiting for the gift of sound and vision and you want to know what that gift is. That's why you're here. You're beautiful. An angel. Stay with me as I try to sing something. Something that feels real. Do you understand? I think you do. Your eyes are sparkling and hypnotic moons, or suns, or Jupiters, or Mars. What have those eyes seen? You were repaired. You said you were repaired. Me too. This place: Berlin. It's where I will be repaired. Brought back to life. I'm sorry about Green. I'm sorry about LA. But look at this room. Blue. Blue. It glows. It sparkles like your eyes. It's Blue. Electric blue. And this is where I will be repaired like you. Here, in this city. Berlin. The strangest, most beautiful city in the world.

'Blue. Blue.'

'Thank you,' interrupted Blue. 'You said my name as if I were really in the room with you.'

'Aren't you?'

'No, not really. I'm back somewhere, I'm not sure where, but I came here looking for you. I escaped.'

'Do you like it here?'

'I do. I think I, as you say, "love it". I love everything about this city: the people, the buildings, the wind, the rain and especially the echoes.

'You hear them too?'

'Everywhere.'

'Even here?'

'This building is a symphony of echoes.'

'Some frightening.'

'And some beautiful.'

Tony Visconti's voice came through the headphones.

'What do you think? Do you want to try something tonight? We've got lots we need to do, so you could give it a go tomorrow if you need more time.'

Bowie continued to stare at Blue. The room seemed to stop. It was a captured photographic moment. The only sign that there was life in the room was the movement of blue blood from underneath Blue's eyes. What shall we do, thought Bowie. Shall we do it tonight? Blue. Blue.

Blue smiled an ocean of hope and love overwhelming Bowie, who was drifting into a mild terror. What do we do? How do we do it? Why do we do this? Help me. Help me. Help me. Blue put out a hand, which Bowie touched and understood immediately what should be done, what needed to be done.

'No, let's do it tonight,' he said with the gentle surge of a man who was digging deep to find a meaning in the slow-falling flakes of dust that ran through the lights, the swarming rain against the window, the moment where something needed to be done against the dancing spotlights of East Berlin that bounced against the walls and windows of Hansa Studios. It was now or never.

This was why Blue and Green had travelled through time and chosen Bowie, the eternal angel. It all made sense now to Blue and Bowie. They were sharing a secret. The pulse. The creative pulse. Unfathomable but physical and it was here and happening in this room.

'OK, let me know when you're ready,' Visconti said with a casual expectancy.

Bowie picked up his headphones, pointed towards another pair lying on the floor plugged into a small box and whispered to Blue, 'Put them on.'

Blue sat on the floor and kept eye contact with Bowie, who lifted his arm to acknowledge he was ready. And then it came. Bowie closed his eyes. Outside the rain streamed lines, fast and furious, down the long window, but inside the dimly-lit studio there was no fury, no angst, no frustration. Everything in the room had settled into a meditative calm. The music jumped out of the headphones in a near-complete state.

The Visconti harmoniser, with its thud and splash reverb, marshalled the Dennis Davis drum pattern into a rolling-thunder pop disco. It was a new sound for a new era in an old world. And then came the Gardiner and Alomar guitar jingle against George Murray's harrumphing, dancing bassline.

Blue smiled into eternity. The music was wrapped in jagged happiness. A riff for all seasons, a movement and a building block for another surprise. This was human alchemy. This was how music touched you inside and outside and somewhere in-between. It was young and vibrant and free and for this night it belonged to Blue. This is what being a fan meant. It was crushingly beautiful and joyously uplifting.

Blue stood and danced as Bowie stood by the microphone, eyes still firmly closed. No words in front of him. Everything was to be in the arms of chance. This was Berlin. It was random and inexplicable but tonight it was about a different kind of energy, positive and unyielding. Blue caught the rhythm with no thought applied, and allowed the body to take over.

Bowie missed his obvious entry point but then came a thin synthetic string section before re-energised backing vocals from Mary Hopkin and Eno ushered you into a Bowie world where storytelling had changed from character to ethereal splendour. Blue of course knew the song in every detail and hummed, ahed and dooooed along with the rhythm slices before Bowie's saxophone prepared the listener for something bold and special.

Bowie opened his eyes. He had found the words, the opening words. He stared straight at Blue who moved in an elegant synchronicity to the drums and bass. They smiled the smile of awakening. They shared the joy of creation. For a moment they were as one as Blue sang the lines along with Bowie as he created them in front of the microphone. To Bowie it was baffling. How could this be? It only encouraged his smile to grow and seize Berlin with a monumental hug as he crooned and half-spoke his meditation on creativity and loss.

The words toppled out as they sang together.

Blue's name became enveloped in the song as Bowie reflected on LA, solitude, sitting alone in dark rooms. Blue felt that it had become a hymn to Green. Bowie was in complete control, he caught the sadness but he also caught the joy. Blue was Bowie's joy; a beautiful creature dancing before him knowing the lines as they left his mouth – singing, swirling.

Bowie pulled the words out of the air. It was automatic but steeped in the blood of near-past delusion. They were together – Bowie and Blue in harmony, on the same journey, searching for meaning where there had been none other than a few fragments of truth.

And now this, this was something deeper, this was something cosmically deep.

Blue's eyes closed as the song began to fade. At last Blue understood that the best creativity came from experience, not sensation. It had happened in the studio. A wonderful tale told in a few words – a near-haiku biography of a man's recent history. The words were echoes: words as echoes.

Blue felt the tendrils of delirium; a happiness that should have been shared with Green. Would Jena understand or would the complexity of the story frighten her? Bowie was not afraid. He understood who Blue was and why Blue was here. The song began to fade but Blue wanted to savour every last note of this experience. It was for Blue the magical world of humans – a world he had joined, a world that he had always been part of. The fade was quick and then there was silence.

Blue tried to remember why he was standing here. In a moment, rich memories began to fade like the song. It was irretrievable. Gone. Soon, Blue understood, there would be no memory of a previous life. Green was slipping away. Blue could no longer picture Green's face. Who was Green? Did Green ever exist? How did I get here? Where was I before Berlin?

Blue had been faded out by Bowie. At the moment they had met and shared something creative, they no longer needed one another, they were both free. Are these echoes, thought Blue, understanding panic for the first time and now afraid to open up to this new reality? What am I looking for? I heard Bowie sing. He sang to me. For me. With me.

Didn't he? I'm here, right now. This is not something I imagined.

Blue's eyes opened. Daylight poured in through the window. The studio was empty. The equipment was gone. Bowie was not standing at the microphone. The control room was in darkness. No Visconti. No Eno. Blue removed the headphones.

From the street Blue could hear people shouting. In the corridors and stairway outside the studio, people were calling to one another with a sense of excitement as they ran down the stairs. Something was happening, a frenzy of activity only a few metres away. Where had Bowie gone?

Was the noise and movement outside the studio door something to do with what had just happened? Was it something to do with Bowie? The night rain had been replaced by a bold sun, white and yellow against fast-moving clouds. The effect brought home to Blue how different the room was to a few moments ago when Bowie had produced the words to 'Sound and Vision'. The room had changed, everything seemed sharper, shinier and polished.

Blue moved over to the window and looked out onto the area around the Wall. People, mostly young, gathered on either side. Some of them had climbed onto the Wall and were hugging and kissing and dancing to a soundless tune that was roared on by a growing number of people who had come to witness the end and the beginning of their city. Blue understood what had happened. Time was slipping. The winter of 1976 had become autumn 1989.

Where was Bowie? Was he here? Did we not sing together? He knew me. He sang my name. And now? And now the end. The Wall is coming down. They told me I was stuck but here I am. Blue no longer understood the reality of the time-shifting circumstances.

Previous time-shifts had happened by design. They had travelled through choice. Blue tried to make sense of what was happening. I was with Bowie in Hansa Studios as he sang 'Sound and Vision'. I wanted to stay there. I wanted to tell Jena. Tell her what had happened. My friend. I wanted to talk more with Bowie. I wanted to understand more. And now.

More and more people surged towards the Wall. Some of them had hammers and chisels and were knocking holes, small but significant, into the concrete. At one point an East German guard looked through one of the holes and had no idea how to respond. The people from the West pushed their arms through and wanted to shake hands with the guard. He held his rifle nervously.

What was he supposed to do? He smiled and listened to the shouts of friendship, of reunification, of being one people again. If happiness had a sound, an ambient sound, then it was here right now at this spot. Human emotion poured onto the streets: this was a special day. Berlin had seen so many 'special days' but this was different, this was harmonious not triumphalist, this was about people being able to breathe again, laugh again, cry again. It was a moment of joy. Unbridled joy.

There were no caveats, no cynicism, no glory or defeat, just simple joy. Blue thought that this was it, this was the moment that pulled his journey together. This was why time had slipped to this beautiful place. It was a moment of reconnection with the human spirit that lay at the heart of creativity. It was creativity that had brought the Wall down. It was art that had brought the Wall down, not famine and tyranny, not ideological experiments, not terror – it was the will of the people, the desire to be heard, to be creative: to be human again.

Blue considered joining the party but thought about the dramatic time-shift that had happened without any design. By the time Blue reached the front door of Hansa Studios, would the timeline have remained in autumn 1989 or would Blue be spun into another period of Berlin's history?

Blue collated the books, essays and movies that remained stored in a memory bank with a now-limited resource. The danger of switching the main memory bank back on was unknown, so not worth the risk, who knows where it might end up – in Prussian history, perhaps, a history of wars: wars against Sweden, Austria, France, Russia and Germany itself. But it was the Weimar period that held the most powerful perfume. A city imploding in economic misery. A city dancing and singing a new hedonism; a city alive with politics and agitators. Alfred Döblin's observations of *Berlin Alexanderplatz* were alive within Blue; Franz Biberkopf's tragic attempt to become a normal member of society was violent yet funny, cruel and endearing. Nothing came close to Döblin's mastery of the streets and its people. The art of the era was crude and dynamic: a graphic illustration of a people seemingly caught in the middle of a Black Mass. It had all the threatening clouds of an end-of-the-world moment.

Would Blue's consciousness pull history about in a confused whirlpool where a random placement was more likely than being 'stuck', as had been suggested by Quangel in Bowie's Hauptstrasse apartment? Nothing was clear. Blue had arrived on New Year's Eve 2015, moved to 1976 and was now watching events unfold in 1989. Berlin accommodated the baffling journey with a casual ease.

The city watched Blue come to terms with Berlin's history and its people. Everything had happened quickly but then again it may have been over a thousand years of Blue's life.

What was this life? Did it exist? Outside, by the Wall, the party continued and had become louder with the roar of hope.

Blue concentrated on the year, the month, the day, the second, the moment. It was all happening right now – out there. Blue was here and it was time to join the throngs on the street. If time stopped again then Blue understood that was the reality of this experience, nothing could be done about it. Blue was in the swirling events of these hopeful joyous people, and until there was a shift, Blue would continue to have Berlin as a home. In three different periods within a short time, the city felt more vibrant and real than London and nowhere on Earth could be as toxic and poisonous as LA. No, this was Blue's home.

The streets had the energy of revolution. Normal public containment: a German rigour and respect for administrative authority had never quite been part part of the Berlin diet since the beginning of what was known as the cold war split the city into two very different parts. The genuflection of ideas as currency in Europe's first and foremost dystopia was always a fire waiting for a wind. And it had come: not cynically or predictably but joyously.

In the years after the Second World War, people in Berlin had starved but survived somehow, through need rather than desire. They had found a way to scramble back some dignity and collect a new identity along the way; they had moved on and rebooted history. But here they were again, with history alive and in the hands of the people, but this time the madness was missing. This time it was the deep embrace of compassion and the end of hurt. They were, on this day, becoming a people no longer broken by revenge-fate – a fetish that had driven the city insane since the days of Napoleon, Frederick the Great and Hitler and then Stalin. The expression of delirium mixed with a shocking innocence prevailed along pathways and side streets that straddled and spun away from the Wall.

Chants: a non-Buddhist but truly German trait enveloped the atmosphere; 'Wir sind ein Volk' melted into the sky along with car horns, banging drums and whistles. People wanted to make a noise – something primitive and protective. The need to share, to engage, to be together was the wondrous alchemy that unfolded from a magical box of tricks nobody could have foreseen. History had no shape, it was a succession of sounds and fateful encounters and shared spaces.

The natural cacophony of an unprescribed event allowed the tuneless and the shy to sing and be happy; it allowed people to touch who would never dare engage their sensuality. But nothing was allowed to be buried, to be hidden. People were free. For the first time in their lives, people were understanding how to be free. It was a mess, a big beautiful mess, nobody knew how it had begun, but they knew it had begun with the people.

The chants moved from a simple polemic to a mighty tune near the

Brandenburg Gate. Blue stood awash in the hysteria and listened to thousands of human beings express their freedom by singing 'Heroes'. They sang in English and in German with a pitch that signalled triumph rather than music. It was a beautiful moment to behold and Blue felt a warmth return that had been missing since listening to Bowie sing in the Hansa Studios. It was an anthem of joy beyond national identity – it was unrestricted pop music as art that lay deep in the soul of the people from the East who embraced their brothers and sisters from the West. It was part of the history of these peoples, the riotous assembly of Berlin who in a stroke had changed the world.

How did I end up here at this perfect moment, thought Blue? Why did fate deliver me to the door of this exhibition of human rapture? Was someone guiding Blue through spatial time, was there a pathway, a route that had been created for this journey? Was Green pointing Blue in the direction of the story they had followed together? Could that be it?

Or was it all accidental fate with no predestined design? Was being part of history in 1989 an example of how creativity affects real lives, the real lives of people who harnessed the sound and words of the music they loved or the performance of men and women on stage who found a way to say the unsayable? or might it have been the paintings, the sculpture, the installations, literature and poetry, architecture and design? Could it be possible that this revolution was inspired by their ability to create and make things?

'Is that why I am walking through the streets watching the very best of the human soul at work? It must be. It can only be. I want it to be,' thought Blue.

Blue climbed through the Wall and entered the GDR in East Berlin. Guards paid no attention as they shared cigarettes and a new nervous banter with the 'ones' from the other side. Blue walked backwards as people ran past like characters in a comic zombie movie: it was unreal. But, in Blue's world, what was real? Who was real? Was this happening? It must be. It was there, right there, physical and touchable. The people running past were focused on reaching the Wall. Their run was staggered, motivated by a nervous system that pounded their heartbeats with a new sound: hope and terror.

Alexanderplatz seemed calm by comparison. The buildings were grey and tired with their windows covered in the slushy spill from many hard winters. The Fernsehturm blinked, unaware of changing history, as holes were smashed into the Wall's concrete face. Blue watched the old people of East Berlin continue to wander through the square with their heads down, businesslike but unhurried. These were people who knew they were being watched and had accepted it as part of their lives. Young men and women jumped off moving trams and ran into Blue. They froze for a moment as they saw the blinking eye high above them. But the energy in the air was too much to stop them.

'Komm... Komm... die Mauer... die Mauer... Komm,' they shouted to a generation terrified to acknowledge that it was possible to raise your voice, that it might even be possible to run to the Wall: an act of suicide, destination death. They didn't want to witness any more carnage.

But there would be no carnage today. Homespun terror had been abandoned against the enormous persuasive will of the people. The word 'no', which had been so definitive in all of their lives, was now part of an ancient language. It meant nothing. Today there was only 'yes', but the older people continued to look away, look down, ignore, hide and slip into the shadows of a life that they had become familiar with. A life structured by banality, a place where creativity, when it existed, was cruel, something people did to each other to maintain that very structure that guided their lives, an empty and graceless position of remorseless justification.

Blue could see it in the faces of the terrified. Faces without a future: hopeless. How could this be? How could they have allowed this to happen? Alexanderplatz became eerily quiet. The young had run to the Wall and into the future, the old were hiding in the past, inside, where it was safe, where nobody was following you, and if they were listening, you simply didn't speak: their world was the world of silence. And out in the vast space of Alexanderplatz, Blue could hear their informed silence alongside the faint echoes of the past.

Blue stood still as the wind picked up speed through the side streets and emerged in a collision on the square. With the wind came the sound of the ghosts of Franz Biberkopf, marching soldiers, drunken prostitutes, fighting Spartacists and eventually rampaging Russians. None of the sounds had gone away, they were as distinct as Blue's first encounter in future years. It was raucous and violent and awash with unfinished turmoil. Nothing ever felt complete on Alexanderplatz. It was an ongoing project that would never change. In the distance, the roar of the jubilant crowds could be heard building towards another chant and another verse of 'Heroes'. From where Blue was standing it could have been another country, another time.

A man watched Blue walk to a bench and sit, eyes closed, listening to the wind pull the echoes of history onto Alexanderplatz. Blue was aware that the man had sat nearby but needed reassurance that this was still 1989. The square was exactly as it had been moments ago, the same exhausted grey concrete and colourless buildings.

High above, the tower blinked in a near-respiratory order of heart and blood; the wind pulled the optimism of the roaring crowds towards them, but the few ageing comrades continued to present the gloom of their lives in 1989 as they stooped and pushed against the wind and the world, looking for the safety of a silent interior. The man sitting next to Blue spoke first: 'I take it you have papers that are in order for you to be here?'

Blue looked at the man's thick, wide-framed black glasses and his small navy-blue felt hat which sat on top of a long horse-like face, ending in a square jaw. The man looked at odds with his physical presence, almost as if he were trying to hide it beneath his quarter-length brown-check coat. His shoes were too shiny for his outfit, too official; this was a disguise that had not been thought through completely, it was flawed. Blue wondered if the man was new to his job.

'Your passport please.'

The man showed Blue his ID in a small brown wallet which indicated he had something to do with the Stasi.

'So you're real. And this is real. All real,' said Blue. 'Do you know what is happening at the Wall?'

'I have an idea.'

'And yet you want to see my papers? My passport and visa?'

'Correct.'

'But why?'

'Nothing has changed.'

'But everything has changed. This is history. You are in it. Part of it, whether you like it or not.'

'Passport.'

'I don't have one.'

They sat silently together. Blue listened to the running tap of echoes spilling out onto Alexanderplatz and tried to catch small thoughts from the man next to him. They were interrupted and displaced by the echoes dancing around them but Blue understood the man's confusion.

Who is this person? I can't even tell if it's a man or a woman. Is that our future? Is this their victory? Men who are women and women who are men? How did she/he get this far? Is he or she a spy? Of course not. A voyeur. A culture tourist looking at how poor we all are. Thinking, where are the cars? Where are the shops? Where's the shiny materialism of our lives on the other side? What do we do here? We spy on one another. We inform. We accuse. We arrest. We interrogate. We imprison our citizens and then we are surprised that they want to leave. To go over there.

But what is freedom? What is this freedom they crave? There is no freedom in their society. They are as much slaves as we are. Why do people want things? To own things.

Things that they don't need. We are equals. In this society we are equals. But, we're not, not really. I've seen the top boys in the firm. I've seen what they have. The lives they lead. I've had a glimpse of their privileges. We are not equal. We are equals in our lack of wanting more. Ambition. Fuck ambition. It's a disease. Who is this strange person in their strange clothes who has no passport? A European, maybe English, I can't tell. I'm tired of following people. Listening in on their private lives. Everything. Every little detail. I'm tired. But what else can I do? They choose us. I was chosen. One of the chosen few.

They give me people to watch. To listen to. To observe. To look for weakness. Once they have been marked there is no such thing as guilt or innocence, only the fact that they have been marked. I'm good at what I do, but recently something happened to me. I didn't want to be good any more. I wanted the people I was following to notice me. Today, for example. Today, I wore my shiny army shoes. A sure giveaway. This person sitting next to me noticed almost immediately. He or she knew I was a mistake. That I hadn't got it right. But that's my way of telling people to be careful. What am I supposed to do with this one? Interrogation? But why? What would they get? Nothing. I'm sure nothing other than the satisfaction that they have control. Control over this man-woman thing who looks harmless.

'What do you do?'

Blue was surprised by the question and had been enjoying listening to the man's thoughts, but was now brought back into the cold winds of 'The Alex'. What would Döblin have thought of this strange meeting on his sacred square? The Stasi man and a new, repaired type of human from the future, gender-free and able to imagine themselves into different time zones. Döblin might have been amused by how both of them were trapped, but both of them were trying to find the route to a personal understanding.

'What do I do?'

'Are you another West Berlin anarchist? The kind of person who does nothing?'

'Everyone does something.'

'I'm not so sure about that, but if it's true that everyone does something, then it's not always something they want to do.'

'Maybe. Maybe that's why some people think they are unhappy.'

'No-one here is unhappy.'

'Everyone here is unhappy. Including you.'

'That kind of statement could get you arrested.'

Blue shared a smile with the Stasi man.

'I've been on a journey.'

'A tourist?'

'No. I came here with my friend to try and understand why we loved David Bowie so much more than anything else in our lives.'

'More than each other?'

'I think I now understand that that kind of love is different.'

'Adulation is superficial.'

'Our love of David Bowie is not superficial. It helped us understand each other. It was an inspiration.'

'Like a religion?'

'No. No, we understood quickly that mankind distrusts its own nature and tries to find stability in religion or philosophy. Love is more simple. Love is our nature. It's what we've been born for. It's what we do best. It's the reason for living. The only reason for living. So, in answer to your question, that's what I do. I love.'

'And that's enough?'

Blue held the man's stare. It was clear the question was not cynical but entirely confused and, considering the man's occupation, innocent.

'It's a start. Something to build on.'

'And this partner of yours feels the same?'

'I think so.'

'And where is this partner? Is he or she looking around our city without a passport or visa?'

'No. My friend has gone.'

'Gone. Gone back?'

'No... actually, yes. Green went back.'

'Green.'

'I'm Blue.'

'The man laughed.

'Were your parents flower people – hippies?'

'I don't think so.'

'The names are very Western.'

'No. They are colours. Like nature.'

'You were individuals?'

'No. We were the same. We are all the same.'

'Equals.'

'Of course.'

'And where is this utopia?'

'Somewhere in the future.'

'So you think we are backward here? You mock me. Us. Don't worry. I would. It would be easy to find this funny if it were not so tragic.'

'No. I don't find this funny. I can see and hear something full of love happening that is making me and many other people smile. People are coming together. They are changing their world.'

'Will it last? This change? Can it last? Is it the beginning of another war? The Russians, what will they do? What will happen? I think we're doomed.'

'No, you're not doomed. You are part of history. Something special.'

'It will be a disaster.'

'I don't think you believe that.'

'The people I work for need to know everything. They will never allow this. This convergence.'

'But they don't know what is about to happen. So they don't know everything.'

'What shall I do with you?'

'Nothing. Think about what you want to do. How do you feel about the world you have been part of? You can change if you want to. You can be creative.'

'Creative?'

'Yes. It's what your soul is.'

The man laughed again.

'Are you sure you are not a hippy?'

'It doesn't matter who or what I am. It matters who you are and what you want to become.'

'I think I should arrest you.'

'Then arrest me if that's what you want to do.'

'No. No, it's not what I want to do.'

They sat in the square as the wind slowed down and the echoes hid in the backstreets, in the shadows, deep underground. This was not a moment for ghosts but one for the people of the future who were represented on the bench on Alexanderplatz next to one another, two strangers – one a member of the Stasi who wore shiny shoes and the other an unusual David Bowie fan who understood at last the point of an incredible journey. The Stasi man got up from the bench and looked down at Blue then turned and walked towards the Wall. He stopped and whispered to Blue, to the city, to the people who were listening, to a suffocated world that had learned to breathe again.

'The irony of all of this is that I always had a dream. The same dream. You know what it was?'

'No,' replied Blue.

'The dream was that someday I would go to New York. Escape. Be part of everything I had been told was wrong with the world.'

The Stasi man gave a small wave as the wind swirled around his feet and walked on. Blue watched him disappear towards the noise. Even here in the impossible claustrophobia of the East, dreams were coming true. This was the simple magic of the human world, Blue's world.

Blue walked along Hauptstrasse and looked up at the sky, quietly understanding that although the firmament was being pulled apart by events at the Wall, the street seemed to be going about its business with its usual anonymity. The Turkish community that had made this neighbourhood their own were collecting children from school, buying vegetables from shop stalls and were almost oblivious to the extraordinary events happening less than a kilometre away. The street of 1989 felt unchanged from the grimy depletion of 1976, but it was the café where Jena had worked that was Blue's main focus. It was unusually empty and looked closed but there was still a light on in the background. Blue looked through the window and saw Jena putting on her coat and wrapping a scarf around her neck. She was older but still retained her easy German beauty. Blue was about to knock on the window when a woman in her late twenties walked past and opened the door of the café. Jena's face lit up as the woman walked straight up to her and kissed her deeply on the mouth. In the dim light inside the café, Blue could see Jena and her lover embrace with the affection and gentleness that could only be shared by these wonderful people, these humans who were yet to be repaired and changed and repositioned and left bereft of the simplicity of emotion.

Blue felt the consequence of a history that had pulled them, Blue and Green, in search of a truth and here it was – a beautiful love. Blue smiled and felt a human tear run down a cheek that had to this point felt fake and unreal and now, here in Berlin, on this monumental day, the tear and the cheek and the skin all felt real. Jena looked up towards the window at the person watching them and a tremor ran through her as she watched what she thought was Blue sending a ghostly smile and wave before walking away.

Jena ran to the door and looked up and down Hauptstrasse but there was only traffic all headed in one direction, the Wall. Had she seen Blue? Could it have been Blue? Was it a ghost? What did it mean? Blue had promised to return. Was that what had just happened? Jena's lover stood behind her and asked what she was looking for.

'An old friend,' she replied.

'Where are they?'

Jena smiled as she held her lover's hand and kissed her and then, with a magical Berlin grace, they both ran with the wind towards the Wall. Blue watched from a doorway as Jena who was obviously happy and in love, ran in the direction of the Wall with her lover. Why had Blue returned to Hauptstrasse? Why would Jena have waited all these years for someone she had met only once? And now Jena was in love. The noise from the drama at the Wall spread across the sky displacing the echoes of horror with a joyful harmony of people and history. But Blue was alone. Would this always be the way? Was this the world that Blue would be part of – singular and friendless? The distant pang of loneliness affected Blue's concentration and allowed another human attribute to invade a near-imperial space.

A car passed with the window down as Lou Reed's 'Satellite of Love' blared out of the car speakers. Blue thought of the Stasi man and his dream of New York. What would he make of this? The driver of the pale VW waved to Blue: today the world was at peace, temporarily, but nonetheless it was magnificent. Blue waved back. Berlin's joy was irresistible and Blue decided to walk back to the Wall, accompanied by the sound of Bowie's backing vocals supplementing Lou Reed's nonchalance in the perfect soundtrack to what Blue considered a perfect day. On the Wall, sprayed with a beautiful clarity, was Rilke's poem 'Liebeslied', which made Blue think of a soul that was alive with the spirit of Green and Bowie and Love and this incredible journey to Berlin, a city enthralled with a new energy for creativity and hope. Quangel was wrong about Bowie being mortal. His work was what mattered and the work would endure far far into the future when even two lovesick repairs will find their reason to exist through Bowie's certainty that life could be truly beautiful even for those who were not part of a preconditioned social order, even for the lonely and alienated who found that love was not ever going to be easy to find, even for those who were scared to tell the world who they really were. Bowie made them brave and stronger and maybe, just maybe, his gift made them smile with a genuine happiness. Blue read Rilke's words aloud and they floated into the crowd then up into the air swirling in the clouds and beyond like a guiding light:

Wie soll ich meine Seele halten, daß
sie nicht an deine rührt? Wie soll ich sie
hinheben über dich zu andern Dingen?
Ach gerne möcht ich sie bei irgendwas
Verlorenem im Dunkel unterbringen
an einer fremden stillen Stelle, die
nicht weiterschwingt, wenn diene Tiefen schwingen.
Doch alles, was uns anrührt, dich und mich,
nimmt uns zusammen wie ein Bogenstrich,
der aus zwei Saiten eine Stimme zieht.
Auf welches Instrument sind wir gespannt?

Und welcher Geiger hat uns in der Hand?
O süßes Lied.

It was then Blue knew what to do. Blue ran, flew after the words
that floated through the sky. Ran after the Stasi man's dream of New
York. It was time to catch the dream, hang onto its wings and find a
way into Bowie's new home, the city where he had spent the major-
ity of his life: New York. It was time to follow Bowie's next stage.
Blue knew that Berlin would be a place that had a special place in the
journey – the feeling of a home – but human instincts were running
through a system tingling with sensation. Yes, it was time, somebody, something, somewhere was calling come... come... come...
I'm waiting for you. It was Bowie.

9 January 2016

'Yes,' a voice replied from behind Blue. 'Yes, at last you've found it.
You've found me.'

Blue stood on Times Square. Traffic poured down and through the
roads and their tributaries and people pushed against the cold winter
wind. The neon lights jingled and the season's grey was blasted with
the colours of New York – yellow and red. Screens ran news stories
and advertisements for entertainment, sport and beauty. A helicopter
drifted overhead and a police siren wailed its way down Broadway. This was organised chaos in comparison with Berlin's calm
reluctance. Blue watched the people wrapped up in the post-Christ-
mas blues and the New Year challenge to find different gears to
power their way through the crowds and sleet-covered cars, buses and
taxis. One of the screens changed to show David Bowie's new video
'Blackstar'. Blue watched Bowie blinded with buttons for eyes as he
asked how many times does an angel fall. Dancers juddered into life
enveloped in a seizure as a solitary candle burned 'at the centre of

it all'. Alchemy, ritual, iconography, a regressive future, somewhere else – all floating in the skylines of a bitter-cold New York night. The world seemed to be passing by without noticing the transgressive magic happening above. Blue was enchanted by Bowie's sense of poetry and childlike fun and awe – was this what truly lay at the heart of creativity?

'So, here we are again. You and me, Blue. Electric Blue.'

'You remember.'

'Of course. Come on, let's take a walk. Let me show you some of my city.'

Bowie put his arm around Blue's shoulder and led them through the throngs of people on Times Square.

'Did you hear me in Berlin? I was whispering into the wind. Telling you to come and join me here. I know what happened to Jena. Your new love. Were you jealous? Upset? Lost? Angry? Disappointed? Or were you happy for her? I think you were happy for her.'

'You can hear me. You can hear me thinking.'

'Yes. Yes I can.'

Up above them the video for 'Blackstar' continued to play on a loop. Bowie smiled and sang along with the line 'I'm a blackstar'.

'Look at us, Blue. We're on Times Square. We're the Young Americans. We're on MTV with *Let's Dance*. *Tonight*. Movies. Theatre. *Black Tie White Noise*. *Outside*. *Heathen*. *Reality*. *The Next Day*. And now *Blackstar*. You see, you understand don't you, that New York has been my home longer than London or LA or Berlin? New York allowed me to be a pop star but at the same time find the space to have a home. To find a wife. To love. To have another child. Make music. Move on. Look at the future. Create my version of the future. Do you see? Can you understand? I could write words. Write music. Act. Curate. Launch ideas. But I could never fail. Failure was a terror. Creativity is held to ransom by failure.'

They both stopped and looked at one another. Bowie hugged Blue. It was a deep, soul-searching grasp that locked them like lovers lost for words but suddenly realising they didn't have to say anything. They both understood perfectly what they were saying to one another. Bowie whispered in Blue's ear.

'Winter in this city is extraordinary. Cold. Bitter cold. The wind crabs up the Hudson from the Atlantic. It never stops. It's vicious. Look, this is 42nd Street. I remember seeing the hustlers in T-shirts in this weather. Can you imagine? Hustling for business in weather like this? Young men and women – some of them so beautiful. I cruised this street in a limousine – up and down – just looking. It was like a Lou Reed song right there in front of you. All of this is now prime real estate; but then, this was a series of fleapits – awful cinemas showing porn. Difficult to imagine now. But then, it was dangerous. Really dangerous. If you had walked down 42nd Street then, looking like you do, then you would have been in trouble. Pimps, hookers, rent boys, drug dealers, gang-bangers, punks, junkies, homeless, voyeurs, out-of-towners, johns and deadbeats. All of them slipping from block to block, cinema to cinema, side street to side street. That's how it was. But now, well, it couldn't have stayed that way. This is Disneyland for the rich. And here we are. You and Me. Can you hear anything Blue? The echoes from back then. I can. I can hear the cars passing with people hanging out of the windows screaming abuse at one another. Music is everywhere. Music is always everywhere. Let's keep on walking Blue. Down Broadway, through the garment district towards the Bowery. I love the Bowery. Always loved the Bowery. I live there and thereabouts. Close enough. The home of modern rock 'n' roll.'

Bowie and Blue drifted into East Village watching flakes of snow float across the rooftop of the Lutheran church towards the now deserted Tompkins Square Park. The one-time punk wasteland had been renovated back to commercial health by the unstoppable march of new money. What was once a ghetto for the nihilists and the lost was now a real-estate opportunity for the latest wave of wealthy refugees from North Africa and Eastern Europe. The remnants of pre-punk vegan cafés from a period when hippy deluxe was political rather than vogue had survived but were now the places of choice for the brigades of yummy-mummies rather than Maoist revolutionaries. The black leather jackets, torn T-shirts and heroin-seared arms were now part of the tourist trail and fashion houses rather than a once-brutal reality. The gay bath-houses had been sealed off like a crime scene in a new era where civil partnerships had crushed the urge for sexual expressionism. A breeze whistled though the park and the single coil of snow was soon glued together with a chain of soft falling ice. The floodlights from the basketball courts created a theatrical backdrop to the silhouettes of Bowie and Blue sitting together on a bench in the middle of the park.

'You created me,' Blue said, watching the snow whirl and dance before falling and laying a thin layer of white over the park.

'Yes,' Bowie replied, holding Blue's hand. 'You were looking for solutions to situations where there are none,' Bowie said softly. 'But I knew you would come. I knew you would come here. I asked you to. I needed to tell you something. But you worked it out. Yes. I created you. You're part of my imagination but I tried to set you free. I couldn't but I will tonight. You've always been with me but a time came when I felt the world was zooming ahead of me. That had never happened before. I was always ahead but then that changed. So I took a moment to consider how to catch up. I started thinking about you around that time. About the people who followed my work. The people who had given me nothing but love. I started to think about the past for the first time. I wanted you to go back and have a look for me. You thought you were making a pilgrimage – an adventure – finding connections, looking for the truth behind creativity. But no. No, Blue. No. It was me. I used you to remember. You were my anthropologist of memories. A place where imagination was better than the event. You and Green. That was you and me. I lost half of who I was in LA. That was Green. A part of me. Quangel was invented to keep you away from me. You were getting too close. Too close to the real me. I suddenly didn't want to see who that was. I started your adventure on New Year's Eve. It felt right. The right time. You Blue. You Blue were my last creation. An idea that has become a living thing.

Look at us. Wandering around New York together tonight. You are my echo.'

'The black star?'

'Yes.'

'What does it mean?'

'It means the end.'

'My end? The end of my story? And when I awake? Will I be alone? Will I have entered the great emptiness?'

'No, quite the opposite. Ideas don't die. Ideas evolve. That's the beauty of creativity. You share it. I share my ideas. I share you. I need you to carry on. Take part of me with you. I want to see what happens to the world. Can you do that for me? I would really like that. Travelling through time, watching the world evolve. I wonder if we will become better at being human beings or was this it? Were we the best examples? I hope not. I liked you from the first moment I created you. Your curiosity refreshed mine. Kept me alive when I was all burnt out, when I had nothing to say. We sang together. You and I, Blue. Friends. We're friends now. You and I. Forever. You will live forever. And I. I will be gone. I don't want to go. I want to be with my family. I hope they know how much I love them. I hope I told them. I did. I know I did. I love them.'

Bowie wiped away the sadness from his eyes. He hummed a medley of pop fantasies that told the story of the world. The dreams of oceans and dolphins and youth and love all swam around his glistening ghostly eyes in the silence of Tompkins Square.

'Tell me Blue. Blue Electric Blue. Tell me about the future. You're my eyes. How will the stars look? How will the sky change? Will it rain? Snow? Does the Sun survive? Tell me Blue. Can I come with you? Like Lazarus. Can we wander the Earth together? Looking at the stars? I don't want to be alone.'

They sat silently together watching the snow fall effortlessly from the dark sky. Blue listened to Bowie thinking about contemporary stories of atavistic civil wars and murderous religious revolutions which were now the common currency of the news gatherer. Nobody had a solution other than meeting savagery with savagery or disappointment with disappointment. This was a world hell bent on mutual destruction. Goodness was outdone by stupidity, hope savaged by ignorance and love outmanoeuvred by hatred. Maybe I, thought Bowie, represent the incapacitated modesty of the meek? The conflict was as old as the planet and through different civilisations they had found no amity that had bonded their future into something less dark and dangerous. And here they were, trying to find the seed of what that solution might be.

Blue looked at the man sitting next to him staring at the falling snow and realised how he had aged and looked vulnerable and weak. Bowie nodded in agreement and held Blue close, admiring the beauty of his last creation. His last idea. He kissed Blue on the lips then stood up and started to walk backwards into the falling snow.

'No Blue, tonight is not about your end. It's not the end of your story. It's mine. My end. I wanted you to take me back into my life and shine it back to me through different eyes. And you did that beautifully. You gave me back my story. Me. I needed to see me as I really am and you did that for me. Thank you. You're real now. Not a part of my imagination but a real idea. You're real, Blue. You can continue and take the idea on to somewhere, on to something – who knows what? That's what's so exciting. Anyway, I've got to go now. I have to die. You have to live. Goodbye Blue.'

Blue watched Bowie fade into the night as the snow thickened around the park and only the faint sound of a car horn or a Tompkins Square bar door closing interrupted the calm that had descended on the East Village. A gust of thoughts swept up the debris of an unforgettable day. Bowie was gone. They would never meet again. His family would be grieving; their loss would be unbearable and deeper than any member of the David Bowie Fan Club could understand. But Blue understood something new. Blue understood the ephemeral nature of their existence was the very thing that gave them their unique strength, their wonderful bond with each other, their desire to create. The snowflakes kissed Blue's pale hand and dissolved into small dots of water that shimmered against the floodlit park.

Blue looked up into the dark, starless sky and considered his long journey to this moment. Blue remained calm and quiet, again wondering if Bowie could hear the thoughts that raged and wept at the memory of the news of Bowie's death. They all die, Blue thought. But somehow I thought that you were different. I know it's foolish of me but after you have lived amongst them for a while you start to believe some of their ideas about gods and life beyond this. This. But they all die, thought Blue again, as if a chorus had been found amongst the thin pickings of the language they were forced to communicate with. I thought that maybe you were one of us. A repair. It would have made sense. The world you created. Sang about. Wrote about. I thought your world was a signpost to ours. And what is that? A better version of this? The best these people can do; their highest achievement is the way they share emotion and care for one another. It's a beautiful thing. I want to be part of that and have been learning how. How to be like them. But... they all die. And now I understand that that's OK. Their end is OK. They live knowing they are going to die. Bowie was not immortal. He had so much more to give. But why go on forever? It doesn't make sense. We are not elemental. We become connected to their story and then we carry on. Today was a shock but maybe the shock lies in the knowledge that I too need a way to say farewell. We all do. I am an idea. He said ideas never die.

10 January 2016

Crowds continued to gather outside Bowie's home on Lafayette Street as Blue stood looking at the various flowers, photographs, drawings, album sleeves and candles that had been left as a testament of people's sense of loss and love. The New York Police Department kept order with a casual nonverbal anonymity as emotions spilled over into hugs and embraces between strangers. New Yorkers stood alongside tourists with a genuine familiarity beyond the usual ersatz cosmopolitanism – common hurt brought people together and this was a city now becoming accustomed to tragedy. The mood on the street was sombre but the bar opposite slung out a montage of Bowie classics from their open door, which cheered the wind that blasted down Houston from the near-frozen Hudson. The mild weather had ended as suddenly as the tragic proclamation that had brought so many people out into what normally would have been a quiet winter evening. People wanted to share something that they were working out together. They had never felt this way before; it wasn't theatrical: it was real.

Bowie had been with some of them for over four decades and for others it might only have been since the release of *Blackstar* a few days earlier. It didn't matter, the musical pedigree of the mourning fans; what mattered was they had something beautiful to share.

Blue understood the innocence of the gathering and felt the genuine nature of their grief. A tall, bearded man stood in front of Blue reading the cards and engaging with different generations of Bowie fans, asking them their favourite Bowie song or era that remained with them at that precise moment. On any other day he might have been seen as a typically deranged ranting New Yorker but today he was a poet of the streets, a documentarian, an archivist, a diarist, chairman of the David Bowie Fan Club and a man trying to elevate himself above an acute depression.

'The thing is…' the bearded man said as he turned to look at Blue. 'The thing is that I just can't get him out of my imagination.'

He stopped speaking as he took in Blue's face. The skin shone against the street light and the veins pulsed a silvery blue liquid in darts so fast that the bearded man wasn't quite sure he had really seen anything.

'Don't you agree, that he's in our imagination? He became part of us.'

'Yes, and maybe we became part of him,' replied Blue.

'Did you know him…? You look like you knew him.'

Blue smiled and shook his head. 'I loved him.'

The bearded man looked around at the crowd, who quietly paid their respects. Some in tears, others looking forlorn and broken mumbled a few words or softly sang their favourite song. People looked down from the apartments above the street: Bowie's neighbours. Was this an infringement of their wealthy privacy? No poor people lived near the Bowery now, which was once the land of the frenzied, starved, drunk and heroin-addicted street people whose stories had fed Bowie's great friend Lou Reed.

Blue looked at the windows and saw the schism of the modern city dweller from London to Manhattan and LA to Bombay – regeneration only positively affected those people with money, lots of money. He had called it a Disneyland for the rich. The people above looking down at the mourners showed no sign of camaraderie or cynicism, only a bland unemotional disconnected interest in the people braving the vicious change in the weather.

Blue had seen TV images of the people gathering in the streets of Brixton in London singing Bowie songs together, and sharing drinks and food as they connected their sense of loss with a wonderful unprepared joy. It was clumsy and British and heartlifting to see warmth and friendship emerging from a day that had started with such a wretched, painful awakening.

'We're the David Bowie Fan Club,' said the bearded man to Blue.

'Look at us. Like some of those kids over there are hardly fifteen, yet here they are weeping with the rest of us. I'm fifty-five and he has never been out of my life from the age of ten. I grew up amongst people listening to cheesy pop music or disco or, even worse, jazz-rock, and then this guy came into my life and everything became clearer, you know what I mean? Like I knew who I could be all of a sudden, no that's not right, I knew who I didn't want to be. I didn't want to be like the people around me. I was different and suddenly that was OK, nothing to be ashamed of, know what I mean? I didn't care if people were gay or straight. I identified with people who were out there trying to grasp stuff. They were brave. I wanted to be brave with them. He introduced me to life as it could be: books, music, movies, art, history; he introduced me to something I had never even considered worth thinking about: science fiction, the cosmos, aliens. I don't know what it was like for you but when I was a kid Bowie made me look upwards to the stars. Imagine, just imagine that there might be something out there for real. How amazing is that? So, I wasn't scared any more. Not scared to have ideas of my own, to believe in myself. That's what he did for me. That was Bowie. And I came here tonight to thank him. Thank him for everything. Thank him for making me unwilling to sit back and be content, to keep looking and searching and listening, to be part of a quest and the quest would make you happy. To still be curious. To care. To want to know.

That's what he did for me. He helped me. Guided me. And his music kept coming. Have you heard *Blackstar*? It's something else. Special. It's demanding and rewarding and pulls you into a world that suddenly makes more sense than it should. A prophecy of this time when Bowie would leave us. Leave us alone. Do you feel that? I feel so alone. Now that he's gone I think I need him more than ever to navigate me through the next period of madness on this planet. We all have our own version of Bowie that means something different to each of us but he was my navigator. I'm sure he means something different to you, maybe only in small ways, but it'll be different. And you may like different periods of the man's life from me. But what we will definitely share in a very specific way, like you said earlier, is our love. A deep, deep love for someone who made us better. Made us better at life. And made us better in our imaginations. So that's why I came here tonight. To say thank you and share my experience with the people whose lives were made better by being part of the David Bowie Fan Club. I'm sorry man, I'm going on and on about me, but I don't know how to feel at the moment, because I've lost something so important in my life. I've never felt this way before and probably will never feel like this again. And...'

The bearded man started to cry inconsolably. He suffered a complete breakdown in front of Blue and a street now crammed full of yearning and loss. His tears streamed down his face as he sobbed outwardly as a tribute to Bowie's influence on his life and very being. His collapse affected the growing crowds, which became reverentially silent watching the dissolution of a man's heroic attempt to hang on to his composure. As the crowd watched on, Blue leaned forward and held the man tight. The sobs became grunts and thunderous evictions from the pit of the man's stomach but Blue held him so he couldn't move as the might of the spasms nearly pushed them to the ground.

The crowd continued to watch this outpouring of grief and were released from their own somnolence to hold and hug and cry and let go a pent-up emotional prism of thoughts. Lafayette Street became a miracle of hope and hurt and unrestrained memory, where the centrepiece was David Bowie; a man who had changed all of their lives and all they had wanted to do tonight was find a way to say thank you; and now they had found the answer through the bearded man and the beautiful creature hugging him tightly as his sobs penetrated the buildings and the sky over New York. The answer was simple. Let go.

Blue held the bearded man tightly and found a way to assuage his terror through gently humming 'Where Are We Now?', Bowie's beautiful, wistful hymn to his time in Berlin. The vibration sang through the crowd like a tuning fork finding its perfect note. And then it happened: the crowd hummed the tune in time with Blue and it grew and grew and soared and then the moment arrived when they all sang the end refrain together. Bowie's last great anthem.

And it was then that Blue realised that Bowie had not gone, that he would live on forever, and that Blue must fulfil a promise that had been made in the desert to Green, a lover who had died so Blue would be able to continue this incredible journey. And Bowie had told Blue that Green was part of him, the part he had left in LA and the desert. Bowie's voice echoed through the icy New York wind reminding Blue of that promise as the crowd continued to sing about a starman waiting in the sky but Blue now knew that the echoes were presenting a route, a map, a through-line where everything would make sense. And it was then that Blue saw Quangel standing on the street corner throwing a gentle wave and smile, then a whisper that slipped through the crowd: 'Hello Blue. Do you remember me?'

Blue released the bearded man into the arms of the crowd, who encouraged him to sing along with their sonorous rendition of 'Ashes to Ashes'. The bearded man turned to thank Blue but the crowd swayed in a tight pack leaving no sign of Blue, only faces lit with eyes that had clarity for the first time that day; remorse and sadness had been replaced with a euphoria that swept Lafayette Street into a clamour that roared with pride.

Blue ran into the wind towards the river. From a window Bowie's song 'The Bewlay Brothers' screamed a demented, haunted insolence – the kings of oblivion were in town. Blue felt no pain from the cold as it shivered against skin that shone in the night air. Quangel was here: the killer of ideas. The natural sounds of New York were diminished, stuck, forlorn in the snow. Bowie's song of madness propelled Blue along Houston to the ice-packed Hudson that reflected a long-suffering contempt for the new inhabitants of the city.

How do ideas survive? Blue shouted into the twisting, dancing snow and across the water, where it bounced back to hug the buildings. The people inside were drawn to their windows not to watch the now-chaotic blizzard but to look for the origins of the question – the sound that had penetrated their castles in the air. But nobody knew the answer and Blue could feel Quangel in the shadows waiting to complete his job: his only reason to exist.

Blue had made a promise to his friend, to carry on. To let the idea grow. Blue wasn't ready for Quangel's art of destruction. Not now. Not ever. Everything had changed. Everything was human. Everything was real.

And as the last few bars of 'The Bewlay Brothers' faded away, Blue looked for that human sensation. Blue wanted to feel reality. Blue jumped into the Hudson, plunging under the ice-cold water.

Patrons

Paul Arnold
Grant Bayliss
Dominic Boyle
Christian Brett
Mick Bridgman
Paul Burgess
Ronnie Connick
Glen de la Cour
Lorna Crombie
Andrew Crooks
Alec Cummings
Anthony Hall
John Henery
Chris Howard
Ali James
Peter Key
Karen Kilroy
Jack Lothian
Richard McLaren
Carlo Navato
Tracey Ann Selmes
Kay Smillie
Susan Waltham